Remind Me Again What Happened

Also by Joanna Luloff

The Beach at Galle Road

Remind Me Again What Happened

A NOVEL

JOANNA LULOFF

ALGONQUIN BOOKS OF CHAPEL HILL   2018

Published by
Algonquin Books of Chapel Hill
Post Office Box 2225
Chapel Hill, North Carolina 27515-2225

a division of
Workman Publishing
225 Varick Street
New York, New York 10014

This is a work of fiction. While, as in all fiction, the literary
perceptions and insights are based on experience, all names, characters,
places, and incidents either are products of the author's
imagination or are used fictitiously.

LIBRARY OF CONGRESS CATALOGING-IN-PUBLICATION DATA
Names: Luloff, Joanna, [date–] author.
Title: Remind me again what happened / a novel by Joanna Luloff.
Description: First edition. | Chapel Hill, North Carolina :
Algonquin Books of Chapel Hill, 2018.
Identifiers: LCCN 2017052406 | ISBN 9781565129221
(hardcover : alk. paper)
Subjects: LCSH: Amnesiacs—Fiction. | Man-woman
relationships—Fiction. | Female friendship—Fiction. |
Self-actualization (Psychology)—Fiction.
Classification: LCC PS3612.U46 R46 2018 | DDC 813.6—dc23
LC record available at https://lccn.loc.gov/2017052406

10 9 8 7 6 5 4 3 2 1
First Edition

For Will

But my grief wanted a just image, an image which would be both justice and accuracy—*justesse*: just an image, but a just image.

—ROLAND BARTHES, *Camera Lucida*

What we, or at any rate what I, refer to confidently as memory—meaning a moment, a scene, a fact that has been subjected to a fixative and thereby rescued from oblivion—is really a form of storytelling that goes on continually in the mind and often changes with the telling. Too many conflicting emotional interests are involved for life ever to be wholly acceptable, and possibly it is the work of the storyteller to rearrange things so that they conform to this end. In any case, in talking about the past we lie with every breath we draw.

—WILLIAM MAXWELL, *So Long, See You Tomorrow*

Remind Me Again What Happened

Claire

The last photo the nurse found on my camera was of an ice cream vendor on a stone street in Mysore. Now that I'm home again, Charlie has printed it out for me. I've placed it in my "Past Life: Work" folder. Charlie hates the way I label my absent memories, but the system has been helping me. All those weeks ago in the hospital, the doctor told me that this photograph helped his staff come up with my diagnosis. Before all of this doctor's sleuthing work, before my induced coma, before all my bumps and bruises, I had been in a hotel overlooking the sea. I had asked the concierge to bring me some tea and Tylenol. I was too tired to move and I felt like I was coming down with a fever, or that's what I'm told I said to the stranger at the other end of the phone line. When the young man from room service came to the door, however, I didn't answer. Instead he heard a lamp break, so he found a maid and together they entered the room with her key. They reported they found me thrashing on the floor. An ambulance was summoned and brought me to the hospital. I don't remember any of this. It remains a blank space in my memory. The hotel staff, the nurses, and Charlie, my ever-dutiful husband, have helped fill in the gaps.

It was only when, days later, Charlie sat by my bedside, showing me the most recent images on my camera, trying to trigger my memory, that the doctor peered over Charlie's shoulder. "How long were you in India?" he asked.

"Close to six months," Charlie answered for me.

"We may have found the culprit." The doctor smiled eagerly, and I suppose we were meant to take this as good news, though I'm sure neither of us felt like celebrating. The doctor patted Charlie's back in congratulations, for us or for him, it was all the same. Two men congratulating one another for their fine detective work. I have to imagine most of this scene, filling out the scribbled notes I've written in my notebook. It would still be a few more days before Rachel arrived. I had asked Charlie to call her. I needed my best friend, and I wanted an ally. It's funny what stays and what goes in a malfunctioning brain. I still had—have—my instincts.

A mosquito bite. A simple nibble, one of hundreds that had poked at my skin, but this one came with a virus. Japanese encephalitis, the doctor explained, as if the news were a gift. I was lucky I was not dead. I was unlucky that I was part of the 30 percent whose natural immunities couldn't shrug off the worst manifestations of the virus. High fever, seizures, damage to the central nervous system. This is why Charlie often answers questions for me and tells me what did and did not happen. Just as he helped me put together the fragments of those first memories in the hospital and the details of the days that followed, he continues to do this now, many months later. There is a smudge where my memories are supposed to be.

THREE MONTHS HAVE passed since that hospital room in Florida. Rachel has gone into town. Charlie dropped her off on his way to the office a few hours ago. They both looked exhausted this morning, and the kitchen was silent as they prepared their tea and English muffins. Now, I am alone in the garage. Rachel is gone but she has left me these neat piles of my life, unpacked from boxes and arranged in careful stacks on the garage floor. She is a better friend than I probably deserve. I am surrounded. There are labels: "Work." "Childhood." "NY Office." "Grad School/Our House." "India/New Projects." When I look out the front window, this is what I see. Every day, I take a picture to help me remember and keep track of reality.

There has been a mosquito buzzing around my head for a while now, and eventually I let it settle on the exposed skin of my calf, just where my rumpled sock leaves the edge of my jeans. It is too late in the year for the insect still to be alive, and I am impressed by its will. I watch it land and poke its little snout along my bumpy skin. Such a small creature, and such a gentle pressure and the slightest sting. How can something so tiny take away so much? I wonder what other blood is mixing with mine, and I wonder what might happen to the next person it bites. Rationally I know I'm not contagious, but there are times when I think my loopiness and my emptiness might infect other people. I let the mosquito think it's safe, I let it have its snack, but I feel the anger building inside me. I am stealthy, and then I strike. My palm comes down hard on its little head, and my blood and the blood of whoever or whatever was bitten before me splatters in a very tiny puddle on my leg. I flick the mosquito off me and rub away the blood with the edge of my sweater. I return to the piles around me.

I'm finding it easy to drift through the stacks of the distant past. My memories open up like old home movies. I see my mother, alive again, and can almost imagine her sitting here with me, going through the old photos, confirming my past. My mother, young, smelling of jasmine and talcum powder. The streets of my old town extend from my memory; I walk home from school along Woodsgate Road, and as I turn the corner toward our house, I see Ralph and Patsy in the window, their little heads bobbing from the force of their tails wagging. Their breath fogs up the window, and I wave to them. My mother will be in the TV room watching *Days of Our Lives* with her anatomy books spread out over the table. She will have given up studying for the day. She has polished her toenails and there are stained cotton balls tossed around on the floor, the couch.

There will be a glass of juice, grown slightly too warm, on the counter waiting for me, along with two Chips Ahoy! cookies on a small plate. Next to my snack, chicken or veal will be defrosting on a platter, assuming it's not pizza night. My father will come home three hours from now. I will kick the soccer ball around in the backyard with my neighbor Jenny or I will do math problems on my yellow plastic desk. My mother will put on a Jim Croce album or Cat Stevens or Joan Baez, and she will hum along to it or talk on the phone or start pounding the chicken with a rolling pin, and sometimes all three at once.

I am a messy kid and I have a clumsily made bed with a rainbow comforter. I give my stuffed animals turns on the bed; they are in constant rotation for the prime spot on my green pillows. I am methodical in my fairness. I have never played with dolls, but I am convinced my stuffed animals have feelings and I treat them as confidantes and I make sure that their feelings are never hurt. I do not play favorites.

I know that my mother is sick; she has cut back her hours in her graduate program. She watches more TV than she ever has before. She talks to herself and I talk to my stuffed animals. My father tousles my hair when he comes home and refuses to look me in the eyes. This is how I know for sure that my mother is not doing well. My father watches her and she watches me. She goes over my math homework, quizzes me on my spelling, and asks who has the prime spot on my bed tonight. When I sleep, I have space under each arm for one of my friends. I choose one and let Mom choose the other— tonight it will be Snowball and Pigsty. Ralph or Patsy hurries around as my mother bends to kiss me good night. She didn't eat much dinner, but still her breath smells of garlic and basil. She leaves the door open a crack to let the hall light in. I have bad dreams and I am afraid of the dark. I will always have night terrors. I will always lose my breath in fear at what I see, eyes open, in the darkness of all my subsequent bedrooms. I listen to my parents' voices and the sounds of the TV. I don't sleep; I only pretend. It will always be this way.

Do you see how much I remember?

SINCE THERE WERE no other witnesses, here is my version of waking up in the hospital, and you will have to take my word for it.

I woke up in a buzzing room and Charlie wasn't there. I still blame him for that. I think it would have helped to see him straightaway. And I wonder, if he had been with me beforehand, in the hotel room, if he hadn't been delayed, would he have seen the signs of my fever sooner, would he have gotten me to the hospital when there was more they could have done? Before the fever spiked. Before the seizures began.

Instead of Charlie, the first thing I saw in that dank, unpleasant room was the shadow of a fan cast on moldy walls. Everything else was awash in blankness. It was humid. Too humid for a hospital, I thought. And then I began to remember that I was far from home. But perhaps *remember* isn't quite the right word. I sensed that I had chosen to go away for a while, back to an old, familiar place. The heat was familiar. Charlie was supposed to meet me here, but he hadn't yet. Later I'd find a crumpled note in my bag that proved it. Written in the concierge's hand and framed with the Lighthouse Hotel border: *So sorry. Something came up. May be quite delayed. Will call soon.* No name, but I assumed from Charlie. The tone certainly carried his abrupt politeness. There are many things I still remember.

And so I lay there in an unfamiliar bed, the sheets kicked down around my ankles, waiting for someone to arrive who would tell me where I was, what was wrong with me, when

I could go home. I had a headache behind my eyes that reminded me of the migraines I have suffered ever since I was
a little girl. And there was something plastic attached to my
neck that sucked and pulled at my skin. My neck, in fact, was
breathing instead of my mouth. I can't begin to explain the
panic I felt. Nor the sense that every time I approached something like a memory, it got blotted out by a sudden shadow.
It's the same kind of sensation that comes after you stare at
the sun too long, and then as you look away, a trailing splotch
of undefined color interrupts your vision. You can sense the
many things that surround what you are looking at, but the
closer you get to the thing itself, the blinder you become.

I tried to remember. Outside this hospital room, I thought,
there is a city that leads to the sea. There is a hotel by the water, with lounge chairs sagging with heavy cotton cushions in
shades of dark orange and blue. I can feel myself lying on one
of those chairs, my fingers drawing shapes in the sand. I am
waiting for something or someone, but before I can remember
who, the sun begins to blind me again and a doctor walks in
and knocks his clipboard against the metal frame of my bed.
He has my attention. He is small and wears a neat mustache.
His skin is dark against the blue white of his doctor's coat.
"Mrs. Scott? How are you feeling?"

"My name is Claire," I answer. "Please call me Claire."

Charlie

When I get home, Claire is still in the garage with her piles of artificial memory. Every time I look at her now, multiple images appear: the Claire in front of me, the Claire I fell in love with, and the Claire struggling against her mind and body in the hospital. Out of the three Claires, there may be only one I am still in love with, and I fear that the one in front of me is not a match. And of course I loathe myself for each and every one of these thoughts.

We are still reorganizing ourselves, trying to get back into some semblance of our old life, a life, I can admit, that has not been right for some time. Our troubles started long before Claire got sick. When the doctors called me, I hadn't been in touch with Claire for several weeks. This was fairly typical. Her assignments took her to hard-to-reach places where phone connections were unreliable, and our conversations felt more like quick check-ins than real exchanges. She would let me know that she was well and whether the story was going satisfactorily or poorly; I would tell her that we had just put an issue to bed and update her on how her plants were faring. Our chats were polite and quick, and then we slipped back into our own, separate lives. Sometimes even her rushed "love yous" got cut off because of the poor connection.

When that phone call from the hospital came, though, in the early evening at the start of autumn, I felt a tremendous rush of fear, love, and confusion, and it took me a few moments to realize that the doctor was calling from the States—Florida, in fact—and not some remote clinic in Tamil Nadu. I had to brush aside a quick beat of anger—Claire was in America and hadn't let me know—as I packed my bags while the doctor went on and on about seizures, telling me that Claire had been in and out of consciousness, that it was touch and go. I had no idea what I was doing in my panic. Somehow or other, there was a flight out of Burlington to New York, and from there a connecting flight to Miami first thing the next morning, and then I would have to rent a car and travel to the Keys, a place where neither I nor, as far as I knew, Claire had ever been before.

I HARDLY REMEMBER the drive from the airport, just little blips of images—the startling blue of the ocean, the narrow causeways that led me to the Lower Keys Medical Center, where finally my vision settled and my mind registered where I was. Such a strange feeling, to follow a driveway lined with palm trees, ending at a white-and-turquoise building, blocky and outdated. The whole place felt out of sync with time. I half expected to be greeted, handed a daiquiri, and led to a lounge chair by some smartly dressed concierge in a uniform of crisp white.

The breezes were thick with humidity; it was still summer in Florida and there were few tourists. The hospital itself felt half-abandoned; the AC was faltering, and the staff had set up box fans here and there to move the stifling air about. I felt caught in its sludge. To be honest, I wanted to return to my rental car, blast some cold air against my skin, and drive away from both that place and Claire, who the doctors had informed me just that morning was still unresponsive.

Even now, so many weeks later, when my mind re-approaches the memory of walking into her room, I want to turn away and run. But instead I find myself there, led gently by a kind nurse. I remember asking, when we arrived at the room, whether we should knock, to which the nurse replied, "No need for that," and suddenly there I was, alone in a room with my unconscious wife. Her hair had gotten long. Someone had tied it into a loose ponytail, I suppose so it wouldn't get tangled in the series of tubes and wires connecting Claire to too many machines to count. Everything in the room seemed to be in perpetual movement except for Claire. A breathing machine attached to Claire's throat. Monitors that beeped erratic lines, documenting Claire's invisible inner workings. A blood pressure sleeve that sighed to life every now and then. I don't know how long I stood there, trying to decipher what these machines were telling me about my wife. I don't know if I spoke to her, or if I just hovered close to her body, silent and waiting. I was used to Claire starting the conversation. I was used to following her lead. Eventually I pulled over a chair and reached for her fingertips. The back of her hand was blackened and bruised from IV lines. Her fingers were cold and unresponsive, so I let them fall away from mine. I was horrified and, yes, a little repulsed.

How can I explain the sick, deep revulsion in my gut that crept up my back, tingled my neck? My sweat, in that humid room, felt icy. I couldn't measure the Claire in front of me with the Claire of my mind's eye. Here was only struggling body, interloper, false double. Claire had always been the strong one. And in recent months she had become so easy for me to identify as the selfish one, the brave one, the bad one, the one at fault, the one who left. And me? I had a script for myself as well. I was the loyal one, the steady one, the one who had been hurt, betrayed, the one who had stayed. But now Claire had shifted my certainties. Her silent body, suddenly vulnerable, weak, guileless, was making demands that Claire would never have made of me. Be strong, Charlie, it said. Don't run away. Say something. Comfort me. Be the first one I see when

I open my eyes. Of course, these were all projections. When Claire finally woke up, she didn't come close to saying any of these things. But she did reach for my hand and say, "Tell me what happened." I didn't know where to begin.

IT ALWAYS TAKES me a little while before I approach Claire when I return home after work. I don't know which Claire will greet me. On some days she meets me with clear eyes, with organized notes, and with a list of questions. What was her first published article? When she next meets with Dr. Stuart, can we ask him to lower the dosage of her prednisone? When we go to the grocery store, can I help her remember to pick up lemon curd? On other days her gaze is foggy. Rachel might be rubbing her back as they look through an old photo album. I know, right away, the days when she's had a grand mal seizure that has left her in bed for the majority of the day, flipping through TV shows or scolding herself for laziness and another memory's escape from her grasp. On other days she's got fury in her eyes. The physical therapist was patronizing or she lost her balance on the stairs or she couldn't find an old postcard from her father that she was sure was in one particular box.

I can tell that today has been a good day. When I enter the garage, Rachel is sitting with her, and together they have been sorting through boxes from our graduate school days. Rachel is wearing a mangy-looking knitted scarf that Claire began, but never finished, when she was asked to join a short-lived knitting group. Claire is sifting through a stack of old VCR tapes. I recognize some of the titles: *Vertigo*, *The Third Man*, *Charade*, *The Big Sleep*. She's unearthed our noir phase, I see. Neither of them looks up from the boxes when I come in. Rachel's chin is resting on Claire's shoulder and they are speaking in hushed voices, a conspiracy of remembrance. I am jealous for a moment before the calm of just watching them takes over. I can pretend, however briefly, that we have all been transported back to a happier time. All three of us coming and going in Rachel's parents' brownstone in Brookline. Watching old movies with a makeshift dinner on our laps. Assignments cast to the side for a spell as we drink wine and marvel at the cigarettes, the femmes fatales, and the thick shadows on the television screen. A happier time for me, certainly. Less so for Rachel, I imagine. I wondered, and even now still wonder, if she was putting on a show for all our benefits, always masking her own sadness for the sake of our shared equilibrium. She may be doing the very same thing in our garage this early evening. Selfless, stoic Rachel. She would probably hate to know I see her this way.

I shift in the doorway, and Claire and Rachel look up at the same time, displaying a little pleasure, perhaps also a little annoyance, in seeing me. Rachel waves and pushes a milk crate in my direction. "Take a seat," she says, leaving her hand on Claire's back.

Claire pushes onto her knees and kisses me on the cheek. "Welcome home, Charlie," she says in a slightly too boisterous voice. She smells of my soap, and also of mothballs. "We thought we could watch this tonight." She places *Vertigo* in my hand. The tape is dusty. I have no idea where the VCR is.

"Seems like an appropriate choice." I find it hard to smile lately, and yet I am always, always trying.

"That's what Rachel said too." Claire smiles at Rachel; Rachel smiles at me. We make a triangle of good intentions. This is a good start to the evening for all of us.

"Do we even have a VCR anymore?" I ask. It is a foolish question. None of us will have the answer.

"We can stream it off Netflix. I have an account." Rachel stands up and unwraps the half-finished scarf. "I'm going to start dinner. I picked up some scallops and leeks at the co-op." She kisses the top of Claire's head as she goes and gently traces her fingers across my shoulder.

When she leaves, Claire studies the neat piles of memories stacked all around her. We are quiet in each other's company these days. There are too many questions we want to ask each other, but I sense neither of us knows how. We both use Rachel to fill in our silences, and we are sheepish with each other when we are alone.

Claire takes the film back from me. She turns it over in her hands a few times. "Rachel says this is an appropriate choice."

I look at her closely. I do this every time she trips over something recently said. It brings out the worst in me. I get impatient. I don't trust her. I don't think she's trying hard enough. I think she's pretending. "Yes, we've already gone over that." I know my words are harsh and I feel guilty immediately.

"Right." She begins to stand up.

I go to her, place my hands into the warmth of her armpits, and lift as if she is a child.

"I can manage, thanks." She smiles but I know she is upset with me. "Let's go get in Rachel's way." She walks to the mudroom door and concentrates on every step she takes on every stair. Every movement comes with a hesitation. She turns to me and waves me toward her.

"In a minute," I say. I start repacking the videos as Claire enters the house. I am not so interested in what fills these boxes that she has put out today. They hold memories that are safe and easy. It is some of the other memories I am keen to have her explore. There are boxes that I want to empty out at Claire's feet, to force her memory to make sense of the more recent past, force her to retrace all the reasons why she left me and all these old boxes behind.

Rachel

lthough it's been several days since I arrived, I still feel strange in this house with Charlie and Claire. I'm used to the three of us being in my house—my parents' house—in Boston. Or I'm used to Claire, alone, being there with me on her quick visits back to the States. Before the hospital in Florida, it had been almost two years since I'd seen Charlie, although we do write to each other regularly and occasionally have halting conversations on the phone that tend to focus on Claire and her absence. I have never told him about the many times Claire came to visit me without him. Nor about the confessions she has made to me only after I promise not to reveal them, usually after we have finished a bottle of wine out on my parents' back porch. It has been my porch, of course, for too many years now, but I am as stuck in the past as my two friends, it seems. Up until recently, Claire had been the one pushing forward and away, and I have to admit, her drifting filled me with a tangle of emotions I'd rather not admit: jealousy, smug satisfaction, anger. She was providing me with a passive revenge, which, if I can be honest with myself, is the only kind of revenge I'm probably capable of.

But then there was Charlie's call from the airport and later his strangled voice on the phone from Florida. Please come, he had managed to say. I need you. And that was all it took to collapse the distance created by all the years that had passed since Claire and Charlie moved away. I made travel arrangements in a blur, much as I imagined Charlie had done, and I felt his proximity, and Claire's too, more than I had in a very long time.

In my memory, I was always the one who needed help. When my parents died and my two best friends moved here to look after me, I collapsed into their care like a rag doll. I don't think I prepared a meal for myself for three months. If it hadn't been for Claire and Charlie, I wouldn't have finished grad school. I wouldn't have clipped my fingernails. I wouldn't have boxed my father's clothes and dropped them off at the Goodwill. If it weren't for them, I'd most likely still be living (if I were living at all) in a dirty heap, surviving off inheritance and take-out food in my childhood bedroom.

NOW, I'M USUALLY the one who prepares dinner in Charlie and Claire's kitchen. I am soothed by the errands I run—to the local co-op, to the farmers' market, to the bakery. I like it when Charlie's car fills up with the smell of sourdough bread and fresh greens and trout. I think back to the meals we used to share, the experiments we tried in my parents' kitchen, all exercises meant to cheer me up and provide me with distractions. I have become a good cook, even though I usually have only myself to feed. Here I make grilled salmon on the back porch; I roast potatoes with rosemary and olive oil. I bake apple pies in the late afternoon, so that the house grows saturated with sweet autumn smells. The nights are getting quite cold, and I like to fill us up with warm, heavy food to help us grow sleepy and quiet as the day winds down.

Even though everyone is trying very hard to be kind and patient with one another, there are sparks of tension that fuse unexpectedly. It happens if Claire has spent too long in the garage and has forgotten to take her nap. If Charlie pushes Claire too hard to remember some event important to him but lost to her. If Claire forgets to take her noontime meds or if Charlie scolds her for misplacing her calendar. And of course there are the triggers that Claire can't possibly understand she is responsible for. She doesn't remember the hurt she caused Charlie with her increasing months away on assignment. She doesn't remember that the last time she came to the States, she asked Charlie to meet her in New York instead of coming home to their house. She doesn't remember Charlie's trip to India to visit her or the reasons why he left early. When she asks Charlie questions about their home (Who chose to put the carpet there? Do I even like antique furniture? Why did we choose to live so far from town?), she can't know the resentments and injured feelings she is drawing out. What is Charlie supposed to do with all that pent-up anger? What am I supposed to do with mine?

I do my best to ignore the old hurts and confusion. I cook and clean and take Claire for short walks up and down the dirt road. We crunch over leaves while Charlie is at work. I help Claire make piles of things from her past, bring her sweaters and hats when the chill encroaches. I try to repay her for her kindnesses to me all those years ago. She is giving me a chance to forgive her, and I hope I am strong enough to take it.

WHEN I GOT to the Keys, I checked into Charlie's hotel and stared at the swimming pool from my window for far too long. Its turquoise water was shimmering from a late summer breeze, and behind it was the sea, dotted with regal sailboats whose grace hurt my mind. I had never been to Florida, nor had I ever looked out on a vacation paradise that offered up umbrella drinks without irony. I remember thinking I should have packed a bathing suit, then hating myself for the thought. My eyes felt too big for their sockets. I had been traveling and crying for over ten hours straight. I turned away from the window, took an icy shower, and then headed out to meet Charlie at the hospital.

When I first arrived, the nurses wouldn't let me into Claire's room because I wasn't family, so I roamed the hallways and attempted to do some work in the waiting room, soap operas blasting from the television, as others received good and bad news around me. The waiting room was a strange place. The other hospital visitors smelled like sunscreen and ocean, their tanned skin suggesting an interrupted vacation. Beyond that room, there was the sea, the tourist trolleys taking people to Old Town, the hum of mopeds and rustling palm trees.

I wanted to explain to the ICU nurses that I was, in fact, Claire's family. If I had claimed to be Claire's sister, would they have asked me for proof? Charlie had made the mistake of identifying me as a friend. The nurse had apologized, explained their policy in the ICU, and directed me to the waiting room with further instructions on how to get to the cafeteria and the guest shop and back onto the streets of Key West, where I might be more comfortable waiting. Claire was in an induced coma, for how long, the doctors couldn't say. Charlie was already feeling guilty for summoning me, but I had told him, truthfully, that I was there for him as much as for Claire. I had never heard him sound so terrified, so uncertain, as when he had called only the day before. Before he had hung up, he managed to say, "She might not make it. I don't understand, Rachel. She was awake when I arrived and seemed only a little shaky, but then, suddenly a switch flipped in her brain and she was gone again." Charlie explained that after her last seizure, the doctors felt it would be safer for her to be kept in a drugged sleep until they got a handle on what was causing the inflammation in her brain.

During the plane ride, I was surprised to find that I was talking to myself, whispering promises that Claire would be okay. She had always been the strong one. This time I would hold her hand and make sure she knew that she wasn't alone, that she would get better and be herself again in no time. Later, in the hospital, I walked through the hallways making similar promises, practicing what I would say to Claire once she opened her eyes and I was allowed to touch her skin, move the hair out of her eyes, help her stand and walk out of that place where none of us belonged.

If the staff had been willing to listen, I would have explained to them how Claire and Charlie and I were family. We had adopted one another more than ten years ago. First Claire had moved in, and then Charlie a couple of months later. Living in what had been my parents' house, we painted rooms and moved furniture and stained the stove with overly ambitious cooking. We filled each other's absences and made a new family in the process. But rules were rules at the hospital, and the only encounter I had been able to have with Claire was a stolen glimpse into her room when no one was around. Charlie acted as my lookout as I pushed against the heavy door and then the dreary curtains. And there she was, almost unrecognizable, a tube hissing at her neck, monitors telling the secrets of her blood and breath. I still wish I hadn't looked in.

In the evenings, I made Charlie leave the hospital with me. We walked through the touristy streets of Old Town, holding hands while neither of us talked. Eventually one of us pulled the other into a fish restaurant and we went through the motions of ordering a meal that neither of us really tasted, while the cheery wait staff offered us another beer or margarita. I could sense their need to brighten our mood, and we tried to smile and be pleasant and might even have grown a little bit tipsy. On the way back to the hotel, we leaned into each other's exhaustion, and laughed at the posters of Hemingway impersonators or the shockingly blue drinks that appeared in the bars lining our walk home, and agreed that only Claire could have brought us to this place.

Claire had always been the one who created our adventures. In our first year of graduate school, it had been Claire who insisted I renew my passport, who then insisted we use our financial aid loans to go to Barcelona, who landed us both jobs at the Washington Square Tavern that summer to pay back some of the money we had spent on our travels. She was the one who had gotten Charlie to travel all the way to the other side of the world, to risk a sunburn, and to taste unfamiliar foods. Even after they had moved to Vermont, she had been the one who was always exploring, her curiosity pushing against the borders of our day-to-day lives. Charlie and I had always looked to her for what came next, and there we now were, baffled and paralyzed without our guide.

It had been a long time since Charlie and I were alone in each other's company. Because we were tired and drunk and because there was such a sense of festive play all around us, for brief moments it almost felt like we had taken a vacation together. I couldn't help thinking about our earliest moments of friendship, a few years before either of us had met Claire. We had wandered a very different coastline together, a colder one, in England, very young and clumsy in our flirtation. I had tried to ignore most of those memories over the years, but there they were, announcing themselves at perhaps the most inappropriate time.

While my mind wandered, Charlie translated the conversations he'd been having with the doctors. Claire had been brought in with a high fever. Her seizures had been severe. The induced coma would allow her body to calm and start to repair itself. Her brain would have been traumatized from all the swelling and the seizures. It would be impossible to know the extent of the damage until she woke up. He squeezed my hand and leaned into my shoulder. He draped his arm across my back.

When we got to the hotel, he left me there and returned to the hospital to sleep beside Claire in a reclining chair. In the morning, I brought him coffee and a pastry from the bakery in our hotel.

Our job was to wait. We were instructed to be patient. In case she had memory loss, we were told to be prepared with photographs and stories. Our presence alone might help her reorient herself. We were told to be prepared for her confusion, her anger, her fear, her anxiety. Our job was and continues to be to remind her that she is not alone, that we are with her to help her navigate from here to wherever *there* might be.

Claire

I have been trying to find my way back into this house. It is filled with things I recognize, but encountering them is like returning to a bed-and-breakfast I might have visited once. The plates in the cupboards have scalloped edges and floral stenciling. There are coasters on every table next to stacks of magazines. I held one of these frilly bits of nonsense in my hand the other night while Charlie and I sat silently in front of the television and Rachel cleaned up in the kitchen. When I asked Charlie if we picked these things out together, he laughed at me. "They're hand-me-downs from my parents' old place. My mother sent them to us after the wedding. Are you serious? They aren't exactly your taste, Claire."

"Then what are they doing in our house?" I asked in return. It seemed like a logical question, and I really don't think I meant to be aggressive when I asked it, but Charlie remained still as stone and kept his eyes on his show, a BBC production, some kind of detective drama. I hadn't been following it very well and had reached for a magazine, which is when I had picked up the coaster and asked my question about it. It is important that I keep track of the cause and effect of our anger toward each other these days, because if I don't, I really can't make sense of it at all. I have been tracking Charlie's sighs, the deep, exaggerated ones he offers while he works hard at not looking at me. On the day of the coaster question, my tally came to six.

The hardwood floors of this house creak underfoot and are scratched with wear. Shredded area rugs cover empty spaces here and there, so torn at the edges that you'd think we had a puppy in the house, but I don't think we've ever had a pet. We certainly don't now, though I think I might like one to help interrupt the careful stillness that exists between Charlie and me. When I go into the kitchen, I open the cabinets and try to guess what I'll find in them. I roam the house, touching surfaces and smelling candles. I have been back here for 23 days, but it might as well be 223. Everything feels like an expected surprise, if such a thing is even possible.

The strangest things to discover are the framed photographs here and there. I look at myself in these pictures. I am in a wedding dress in one, and in another I am sitting on a beach in an orange bikini with black flowers. I touch my belly, feel the contours of my body, and wonder how long ago the picture might have been taken, whether my body might fit into something like that bikini today. On the bookshelf I see a photo of myself wearing a dusty smile, a camera around my neck. I look fearless. I see Charlie as a child, his parents on either side, hands resting on his shoulders. He looks just as serious then as he does these evenings. I want to tell his younger self a joke; I want to tell him he needs to loosen up a little.

I think to myself that I could never have chosen this house that talks to me with every step I take through it. I would not have arranged these photographs in such perfect order along the bookshelves. I would not have minded the stains left behind on countertops from perspiring glasses or the dribble of wine. I am not allowed to drink anymore. My medications won't allow it—the antiseizure "cocktail" (isn't that funny?) that my doctors have come up with does not mix well with alcohol. Once we fine-tune the cocktail, they tell me, I'll start to get my energy back. I'll be less loopy and sluggish. The things they warn me I'll never get back: my driver's license, my hand-eye coordination, and most of my memories from the age of seventeen to thirty-four. We call this memory loss my black hole. We try to laugh about it, all of us—the doctors, Charlie, Rachel, and me. But at the same time, we are skeptical and hopeful. Perhaps there is a way back to those memories, after all, we think. Charlie, for one, is insistent about it.

I HAVE A bald spot. I fell down in the kitchen a few days ago and I hit my head on the tiles and split open my scalp. Charlie was beside himself. "Dear God, Claire. What have you done? Hold this; press it here. Get in the car." He drove with his jaw clenched, sweat collecting at his temples. I wish it had been Rachel who took me to the doctor. She has remained strikingly calm and dependable over these past weeks. But she let me go alone with Charlie after draping a shawl over my shoulders and kissing my cheek.

In the car, I reassured my husband. "I'm fine, Charlie. Really. It doesn't even hurt that much." It actually felt good to be out of the house. I opened the window to feel the speed of Charlie's driving. It is terrible of me, but I enjoyed his sense of panic. Sometimes I strive to get a reaction out of him. He is calm in a much different way from Rachel, as if he is perpetually gritting his teeth to keep some secret words from getting out.

"Do you feel faint?" Charlie rolled all the windows down. My hair twisted in the wind, wrapped itself around my neck. I was writing everything down in the dark of the car in fumbling lines, with one hand still pressed to my head.

"Must you write in that thing right now? All the time?" Charlie stared at the road in front of us.

"You started it, Charlie. You can't be angry with me now." I took the dish towel from my head. It was saturated.

Charlie looked at me. "Good God," he said. "Please stop writing. If you forget anything, I'll help fill in the details later."

I put the journal away to calm him, but I wouldn't ask for his details later. It didn't work that way.

THE DOCTOR GAVE me five stitches and some ibuprofen, consulted with the neurologist, and discussed my antiseizure "cocktail." Up the phenobarbital. Reduce the prednisone. Let's not go back to the Dilantin. I have it all written down in my meds log, but Charlie is the one who fills my daily pills container. The nurse shaved off a patch of my hair so that the doctor could put the stitches in.

The next day, I asked Charlie to take me to his barber so I could get my whole head buzzed. It would feel better that way, I said. More symmetrical. I thought it would look good, but Charlie clearly was trying hard not to be appalled. "But your hair, Claire," he said. "It's always been so lovely."

When we got to the barber's, I met Charlie's troubled gaze in the mirror. "It'll grow back, Charlie. Don't look so glum. It's only hair, after all."

Even the barber looked uncertain. "Don't mind him," I told the barber. "It's my head. He'll get used to it." The barber shrugged his shoulders and offered Charlie a quick apology.

And so my hair was all shaved off, and there was my face, staring back at me. What can I say? I looked a bit strange. My ears seemed enormous and my mouth was so very small. The scar on my neck seemed even more pronounced. I touched the soft fuzz of my neck and smiled. "Now we get to watch it grow back!" I was trying to make all three of us feel better. The barber looked guilty; Charlie looked anguished. But I felt worlds lighter.

THE FEELING OF lightness was short lived, though. I always feel even more restless and burdened when I return from my visits with Dr. Stuart. His questions race around my mind. Who is the president? What do you remember about your job? Did you like being a journalist? What was the weather like in Pondicherry? What was the name of your first dog? When did you first feel guilty about hurting someone else's feelings? What is your favorite flavor of ice cream? I feel like I am answering a questionnaire or maybe taking some kind of psychological torture test that will somehow dictate the rest of my life. What if my favorite flavor of ice cream is strawberry and not coffee as I answered? What if making Stevie Norris cry on a field trip to Old Sturbridge Village wasn't something that I did that made me feel guilty? I get impatient with the questions and I fear I am a terrible patient. During my last visit, I think I even shouted at my poor doctor. "So, what you're telling me is that I may never drive again?"

He shrugged his shoulders. Like a lot of people lately, he sometimes looks a little bit frightened of me.

"What does that mean?" I exaggerated his shrugging. "You've got to keep me hopeful, Dr. Stuart," I said, trying to smile, to calm both of us. "Go ahead and lie to me if you have to. I need to believe that I'll be able to drive again, get on a plane again to another time zone, go swimming in the ocean."

The doctor nodded and looked at my chart. "The important thing is that you're making progress, Claire. Try to be patient. The other things will come when your body is ready for them."

He is trying to be helpful and kind; I know this. But I am not good at being patient. I am angry ("This is normal,

Claire") and frightened ("Who wouldn't be, Claire?) and growing increasingly resentful about his notes and my mysterious chart and the directions he murmurs to Charlie when they huddle in the corner as I politely sip water in the waiting room. ("Don't blame Charlie. He's only following the doctor's orders.")

I keep notes of our conversations so I don't forget them. Before Charlie comes to pick me up, I scribble them down so that I don't forget what the doctor has forbidden me to do or, on rare occasions, reluctantly allowed me to start trying. Like drinking a little bit of caffeine now and then. A sip or two of wine is fine, but just a sip. A longer walk if Charlie or someone else is there to keep me company. I take notes like a good student, and I nod to show how eager I am to take on more. "Baby steps," I echo, sounding a lot like a baby, in fact.

Here are some of the facts associated with my misfiring mind: Japanese encephalitis is transmitted to people through a bite by an infected mosquito. This mosquito had probably nibbled on a pig or a bird wading in still water before snacking on me. I was probably bitten while on assignment in Tamil Nadu, perhaps alongside a rice paddy or along the irrigation canals that had almost, but not completely, run dry. The minuscule remains of the flood catchment area, the focus of my article, were also most likely the source of my virus. From 1973 to 2010, there were only fifty-eight reported cases of the virus among travelers living outside Asia. Many of those travelers died; others were lucky to have immune systems that fought off the virus. I am part of the 30 percent of survivors who suffer lasting damage to their nervous system. I am both lucky and terribly unlucky. I have survived, but I am forever altered.

My doctors inform me matter-of-factly that it makes perfect sense that I have my black hole. They talk about my brain as if it were a mesmerizing discovery, an uncharted, unpredictable planet. The virus and all those subsequent seizures damaged my temporal lobes. They tell me that these lobes are responsible for forming new memories ("a process called consolidation"). This area of the brain also stores memories, hence the soupy nothingness that has replaced where my twenties should be. The doctors reassure me that all my symptoms make sense! Some days, the doctors tell me, I won't remember their names. They won't be offended, they say with a laugh. Some days, I won't remember my honeymoon no matter how hard I try, they say. But you must try. Every brain is different in how it responds and how it copes. Charlie nods along with them. When I come home to Rachel, she fills my sensory world with memories to help me remember my honeymoon and many other things. Research has told her that smells and sounds can trigger recollection, so she prepares meals from the days we all lived together; she tracks down old CDs—the Breeders and Mazzy Star and Luna—that echo the shows we went to at the Paradise; she spreads out photo albums for us to sort through together.

I CAN TELL you, even with this black hole of mine, that I know I have always been a messy person. I like a little clutter and dust on the edges of things. I have always had the tendency to misplace a single shoe from its pair. I leave dishes in the sink and keep the radio on even if I'm watching TV. I am committed to my mess and that is why I can say with complete confidence that I don't belong here. This place doesn't feel like home. Charlie doesn't feel like home either. I think he is determined to make me feel like a stranger here.

Charlie told me that I was delusional in the hospital. He explained this to me after he returned from work last Friday. He said that for several days I accused him of trying to kill me, of imprisoning me in a jail that was only made to look like a hospital. I accused him of hiring actors to play the roles of doctors and nurses and slowly poison me. The real doctors couldn't figure out what was causing these paranoid notions—whether they were muddled aftereffects of my seizures, or some kind of drug fever from an allergic reaction to one of my medications, or ICU psychosis, a not-uncommon phenomenon among patients who linger in the ICU too long. "It's meant to be a transient place," Charlie said by way of clarification as he continued to describe my unruliness. I hate when he talks to me like I'm a child.

I snapped back at him, "I know, Charlie. People either die there quickly or recover enough to be transferred to a main floor." I imagine myself in that windowless room, a breathing tube coming out of my neck, and restraints on my arms. Charlie thinks I'm lucky that I don't remember any of this. Perhaps he is right. And yet he insists on filling my head with his memories. What I find amazing is how I can feel so much guilt and humiliation without my own memories to attach these reactions to. Charlie is a very good storyteller.

I CANNOT TELL you much about last week or the week before, but the doctors insist that my short-term memory will improve with time, as they keep tinkering with the balance of my medications. I can tell you that it is autumn in Vermont—I can see the season outside these windows, the leaves just past their radiant brightness.

I cannot tell you about unpacking my bags or if I asked where all my things are, because frankly I am not certain what things I have or what things I should be searching for. But I do remember Charlie pouring us some tea on our first evening back here and adding a few drips of honey and milk and then taking mine away before I could protest, murmuring, "I forgot you prefer yours with lemon." I really couldn't say if he is right. But I did end up drinking my tea with lemon and enjoying it.

I know that my parents are dead. I can describe the house I grew up in, nestled into the Berkshires. I can tell you the name of my second-grade teacher—Mrs. Pierce—and I can tell you the name of our class bully—Freddy Maloney—who had shockingly red eyelashes and eyebrows. I can tell you how I got the scar in the very center of my forehead, but I was too young when it happened to remember the fall itself, which sent my head into a stone stair.

But I cannot tell you about my last work assignment or the half-finished story on my computer that Charlie presented me with today. "It's quite a good story, Claire," he said as he pulled a chair up to an old desk in the study. "I think it'd be good for you to read it and see what you'd been up to before this accident." Charlie talks about my fevers and seizures and still-to-be-determined diagnosis as if I had been injured in a car accident. He is having trouble accepting that the tiniest mosquito bite could overturn our lives. I am a mystery to my doctors and to Charlie and Rachel, a puzzle to be worked out. You have always been so lively, so healthy, so strong, Charlie tells me. It just doesn't make any sense. Here is one thing we can agree on.

I AM A clumsy typist, but amid the typos, my article describes a hunger strike in the province of Karnataka in southern India over rights to a waterway. After reading this, I can tell you that one senior official from the BJP believes that water will become a life-and-death issue for the people of Tamil Nadu, and wars may be fought over the Cauvery River. I can describe the photographs that accompany my incomplete story—the rich, green paddies and farms of Kerala, which, downriver, become the arid, yellowed landscape of Tamil Nadu. In one photo, a young boy, shoeless, leans up against a hoe and squints into my lens. I listen for my own voice in this distant story and I seek my own internal eye, which snapped these images and has them tucked away somewhere in my misfiring brain. But there is nothing here that I can confidently claim as my own, nothing apart from a vague sense of familiarity, no different than coming up

against any famous image—the Dorothea Lange photograph
of the migrant mother, for instance, or the naked child running down the streets of Vietnam, or Avedon's photograph of
Marilyn Monroe. None of these would seem more personally
my own than the next.

Today is Monday, and Charlie went to the newspaper offices, and Rachel joined him in town to catch up on her own
work, and even though I wasn't supposed to I took a walk on
my own. I rummaged through a bin of old clothes—for some
reason, everything of mine is boxed away in various closets—
and created a mismatched outfit of wool and corduroy. It
looked cold outside, sunny but breezy, so I put on Charlie's
too-big hat with its flaps over my ears and his too-big gloves
and smacked my hands together to encourage myself. I
thought about leaving behind a trail of some kind—marbles
or stones—but I wanted to prove to myself that I could still
get from here to there on my own. No one seems to trust me

these days; the least I can do is to try to trust myself. I put Charlie's digital camera in my pocket.

Charlie's house—our house—is nestled in the woods. Aside from the farm across the road, we are surrounded by oaks and maples, and today the colors were almost shocking. It is the second week of October and the sluggish afternoon light slanted through the trees, leaving half the landscape in shadow and the other half brilliant with foliage. I took a picture of our house in the angling light, the spindly shadows of trees hugging the roof. It was still warm when I left, but I knew it wouldn't be for long, and when I got to the dirt road, I chose left, the direction I thought would lead me toward town.

What I imagined, or perhaps remembered, was that the road went on like this, dusty and pebbly and rutted, for a mile or so, and then it would meet a bridge where it would become paved and drift down, down, down, always shifting left, until it met another road, and then a covered bridge, and then some semblance of a village center. As I walked, I pieced this town together in my memory. An antique shop that was almost always closed that had once been a mill of some kind. A little white house with green shutters that claimed to be the post office. A full-service gas station with a little café inside that always smelled of fried eggs and bacon. I walked, and with each step I kept enlarging this town in my mind. I kicked at the dirt under my feet and snapped an image of the poof of dust that hid my hiking boot. And then I shot an image of my footprint in the dried-out road.

I walked up to the neighbor's fence and took a picture of

their sullen-looking horse, a gray-white wreck of an animal, who was standing, inexplicably, in an empty water basin. I took a picture of an orange leaf swimming in a puddle. I rested the camera on the fence and set the timer and stood in front of it with the road and the forest behind me, and I grinned, stupidly, at nothing.

I must have gotten a little farther down the road and as far as the bridge before . . . before what? A seizure? A fall? I don't know. There are a few more pictures on the computer screen as I scroll through them this evening. I am holding an ice bag against the bump on the back of my head. Charlie is downstairs, watching the *NewsHour*. He isn't talking to me right now.

I never made it into town, so I don't know if I was right to turn left or if the antique store was open or if it exists at all outside my imagined memory. There was a neighbor, an older woman named Mrs. Culver, who nearly ran me over—her words—on her way home. I was lying in the middle of the road, staring up at nothing—her words again—and nearly scared her to death. She sat me up and slowly helped me into her car. She must have known who I was, where I lived, because she deposited me here, on this couch, and called Charlie. Charlie has repeated this story to me more than once tonight, because I can't quite keep it straight in my head. But he has gotten exasperated now, and he is angry that I tried to take a walk on my own, and I feel sorry that I've made him so worried. It took a lot of arguing before he agreed not to take me back to the hospital.

I believe Mrs. Culver, and I believe Charlie, of course, but I keep seeing myself in town, sitting at the gas station café, drinking a strawberry milkshake. I can see myself taking a picture of the milkshake, but it is not here on the computer in front of me. Charlie uploaded the photos and sat me here about an hour ago before he went downstairs. He did all of this without speaking. He is frightened and angry and has left me with my pictures. The neighbor's horse is staring at me from the screen. His gaze is full of accusation too.

Charlie

Claire is obviously restless and I can't blame her. Her body, even if her mind doesn't remember, is used to movement. She is always tapping her feet or shredding scraps of paper with impatient fingers or biting her nails, getting up and then sitting back down again, seemingly forgetting the task that set her in motion in the first place. She can't read a book—she tells me that she loses track of characters, plots, names. So I give her the newspaper, and she complains that all the current conflicts, leaders, villains, heroes, even some of the places, are unfamiliar to her. It took me fifteen minutes the other night to fill her in on the conflict in Syria.

These games of catch-up are quite shocking to me, these gaps in her memory. She's the one who used to lecture me on my current-event laziness. Your curiosity doesn't extend beyond the Champlain Valley, she used to say to me accusingly as she listed the junior senators from South Dakota and Virginia as quickly as she named the candidates in the race for Bangladesh's most recent elections.

When I hand her the paper lately, she takes it as if it's her punishment. She scowls at the headlines and contemplates her ink-stained fingers. All the while, she keeps her notebooks near her, and writes down the names of politicians, and documents a running list of conflicts, organized by region and then by country. She sits with her feet tucked up under her and a pen sucked between her teeth. She is still recognizable to me, even if she feels like a stranger to herself. She has sat like this, contorted and in deep concentration, for all the years I have known her. All her pens have bite marks on them. She has always worn trousers under her skirts so she can sit at any angle she wants. I point these things out to her, in the hope that the continuity, even if it comes only from my memories, will soothe her, but she seems to resent my knowledge of her. Who am I to tell her who she has been over time? This is our present tug-of-war; the line in the sand is our shared past, and each of us wants to tug the other across to see it our way. I admit that I do have the upper hand these days.

She distrusts my answers, and yet she keeps asking these questions of me. Where was her last assignment? When did we last visit my parents? Where does her cousin Charlotte live these days? When did the two of us last go on vacation together? I come to her with proof in my hands: I give her the article about the fight over the Cauvery River in India, the first half of which was printed only weeks before she became ill. We have been over to see my parents only once, on the way home from our honeymoon. I show her the pictures; she is tan and I am sunburnt, and my parents smile awkwardly at the camera on its timer. Charlotte lives in Tucson these days; I hand her the Christmas card of her family, an infant whose name I forget and a small dog whose name I remember—Yapper. We have not gone on vacation together for a long, long time. My hands are empty; there are no pictures to offer her of broken plans. When she looks at me with that flash of impatience in her eyes, I want to tell her, You think I know all these things about you, Claire, but you have left me too much in the dark. I could make a long list that would rival the current events listed in your notebook of all the ways you have kept me ignorant of what was really going on in your life.

The doctors tell us to be patient, because little bubbles of memory may rise to the surface. The brain is mysterious and unpredictable, they say. They warn us that we shouldn't count on Claire's filling the black hole completely, but that we should keep trying. Claire keeps her journal and I answer questions. I have questions of my own, but I keep them to myself. I learned a long time ago what a coward I am. There have been so many times I would have liked to punish her, but now I wait for her to remember the slights and the deceit and the silences. I wait, for now, to see if she might feel a greater responsibility to me the second time around.

PERHAPS BECAUSE I have always let Claire direct things in our lives, I am not very good at being in charge, now that she is back home with me. Even when she still lived here, her daily calendar was always scribbled full of notes for conference calls, lunch dates, visits to UVM's library, and interviews with scholars in residence. I don't recognize the old Claire in this new version, confined to a chair, half-read books with broken spines spilled at her feet. She waits for me to tell her what the day's plan is, looks deflated when I tell her that we haven't much scheduled but that we could go for a quick stroll through the woods if she's up for it. We could meet Rachel in town, where she is finishing some edits on a textbook. On a daily basis, I thank God for Rachel. Without her, Claire and I would have strangled one another weeks ago. She is a quiet, patient presence around here, and I try to model myself on her kindness as much as I can. When she takes her rental car into town, as she does from time to time, I have to swallow my panic.

Our days revolve around Claire's pills. We mark time by her medicine box, two pills before breakfast, one midmorning, two more during lunch, in midafternoon, at dinner, and before bed, and suddenly the day is over without much to speak for it. I have limited my time at the paper to two days a week for now, but I think for all our sanities, I should increase it to three as soon as possible.

Our trips to the hospital break up some of the monotony. She has visits with physical therapists, occupational therapists, neurologists. I used to accompany her at these visits, but they are too depressing for me and too embarrassing for Claire. I used to try to protect Claire from whatever shame she might have been feeling as I watched her fight against elastic resistance to strengthen her atrophied muscles. Or when the neurologist asked her to walk in a straight line, toe-to-toe, as if she were a drunken teenager meeting the demands of the police officer who had pulled her over to the side of the road. The doctor would then ask her to list the names of the presidents from the present back through the past, and there was that black hole that spread open wide again, swallowing Bill Clinton and the first Bush and, lucky for her, Ronald Reagan. But now I retreat to the waiting room or take a walk to the nearby café to wait out her appointments. My presence seems to be a constant nuisance to her.

In the early visits, when pushed, she would occasionally catch a spark of memory, describe the argument her parents had over whether to vote for Jimmy Carter or the Independent candidate, Anderson, and how her mother blamed her father and people like him who voted for Anderson, and who, as far as her mother was concerned, were responsible for Reagan's taking over our sad, frightened country. She would tell me these things after her visits, her energy reawakened by the doctor's questions, until I forced her to lie down for an afternoon rest, which the doctors all urged on her, at least for the next few months. She swallowed her pills dutifully and always thanked me with careful politeness. "Thank you for taking such good care of me, Charlie," she whispered just the other day. Was there sarcasm in her voice, or have I just conditioned myself to detect it in our conversations?

"Don't be silly, Claire," I answered. I looked at her face for any kind of clue to what she was truly feeling.

"Dr. Stuart thinks my motor skills are improving."

She rested her water glass on the table and all I could see were the little tremors coursing through her fingers. I nodded.

"What do you think, Charlie? Do you think they might let me drive again soon?" Her eyes held my gaze. She was—is—so striking. Eyes that change color in the light, set far apart from each other. A slightly too-big nose. The softest fuzz along her earlobes. Crooked bottom teeth. Looking at her makes me want to weep. Or shout something awful.

I sat on the bed beside her. I hated this feeling, of somehow being the gatekeeper to her independence, even if it really was the doctors determining when certain freedoms could be offered again. "Let's just hope the seizures keep themselves at bay, and perhaps, yes, soon, we will know more about driving." A catalog was developing in my mind, of all the other things Claire hadn't mentioned, things that had always been important to her, things now forbidden. Swimming. Cycling. Long-distance travel. Bourbon with ginger ale. Late nights of animated discussions. Did she even remember any of these things enough to miss them? I must have been silent a long time.

"You can't keep me trapped here forever, Charlie," she

said. I think she was joking. "I'll find a way to escape even if they don't give me my driver's license back."

"And where shall you escape to?" I asked, not quite joking myself.

"How about first to Rachel's—I will steal her away with me—and then who knows from there. You'll have to come hunting for us. It will be like a game. Perhaps we will leave clues, or perhaps you will have to find clues on your own." Claire laughed. She had no idea what she was saying to me. I patted the bed and turned off the light and held my tongue as usual.

LAST WEEK, AFTER her fall, when I managed to calm myself enough to bring her evening meds and a cup of tea, she asked me why all her things were packed up in boxes. She didn't turn away from the computer when she asked this. A forlorn-looking horse was eyeing her from the screen, and I was struck by his relentless gaze. "What is he standing in?" I asked as I bent closer to the image. Claire smelled metallic, of dried sweat and iodine.

"A water basin, I think. It was empty. Do you think I embarrassed him?"

"He does look a bit accusatory in this shot, now that you mention it."

"That's what I thought too!" Claire laughed at the horse. "I think I humiliated him. Somehow it would have been okay if there had been water in the basin, don't you think?" She turned to me. "That way, it might have looked as if he was trying to cool himself off. But with its emptiness, he looks as if I caught him in a clumsy mistake." She turned back to the photo. "If only I could have explained to him how embarrassed I was too, unsure of my way to town."

I put the tea on the desk and placed my hand on the back of Claire's neck. She was warm and I worried that she might have caught a chill in the time it took Mrs. Culver to find her. "You feeling all right? You seem a bit feverish."

"I'm fine." She put her hand on top of mine and patted it once before peeling it away. She swiveled in her chair. There were dark circles under her eyes, and her face had grown so thin over the past weeks. "You didn't answer my question, Charlie. What's with the boxes?"

Sometimes, in these days since Claire left the hospital, she will get a knowing look in her eyes. I can't explain it exactly—just a small glint of teasing or mischief that will set me off, wondering all over again if she might be pretending, if she has built up a secure wall of innocent ignorance, of emptiness, and she has been fooling us all. And there, in front of the computer, the look had appeared again, a flicker of awareness that she was putting me in an awkward position. She was forcing me to answer a question I didn't want to confront, or, worse yet, perhaps she was making me tell her a truth she already knew, a truth she had in fact created.

"They hold your things," I answered blankly. "You and Rachel labeled them yourself, so you should know."

"I know that, Charlie. What I mean is, why are all my things packed away in the garage?"

"Part of a spring-cleaning frenzy," I said, lying. "Anything that hadn't been used or looked at in over a year went into a box. That was the decision."

"Yours or ours?" There was that smirk again.

"I believe it was your decision, Claire," I said. I looked into her face for some kind of reaction, but she just wrinkled her nose and shrugged. I sat down in the other desk chair and watched the back of her neck as she returned her gaze to the computer.

THE DOCTORS HAVE urged us to keep Claire as calm as possible, to keep her in familiar settings, to keep company to a minimum, to keep her from troubling thoughts or confusion. She should be stable, they have told us. The medicines will help. But she has brain damage, they remind us, as if we are small children. Returned swelling is a danger; she should remain as still as possible for now. They have no sense of what an impossible task this will be for us. Claire has no familiar setting. She was always off and away, two weeks in India, followed by three in Iraq, followed by a few days in Turkey. She had taken a position at the *Globe*'s South Asia desk two years ago, and for her few trips back to the States she had rented a studio apartment in Manhattan rather than choosing to return to our home. It was just too much of a hassle, traveling all that way north, she'd say by way of explanation or complaint, depending on her mood. She'd insist that I come to her, and when I protested and reminded her that I couldn't leave my job at the drop of a hat, she'd say, "Suit yourself," and a few days later, she'd be off again into a distant time zone, starting her day as I'd be drifting off to sleep.

The doctors insist that Claire can't be alone, so the closest thing she has to a familiar setting, her studio, is out of the question. I've thought about subletting it—Claire probably wouldn't know the difference—but it feels like a trespass all the same. All her former possessions and autonomy are now in my hands: her apartment key, her mailbox key, her bills and doctors' appointments and medicine vials. Her work folders and office files—her editor has sent all these things here and I have stashed them in the garage. I could go hunting if I chose to, search out the silences that have built up between us over the years, the smaller and larger lies, but for now, I'm waiting. As I said, I'm a coward.

"DOESN'T SEEM LIKE something I would do, put all my things in boxes. Rachel tells me I've always been horribly messy. That you and she were always cleaning up after me. She said you both used to complain about it, but you didn't really mind because I was the one who used to do most of the cooking and plan the parties and instigate late-night drinking games around movie trivia." She pointed to her notebook and tapped it with her finger. "Rachel says that you would have been bored out of your minds without me around, so you

didn't mind scrubbing the dishes or dealing with the laundry."
She turns the chair and smiles at me. "Looks like I'm providing entertainment for the two of you again."

And for the hundredth time that day, I tried and failed to
smile at her in return.

"Charlie, please." Claire nudged me in the side. "The
boxes? Were you kicking me out or something?"

"That's an interesting theory." I imagine my smile looked
more like a grimace. "You hadn't been home for a while." It
was all I could muster.

"Where is all my stuff, then? Where have I been?"

"An excellent question." I was still good at sarcasm when
I wanted to be. But Claire's mischievous expression had faded
away and I immediately felt guilty. "Do you remember your
apartment in New York? I was talking with you about it a
week or so ago? You kept most of your things there so you
could grab them between assignments."

"Why couldn't I just come back here?"

"It was more convenient for you to stay in New York. Your
editors were there, the main office, and your colleagues." This
was too much for me. Claire's old explanations coming out of
my mouth so that I could try to make her feel better for never
returning to me.

Claire nodded her head, but I could tell she was drifting into confusion. Perhaps it was lucky for us both that she
looked so momentarily helpless and lost in the absence of her
own memories.

I leaned over her and turned the monitor off. "You look

tired, Claire. We can talk about this more tomorrow, if you'd like. Do you think you might be ready for bed?" I never imagined that I would ever address Claire as if she were a child. I waited for a look of scorn or a roll of the eyes or anything that could point out our shared embarrassment and throw us back into our own flawed version of equilibrium.

But instead, Claire wrote something in her notebook and then held out her arm to me. "All right," she said. "You coming along too?"

"I'll help you get settled and then I'll join you a bit later, after I finish up some work."

"I know you and Rachel stay up late, playing cards and gossiping about me over several glasses of wine. I'm jealous." Claire leaned her body against mine as we shuffled to the bedroom. She stepped out of her clothes and left them in a bundle by her feet. She has never been good at putting her things away at the end of the day. She creates piles wherever she goes. When we first moved in together, I grew used to the mountains of discarded outfits that would build and build in the corners of our bedroom. And finally one day she would open her bureau drawer or stand in front of the closet, sigh into the emptiness, and then methodically fold and straighten and hang all the clothes from her piles, only to start the process all over again. She baffled me, even then, and I was amazed at the differences between us as much as I was awed by the desire that drew me toward her.

But now I can't even get used to her in my bed, the bent angles of her body taking up the space where I am accustomed to sprawling. She's right: most nights, Rachel and I stay up beyond midnight at the kitchen table. I always let Claire fall asleep before me, and when I return and watch her there in my bed, I feel like running away. Instead I grab my pillow and the flannel blanket and head for the downstairs couch. I wake before her, and when she approaches me in the morning, still bleary, and asks when I finally came to bed, I tell her that I slipped in after midnight and that she had been sound asleep. Over the years, I have become quite good at lying too.

THAT NIGHT, AFTER her fall, I stood there, watching her uncertain presence as she stood in the center of our room, her clothes at her feet, and contemplated how shrunken she had become, her belly dimpled and her socks scrunched down at her heels. I tossed her one of my old T-shirts, and as she put it on and her breasts disappeared under the BU letters, I wondered if we might ever desire one another again. These days, she looks at me with curiosity when I get out of the shower or change my clothes, but I don't sense any longing in her eyes. And as for me, I am still too twisted up with old angers and hurts. More than anything, I want her to really remember me, to encounter me with a look of real familiarity and recognition, and perhaps even regret, and maybe then I will be able to approach her again and call her to me. My Claire.

Rachel

It has been over ten years since Claire, Charlie, and I lived together. After my parents died, the two of them swooped in and took charge and helped me put my life back together. I will always be grateful to them both for getting me upright again. It is not an exaggeration to say that they saved my life.

When I returned to graduate school in Boston, my parents offered me the attic of their old brownstone to make into my own apartment. I argued with them about it, saying things like, I'm an adult now and need my own place. I needed my independence and my space. I was stubborn and ungrateful until I saw how far my stipend would go in the city, and then I reluctantly unpacked all my college things and moved into a bedroom one floor above the one I had grown up in. I was relieved and resentful at the same time, and I still feel haunted by my coldness to them when I first moved in.

Once I had made some friends and had gotten settled into my graduate school life, I condescended to sit down for a meal with my parents or join them in front of the TV for a Hitchcock marathon or join my mother for a trip to Stop and Shop. And once Claire started coming by, charming my dad with her Red Sox trivia or helping my mother set the table for a Sunday night meal, I started to appreciate my parents again. They were smart, loving people, and they made Claire, and later Charlie, feel right at home. I think they sensed, long before I did, that my two best friends were craving a sense of family. I can still picture us all together in their house that is now only mine. My father on the balcony with his pipe, Charlie at his side, arguing politics, politely coughing away the smoke that drifted toward him. Claire perched on the bar-stool, asking my mother for advice about her next semester's classes even though she had registered several weeks before. And me, trying to translate the space between past and present that had led to all these conversations circling me. I was happy and simultaneously embarrassed by my happiness. And then, only a year or so later, those moments became echoes.

After my parents were killed by a drunk driver on the Mass Pike, I locked myself in the attic and wouldn't come out. My aunts came by, opening the house with their spare keys, and banged on my door, but I wouldn't budge. My cousin Sam called to me from the other side of the door, begging me to eat some toast, take a shower, walk around the block, but I ignored her. I listened to their shuffling below me. I heard their concern and their exasperation, but I didn't care. I wanted to disappear into my covers; I wanted my bed to swallow me up and bring me to my parents. I wanted to disappear from my life. I hadn't spoken to anyone since the hospital, and I wasn't even certain my voice worked anymore. I had stopped eating. I lost track of the hours, days.

Claire kicked my door open. I remember the sound of its crashing. My room was dark, but she was illuminated by the hall lights. She smelled like the outside, early winter. She sat down on the side of my bed and told me that she wasn't leaving. Charlie was downstairs and he wasn't leaving either. He was making some tea. Then she slowly peeled away my sour clothes and led me to the bathroom, where she filled up the tub with steaming water and lavender oil and watched me as I dunked my miserable body down under the water.

OVER THE NEXT couple of months, first Claire and then Charlie moved in. Little by little, they filled up my parents' house with conversation and bustle. While I sat, despondent, on my father's favorite couch, looking over my course readings without registering a word, Claire busied herself in the kitchen and Charlie shouted at an op-ed article from the *Globe*.

These days, as I straighten up their kitchen, I think about

my mother's kitchen, which is of course mine now. I inherited my mother's slate counters and gas stove and cast iron pots too soon, but we all eventually made a home there. To repay their kindness, I am trying to help forge a peaceful ground for them in their own house.

Claire and I had met less than a year before, in our research methods course, and Charlie I had known back in England, but he was a new arrival to Boston, just like Claire. We called my parents' house, which had suddenly become my house, the Orphanage. It is an unassuming brownstone tucked away in Brookline, in the shadows of Boston. It is made of bricks and it is sturdy and there is a garden out back that I share with my neighbors and their gray tabby. Claire was the first to name the house, and she didn't mean to be cruel. She has always been matter of fact and unsentimental.

I was two years into graduate school when my parents died. Claire had lost hers long before in quick succession—her mother from cancer, her father from the strain of that loss. Charlie's parents were the only ones still living, but they were hidden away in a sleepy village in northern East Anglia. There was only one shop and one lone pub in their town. They rode their bikes to and from their little stone cottage when they did choose to venture out. I had visited them once, the year Charlie and I met, during my junior year abroad. They still remember me. They send me Christmas cards every winter. Charlie hasn't seen them in at least five years, I think. I don't know if he's told them about Claire.

Claire moved in with me, into my parents' house, when I

returned to school. She was just finishing up her degree and had been hired as a freelance journalist for the AP's Boston bureau. I changed my studies from journalism to publishing then. I found that I had lost my curiosity and my willingness to talk to most people. I got an internship working for Houghton Mifflin in their language arts section, and I still edit high school English textbooks for them, sitting at a desk next to a window that overlooks Copley Square.

Claire took possession of my parents' bedroom, an act I was grateful for, and I moved back into my childhood room. Charlie came over on the weekends and helped us with the larger projects, stripping hardwood floors, repainting all the rooms. Forest green in the dining room. A burnt orange-red in the kitchen. The smell of paint lingered in the house for a long time. It smelled of newness to me, and that, in and of itself, was a relief. I followed Claire's lead in her rearrangement of loss. As if by changing the shapes and patterns of things, we could carve out a present from the past. It wasn't exactly an act of erasure, but it was close.

I let Claire help me believe that we were all a family then—Claire, Rachel, and Charlie. The orphans. I loved them both very much.

WHEN CHARLIE AND Claire returned from Claire's hospital visit this afternoon, Claire seemed unsteady and Charlie was chewing on the inside of his mouth, never a good sign. Claire kissed me on the cheek and announced she was heading upstairs for a nap. Charlie collapsed on a chair and ran his fingers roughly through his hair. "I'll wake you in a couple of hours, then?" he called out to Claire, who was already halfway up the staircase. She stopped and stretched her torso over the banister. She winked at both of us and extended two fingers. A peace sign. And then she retreated up the stairs and Charlie let out a sigh. "I don't know what I'm doing, Rach."

Charlie hadn't held my gaze for more than a few seconds since their return, and now was no different. He rested his head in his hands and muttered toward the floor. "Tea?"

"All right," I said. "Come with me to the kitchen."

While I filled the kettle and set some crackers and cheese on a plate, Charlie sat down on the counter, his long legs dangling over the silverware drawer. The flash of him in this same position ten, maybe twelve years before, sent a pulse through me for a moment. Oh, innocent, helpless, sincere Charlie. I might not trust you this time.

"Was it a difficult day, then?" I passed Charlie the crackers. I could be patient. I'd wait for whatever information he felt like sharing with me. So far he had been pretty reticent. "Black tea or chamomile or peppermint?" I don't know why I offered these choices. Charlie has always thought that herbal teas were criminal. I placed a bag of Darjeeling into his cup before he answered.

"Black. As if you had to ask." Charlie picked at the plate of cheese. "And not that difficult, I suppose. But I swear, Rach. It's like she's testing me. I watch her and I don't believe her. I think she's playing with me."

"Playing with you how?"

"I think she remembers more than she lets on. I think she's trying to rewrite everything."

I THINK ABOUT this comment of Charlie's. This word, *rewrite*. I think about Claire, the way she appeared as she walked in from the garage. A bit haggard, certainly, but fierce and determined as ever. Her eyes, always enormous and searching on her otherwise small face, were almost defiant. Don't you dare treat me like a sick person, she seemed to be warning me. And I wouldn't ever have dared it. Claire, in a way, has always written our stories. Charlie and I have both always looked to her to tell us what comes next. I am waiting for her to show us how to go forward from here. I sense that Charlie is waiting for the same thing.

But if Charlie is right about Claire's acts of revision, then our next step may actually be a step back into the past. Perhaps I am even more eager for her to lead us in that direction. Maybe she will crack open the truth of what happened to us. I've been waiting all these years for her merely to explain why. I'd forgive her if she'd help me understand.

AND WHY, EXACTLY does Claire need to be forgiven? Charlie, of course, has his own answers. And if I'm completely honest, I probably owe Charlie an apology or two. I have to admit, it is so strange to see Claire and Charlie together again; I had grown used to visiting with Claire on her own, when she swept into Boston or invited me down to New York on one of her short stops there. I kept Charlie company through e-mails, and we had recently got ourselves caught up in a postcard-sending ritual. He sent me, first, an old card from Niagara Falls, probably printed in the 1940s or early 1950s, and it had one line of text on it that I didn't recognize at first, until I sat with it for a while and realized it was a line from an Elizabeth Bishop poem: *A dreamy divagation begins in the night, a gentle, auditory, slow hallucination. . . .*

It was winter and the quote was from "The Moose," and I felt a little jump in my belly, thinking that Charlie had remembered that it was one of my favorites. So I had trudged in the snow to a junk shop in Jamaica Plain and found a water-damaged, musty old card with a faded greeting on it: WELCOME TO HYANNIS! HAVE A SWIM! A group of young girls with arms locked like paper dolls gazed out from the postcard. They wore bathing caps and modest suits that covered the tops of their thighs. The girls looked shy, a bit ashamed even, in front of the camera, and the exclamation points in the greeting seemed to taunt them. On the back of the card I scribbled a line in return.

> January jumps about
> in the frying pan
> trying to heat
> his frozen feet
> like a Canadian.

It was from a George Barker poem. Charlie had always insisted that the writers from Norfolk always got ignored by the rest of England, so he had forced me, during our time together in East Anglia, to listen to him recite lines from Barker and William Cowper and even John Clare, who wasn't from Norfolk but was overlooked nonetheless because "he wasn't Byron." I hoped the lines would remind Charlie of that cold winter we had spent together in Norwich and how we had looked forward to the spring months, when Charlie had promised to take me on a trip along the Broads and to the old port towns of Southwold and Lowestoft. I liked that there were summery bathing girls on the front of the post-card, while the text reminded of the long winter ahead. As I mailed off the postcard, I had a giddy feeling in my gut—I wondered what he'd send me next.

Looking back at these cards, I am amazed at how little we've all changed. Charlie and I have always been better at communicating in silence or with other people's words. Claire took over from the poets and novelists we had read aloud in those smoky Norfolk pubs. When Charlie moved in with us, he took on the habit of using Claire as his mouthpiece. "Claire," he would say, "you know what I mean. Tell Rachel why it's a terrible idea to replace the tiles in the upstairs bath." Or "Claire, you'll explain it better than me. Tell Rachel why Al Pacino's character lost all plausibility in that scene at the diner."

And it wasn't only Charlie. I told Claire things that were always meant for Charlie's ears; I told her in the hope that she might translate my indistinct feelings and make them more decipherable. And then, of course, I had told her the most important thing of all and she promised never to tell Charlie about it, but of course it was the thing he most needed to hear. But I was frightened and I wasn't sure that he loved me, and Claire had been so protective and so very certain and she handled it all, the appointment, the counseling, but most of all, she handled the silence for us. After being our voice for so long, it was a bit of a surprise, I suppose, that there were things she would never reveal.

I thought at the time that she was being the very best kind of friend, and I still do want to believe that. I don't think anything that was to come was planned, that Claire used this secret pact to her advantage, but of course it can look that way now, just as it looked that way then, when I watched Charlie kissing her up on that ladder, spying on them from the doorway, my own silence twisting up in knots, settling in for the long haul.

When I am completely honest with myself, I have to contend with my own memories, of how I explained things to Claire, how I erased the truth. When I had told her, she asked me, "Do you love him? Is he the man for you? Can you imagine your future together?"

I had dismissed her questions. How was I supposed to imagine a future with Charlie? We were only twenty-three years old. But there was a lot I didn't say because I was embarrassed by my feelings. Claire and I had spent so many evenings planning our future, our careers, our future travels, that I was afraid to tell her that the idea of raising a family with Charlie filled me with comfort. I had fallen in love with him in a rowboat on the Broads, and I had been denying it ever since. Claire, it seemed to me at the time, didn't believe in love or sentimentality or nostalgia, and I needed her to see me as an equal and an ally, so I lied. "I love Charlie as a dear friend, just like I love you, Claire," I answered stupidly.

She had joked with me then. "Well, not entirely the same, Rach. We don't sleep together."

I laughed with her and exaggerated my ambivalence. I'm not sure I'm in love with Charlie, I said, when what I really meant was, I'm not sure he's in love with me. We all have so many plans, and a baby would interrupt them, I said, when I really wondered if we could all still live in this house, Claire, Charlie, me, and a baby. Could we all raise this child together? Make new rules that didn't follow a particular order?

When she asked, Do you want to tell him? Do you want me to tell him with you? I had answered, No. I thought I was being grown up about the whole thing, stoic even. Charlie is so dutiful, so serious, don't you think, Claire? He would offer to marry me and make things right, but later he might start to resent the limitations, the constraints. I don't want to be responsible for his future disappointments.

Eventually it was my own words that came out of Claire's mouth.

IT IS HARD for me to look back and try to figure out what in fact I had wanted from Charlie. My parents were dead and I was pregnant and Claire seemed so certain. We had our whole lives to think about, she said, just as I had said moments before. Charlie was my good friend, but hardly my boyfriend, and so on. Her words took shape in my mind, alongside my own, even though in my heart I believed we really could raise the baby together, in my parents' house. We were already a family. I had lost my parents, but we'd all raise their grandchildren in their bright kitchen, cozy living room, book-filled attic. I didn't care if it seemed strange to other people; we could all be a family together.

I never did explain all of this to Claire because I knew she'd think it was foolish. She'd think I was foolish, unreasonable, selfish even. She certainly wouldn't be putting her life on hold for anyone, and I shouldn't either, nor could I ask that of Charlie. We were so young. I heard her voice in my head. What on earth would we do with a child? What would I do with one? Because most certainly Charlie and Claire would want to leave one day, and then I would be alone with him or her, and it was this thought that made me feel panicky. I erased my fantasy and replaced it with Claire's sensible advice, which she had translated from my own words.

The timing was excellent, she assured me. Charlie was leaving for a conference in Chicago. She would make the appointment at the clinic. She would hold my hand; I wouldn't be alone. I'd have a full week of rest and time to think before Charlie returned, and he would never have to know. As Claire and I mapped out our plans, Charlie was most likely on the tenth floor of an old building on Comm Ave, his head cocked in attention as his professor lectured away the afternoon. Claire had held my hand between hers, and two cups of untouched tea steamed in front of us. "Oh my sweet Rae," Claire whispered as a Syd Barrett album crackled from the living room, and then she told me not to cry, that it would all be okay. We were only twenty-three years old, and someday this would all feel like a very long time ago and I would know that it had been the right thing to do.

But now I know she was wrong. I was wrong. Nothing feels like a long time ago, because Charlie started sending those postcards that I taped to the wall over my desk, and I started to anticipate them in my mailbox and I began driving to antique markets in Essex and Amherst to look for old postcards and I would send them, hoping for a quick reply. They were important to me, even though they made me feel guilty, even though I knew some of the secrets now tucked away in Claire's boxes. I started to believe that the postcards were filled with secret messages. For Charlie, though, I think they were merely a playful distraction built on other distractions and denials that helped him manage Claire's disappearing acts.

Besides, it was too late for an explanation now, too late for an apology for the many lies we told him, all those years ago. Perhaps if he hadn't climbed up that ladder to kiss our best friend, perhaps then I would have felt more of an obligation, but I took that first betrayal and all that came from it as my punishment. It's awful of me, but when I first learned about Claire's being sick, I thought that her own punishment had finally caught up with her. But now I'm not so sure. Perhaps her good fortune has won out again and she's going to be given a second chance with Charlie. I have become a bitter and angry person, I realize, because I'm not sure I'm willing to let that happen, for any of us.

"WHERE ARE YOU, Rach?" Charlie asked over his tea. "You traveled far away for a moment there," he said.

"I'm drifting," I answered him. "Going through boxes, looking at old photo albums, you sitting there, banging your legs on the counter like you've always done."

Charlie put his cup down. "At least two of us remember things." He smiled and scowled at the same time.

"What did the doctors say this time, Charlie?" I passed him another cracker.

"Much of the same. Patience. Exercises. No stress or exertion. Who knows. We'll see. Unpredictable. Time will tell. It's amazing, the clichés that come out of these doctors mouths."

Always the editor. Charlie has always hated sloppy arguments. "One step at a time," I said, smiling.

"We'll cross that bridge when we get to it."

"It'll be a long road ahead."

"We must prepare ourselves for whatever comes next." Charlie laughed and reached for a bottle of wine.

"We'll help her remember, Charlie." I grabbed two glasses from the drain board and watched as Charlie's heels hit the counter in anticipation. I wondered if this is how he and Claire used to sit in our kitchen while I buried myself in blankets in my room. Did their courtship start this way, over wine and gentle teasing? Who was the first one to edge a bit closer, brush an arm or a leg with a hand?

This time, I pulled myself up onto the counter next to Charlie. I clinked his glass with mine and rested my head on his shoulder. We would sit like this for a long time until I headed to the guest room and Charlie pretended to return to Claire before making his bed on the couch.

Claire

Charlie and I both try to keep busy, in and out of
each other's company, and attempt to keep Rachel
nearby as much as we can. Just last week I told
Charlie that I wanted to bring some of my boxes into the
office so that I could sort through my research and maybe
find my way back to the stories I was working on when I
got sick. Charlie agreed that this was a good idea, and he
cleaned out the office to make room for my things. He placed
a jar with my favorite pens (felt tip, fine, black ink, he assures
me are my favorites) on the corner of the desk. Meanwhile,
Rachel helped me organize a folder with clips of my articles

from the past two years. This is in the top drawer. Charlie has moved all his things—the desktop computer, his folders of tax forms, travel receipts, and who knows what else—into the filing cabinets downstairs, where I know he sleeps, even though he pretends, sometimes, to join me in bed. He has left the wall calendar (botanical theme, November has an image of an orchid) and a photograph of the three of us—Charlie, Rachel, and me—standing in front of Rachel's brownstone. The sun is in our eyes and we are squinting, and we are obviously happy. Our arms hidden behind one another's backs, me in the middle.

So I work in the office and listen to the distorted sounds of the TV drifting from downstairs. Just last night, when I came down to the kitchen, Charlie nodded at me and asked how the work was going. I told him that it was going well. "There is an intriguing story I found about a commune of sorts outside Pondicherry. A French woman started the place and it's rather self-sufficient, like a village from the eighteenth century or something."

"Hmmm," Charlie said, as he kept his eyes fixed on the TV. "Is there a blacksmith and a baker and single-room schoolhouse?"

I stared at Charlie. I tried to gauge whether he was making fun of me or was merely uninterested. His face was pink from recent shaving and he rubbed at a little nick on the edge of his chin. I wanted to hit him, and I had no idea why. Instead of throwing the pen I was clutching in my hand at his face, I walked into the kitchen to heat some water. I sat on the counter and peeled a banana, and without really thinking about it I kicked my legs against the counter sides.

"Will you stop that, please?" Charlie called from the living room. "It's incredibly annoying."

I thought about keeping it up. I felt like a petulant teenager. But I stopped and fixed my tea like a grown-up and then made my way back upstairs. I felt Charlie's eyes on my back as I walked up the stairs, but I wouldn't look at him. Later in the evening, I heard him pass the office on the way to the spare bedroom. His computer groaned to life, and I switched mine off and headed to the living room. I turned on the TV to some medical drama that I couldn't follow, wrapped the quilt around me, and closed my eyes. Charlie might have come to wake me later in the night. Or perhaps it was Rachel who reminded me to take my last doses of medication and ushered me up the stairs. Or maybe I remembered to do these things on my own, but I woke up in our bed, alone, with the alarm beeping away.

Charlie emerged from the bathroom, a towel wrapped around his waist, his hair dripping water into his eyes. When he isn't wearing his glasses, he squints and his face looks much younger. His body is still thin and pale, almost hairless, and in the outlines of the early morning he could have been taken for a ghost. "Sorry about that," he mumbled. "I got up early and forgot to turn the alarm off."

"It's okay." I kicked the covers away from me. "I should get up anyway. I thought I'd come into town with you and Rachel today. I feel like getting out of the house."

"Of course," he said. "I'll finish up in here and leave you to it. Think you can be ready in an hour or so?" He was back in the bathroom before I could even give him my response.

Mornings are difficult for me. The phenobarbital and steroids I'm on make me sluggish and hazy. Tasks I know should take me only a few minutes seem to take forever. I'll stand in front of the closet for a long while, occasionally forgetting if I've already picked out a pair of pants or a sweater from the drawers on the opposite end of the room. I'll wonder what the weather might be like, and then Charlie's voice will startle me from downstairs. "Claire, what's keeping you? I've got your tea in a travel mug and some toast with jam you can eat in the car. Let's get a move on." And so I'll grab a pair of jeans and one of Charlie's sweaters and race down the stairs. I fear I wear the same clothes almost every day of the week. The pretty skirts and blouses Rachel helped me pick out are still in their shopping bags. They seem inappropriate for my lazy life. Who would I be getting dressed up for?

ON ANOTHER OCCASION, Charlie has the idea of taking me to work with him. After my unsuccessful attempt at getting myself to town, I think he has become worried by my restlessness, but he continues to worry about leaving me alone, unsupervised. So he suggested that I join him at the office today, meet the newer staff, take in the renovations. When I tried to picture the little news office that had been under Charlie's supervision for eight years now (he constantly reminds me), all I could envision was a 1950s newspaper room, abuzz with clicking typewriters, men shouting orders at one another or at girls with notebooks and pencil skirts who wear a look of urgency and efficiency. Who knows where these girl Friday images come from? I think I remember movies better than our own lives.

Even though Charlie works for a small, local paper, I knew the place would be filled with computers and blinking phone lines and glass-walled offices where men and women alike share space and pursue their assignments. But still I pictured an old-fashioned landscape of bustle with Charlie at the helm, measured, fair, diligent. The chief editor, the boss, the man who keeps things orderly and on-task. However fuzzy the memories of his office, however they shift in and out of focus in my mind, Charlie continues to appear, unchanging—stoic, responsible, tight lipped. You can count on Charlie for anything; he is nothing if not reliable.

A memory comes to mind as we sit over breakfast; it is hazy at its edges. I am on a ladder at Rachel's house, dressed in paint-spattered clothes. I hold a brush clumsily and blue paint is trickling down my arm. It has already covered my shirt, my shorts, the ladder. Little dribbles of blue fall from my brush to the tarp laid out on the floor. I think Rachel has just been in, scolding me for my mess, and I am feeling wounded. And suddenly Charlie is there at my feet, his warm hands encircling my ankles, a crooked smile of uneven teeth on his face. He is gazing up at me. Did he wink? It seems out of character somehow, but I see a quick crinkle at the corner of his eyes as he takes the brush from my hands, lays it carefully on the paint can, and changes positions with me on the ladder. Charlie seems impossibly tall in this memory. With a turpentine-soaked rag, he rubs away at my mistakes. The ceiling splatters disappear and all the uneven lines of drying paint get smoothed over by his roller. I look up at him, his brow wrinkled in concentration and the afternoon light casting shadows into the hollows of his cheeks. I can see him older in this moment; I can see him as he appears today, at least twelve years later, as he wipes a napkin across his lips after a final sip of coffee. When he climbs down from the ladder, he stops in front of me and moves a stray piece of my then long, straight hair. And quite unexpectedly he kisses me just above my collarbone, the tickle of his beard lingering on that vulnerable stretch of skin. Where do these memories come from? They, too, feel borrowed from a movie.

I touch my collarbone now and perhaps I even blush a little at the memory. Perhaps I am remembering the first kiss Charlie ever offered me, that gentle graze against my neck, sheepish and quick, testing my reaction. How did I react? The memory is frayed. Did he leave the room? Did Rachel enter? What would her expression have been as she caught Charlie and me in this moment? There is guilt attached to this memory, something I most certainly feel, although I can't be sure why. Did I hurt Charlie by not responding to his kiss? Did Rachel take offense at this small act of intimacy?

I'd like to ask Charlie now, as he bends over his newspaper at the kitchen table, whether he remembers our first kiss, but I worry he might take it the wrong way. For me not to remember such an important moment would be yet another betrayal of our shared past. The question would make us both awkward and I want this day to go well. If Rachel were here, perhaps I would ask her instead, but she has already left for town. She has become the keeper of our shared memories. Unlike Charlie, she is generous with her stories. She lets me see myself with her over the years and she is not afraid to talk about the unhappy, angry moments too. I set aside the question for now, knowing that in a few hours, if I remember to ask her, she can confirm or deny it for me and another memory can be put in its proper place.

Charlie raises his eyes from the paper and checks his watch. For just a brief moment he seems surprised to find me here, across the table from him. "You about ready, then?" he asks, and before I can reply he's pushed his chair back and brought his mug to the sink.

THE NEWSPAPER'S OFFICES are small, a cluttered wing of a large warehouse building in downtown Burlington. The directory has a long list of businesses: a massage therapist's office, a few accountants, lawyers, counselors, and the mysterious F. D. Brown, Finder of Folks, Facts, and Falsities. As Charlie and I wait for the elevator, I ask him if there is in fact a real life private dick working in his building. Charlie's face lights up at the question. "Ah, the infamous Mr. Brown. He is a walking noir movie. You've got to remember him, Claire. He's been here for ages—fedora, mustache, buffed wing tips?"

I shake my head. The only image that comes to mind is Cary Grant in that movie—what is it called? I am still trying to come up with the title when the elevator dings its arrival.

"I can't believe you don't remember him. He's a real character. Maybe we'll take a pass by his office later today so you can at least catch a glimpse of his secretary. Her name is Lollie! It's tremendous, really. You'd expect their lives to take place in black and white with a machine pumping fog into the office."

"What does he get hired for?" I am intrigued by Mr. Brown and Lollie. And I am glad to see Charlie so animated. I begin to imagine offering up my photography services to them. I could knock on their door and play right into the mystery. I could tell them in a cryptic voice that in the past I did investigations of my own, that I have traveled and seen much of the world, but that now I have returned to small-town life, carrying old wounds. I would be the perfect spy, forgetting immediately whatever it was that I had seen, so their clients' privacy and nasty little secrets would quickly disappear into the black hole of my mind. Perhaps I could even hire Mr. Brown to solve the mysteries of my own past. Out of professional courtesy and gratitude for my discretion, he would offer his services for free, and then Charlie would be under the watchful eye he so frequently places on me.

Suddenly, in my mind's eye, I become the femme fatale, the woman with the red lipstick and the stiletto heels and husky voice. I will ask for a cigarette and pause provocatively between words. I will ask for an ashtray and push a neat pile of twenties across the office desk. I have secrets. I will leave in a perfumed cloud of mystery.

"Claire, are you coming?" Charlie is standing outside the elevator, looking at me with that bewildered gaze that has become so typical lately. "We don't have to do this, if you'd prefer not to. We can always visit another day."

Charlie has taken my daydreaming for hesitation, yet again. He is worried about my potential embarrassment at not remembering all the old, should-be-familiar faces. He has quizzed me several times on our car ride here. Henry is a features editor—forties, beard, ex–football star, broad shoulders. Emile—the arts editor, a transplant from Montreal—talks with his hands and with long pauses. Nolan—the sports editor, unexpectedly frail and freckled, redheaded. Chessboard on his desk at all times. Nancy—obits and marriage announcements. Grandmother of ten, loud talker, smells of rosewater. A hugger.

I'm intrigued by Charlie's descriptions of other people. He looks carefully and critically at the world around him and offers up his inspections and evaluations as if they were the result of prolonged research. He'll wrestle with just the right details. Henry isn't quite "rude," he's merely "effortlessly belligerent." Emile isn't quite "effeminate"; he "is comfortable with his feminine side." Nancy isn't "a gossip"; she is "enthusiastic about the narratives of others' lives." If I thought Charlie would handle it well, I'd tell him that he could use an editor himself to help him cut to the chase. Let's get that word count down, Charlie. We've got only two columns to work with.

It's bad timing; the moment Charlie opens the door to his office, I remember the movie I was trying to think of, and before I can stop myself I shout out, "*Charade*!" and punch Charlie on the shoulder. He is blushing to his ears, and I quickly whisper, "The Cary Grant movie." Charlie looks at me as if I've really lost it.

Of course, I've realized too late that Charlie hadn't been a part of my internal conversation about private dicks and perfumed smoke and I want to fill him in so he won't carry that "she's crazy" look on his face for a minute longer, but suddenly there is a young woman standing in front of us, handing Charlie a stack of mail and some memos and a schedule for the week. She identifies each packet as she loads up Charlie's arms, and if I could describe her voice as a food, I would choose cotton candy. Charlie has not briefed me on this employee of his. She is lovely and I am suddenly aware of my dingy corduroy pants and pilled, roll-neck sweater and bitten-to-the-quick fingernails.

She holds out her now empty hand to me, and I am running through Charlie's list in my head just in case I'm missing someone he mentioned, even though I'm certain I would have remembered a description of this woman. She rescues me.

"It's been a long while," she says. "I'm Sophie."

And I am suddenly relieved. She has a kind smile and her hand is small and cool in mine. "My God, your teeth are perfect." I don't know where this comes from. This is my tendency these days—to blurt things out without thinking first. Perhaps I've always been this way. I am sure I have never seen

teeth so white and uniformly perfect as the ones offered up
by Sophie's smile.

"Thanks." Sophie laughs as she takes her hand back.
"They run in the family. No braces even."

I look to Charlie for help, and for a moment he seems flus-
tered too. I have become paranoid in an instant. Look at this
girl. Everything about her is contained and in place. Her short
bobbed hair and uniform bangs across her pale forehead, dotted with freckles. Eyebrows plucked to perfection arched over
brown, cow-like eyes. Her lipstick, a muted pink, traced me-
ticulously around well-shaped lips. Every color of her stays
within its lines, right down to her painted toes peeking out of
her tasteful green heels. Oh, how well she suits Charlie and
his own version of tidiness. And how I must always appear to
him like a messy scribble.

I sense immediately that Sophie and my husband must be
having an affair. What I can't determine is whether I feel any
jealousy or instead feel like giving him a celebratory punch
on the shoulder.

But then I realize that I'm meant to be a part of the conver-
sation, and I remember to tell Sophie that I am Claire and that
I'm happy to meet her, and I apologize for the teeth comment.
These days, I say, I seem to have lost any kind of filter.

"Oh, you should never take back a compliment." Sophie
smiles at me. She is trying so gamely to make things comfortable in this impossibly tiny office. I feel a little bad for all
of us.

Meanwhile, Charlie has snapped back into some sort of

efficiency. Before I know it, he has guided me through his office with his hand gently pressing between my shoulder blades.
We have greeted Henry and Emile, and Nancy has given
me a hug and a box of macaroons. I collapse into Charlie's
chair and kick my feet up onto his desk. Next to his computer,
there is a picture of the two of us, squinting with the sun in
our eyes and our backs to a turquoise sea.

"Honeymoon," Charlie says as he follows my gaze toward
the frame.

"Before the sunburn," I add, and there is such a look of
relief and pleasure on Charlie's face, I almost want to take
it back—this little glint of memory that always sets up false
hopes for us both.

Charlie leans over to give me a quick kiss on the forehead.
"You smell like Nancy." He is feeling better. The earlier moments of awkwardness, perhaps even guilt, have passed. "Will
you be all right in here if I go chat with Henry for a bit? There
are a bunch of magazines in here or you can use the computer.
I've pulled up some of the articles you were researching before
you got sick, if you're up for having a look. Only if you want
to, of course. I noticed earlier this week that there have been
some developments in the hunger strike. Anyway, the password is Maldives if you want to have a peek."

"Of course," I say. "Take as much time as you need." I
smile, and Charlie is relieved. He feels he has done the right
thing, bringing me into work, helping me get started up again
with my research. Maldives. As he closes the door behind
him, all I can think is, Poor Charlie. How much injury do I

cause you by no longer fitting into this past of yours? I turn on the computer and type in the country of our honeymoon and start searching for some of my own memories.

AFTER SOME TIME in Charlie's office, I leave him a note and journey back to the street. There is a café downstairs from Charlie's office, and it seems like a good spot to stop and sit and read and organize my wandering thoughts while he bustles around a few flights up. Charlie and Rachel are always encouraging me to write, to keep writing. You have so much material, Rachel tells me, you could write a book. I have spent the past weeks copying my notes onto my computer (Charlie has given me a laptop, on loan from his work), and I have been searching for ways to make something whole come out of all these notes. Rachel has been keeping me company, although sometimes she'll do her own work over at the library, where she is now, and where I imagine she prefers the quiet and lack of distraction.

There are a few articles here and there within my files, longer feature pieces that have some substance to them—the river protests, the utopian community just outside Pondicherry, the residue of French colonialism in the restaurants of the old quarter—but I don't know where to start. Even after two hours of work yesterday, there are only three paragraphs littered on my screen.

IN ONE OF my boxes, I found a fragment of a menu that announces BOUILLABAISSE! in bold, black letters alongside a list of familiar Indian curries—vindaloo, chana masala, dal makhani. I brought this scrap with me today, along with some notes about the Mother, a French woman who founded the Pondicherry commune. As I sit outside this café—it is really too chilly to be out here, my fingers are stiff with cold—I can see this town in fragments from the photos I've found and the memories I've stitched together: the Mother's devotees dressed all in white, drifting in near stillness through the streets; the pastel-painted houses of the old French Quarter; the smell of croissants newly baked, coming from the shadows of storefronts. And I can picture this restaurant with its whitewashed walls and art deco font LE GOURMET, and quite unexpectedly I see the outline of a man's face across from me. He is there in my memory, holding my hand, and a candle's light flickers shadows onto his face. He is smiling and brushes a stray hair from his forehead. We are on a terrace and the breeze carries the sea toward our table. The waiter, who is dressed in a crisp white uniform, puts down a plate of steaming stew, with rice and naan on the side, and then whispers, "Bon appétit." He disappears with polite efficiency. And then the man across from me vanishes too, and I look up from my computer. All I can write about are these hazy disappearances. I delete the three paragraphs so Charlie won't see what I've been writing.

And I think I may in fact be going crazy, because when I glanced up from the screen, I saw the man from the restaurant, the man from my memories. He was looking at me from the window of the bookshop across the street. He held up his hand for a moment, and I wondered if he was waving at me, if he was beckoning me over to him, if he was really there at all. All the remaining warmth of my body traveled up to my head, and the rest of me turned icy. I told myself to calm down, breathe deeply, and focus on something specific in front of me, as the doctors had told me to do. The best way to prevent my seizures, I had learned, was to keep myself from stress, to keep myself from getting too tired, to "turn my brain off" when I started feeling too overwhelmed. And so I stared at my hands and counted to twenty, slowly and deliberately and out loud—I didn't care if I looked like a mad person—and tried to keep the static in my head at bay. When I looked up, the man was gone from the window. I looked down the street in one direction and then the other, and that's when I saw him again. He was walking away, but he momentarily turned to me, and in this instant I thought to call out to him to watch where he was going, and it was as if he heard me. He smiled or grimaced, it was hard for me to see, and then turned around and entered the crosswalk and the crowd of people moving on their way.

I got up from the table and left the shop, off to follow this man who I was absolutely convinced I knew. How can I explain my electric and malfunctioning brain? I heard my own voice in my head calling out, Michael! and I could smell the steamy bouillabaisse, and the cobblestoned street underneath my feet now merged with the cobblestoned streets of the old French Quarter of Pondicherry. Michael was wearing a green jacket and brown pants and a tan scarf spun loosely around his neck and he was walking away from me. I followed him down Church Street, and I willed him to stop. I ran after him, even though I knew I wasn't supposed to do these things. I ran and stumbled in my clumsy boots and I searched for him in the swell of people meeting their friends for coffee and ducking in and out of stores. Even as I ran, I knew I had lost him again. He had disappeared into this ceaseless flow of strangers.

When I walked back to the café, I whispered to myself over and over again: You are not crazy, Claire. He was here; he was across the way in that bookstore and he waved at you. You know this man, and he knows you, and he came to tell you something. I arrived back at my table, and my computer was gone. I had left it there, along with my bag, which was also gone, and my papers and my photographs. I sat down in my chair and I thought about crying.

Somewhere in myself, I knew that I was panicking, but I felt completely emptied of feeling. I put my cold hands to my temples and rested my head in my palms. And then I felt a shadow fall across my body. Please, please, please, I whispered into my lap.

"What is the matter with you, Claire? Have you gone completely mad?"

I looked up. There was Charlie, my computer in his arms, my bag dangling stupidly from his shoulder. And all I could think, in my typically ungrateful way, was, How can I make you disappear, Charlie?

Charlie

Claire and I drove home in silence. I knew why I was furious. I had told her to stay put in my office, that we'd go get a late lunch together. She knew how frightened I'd been after her last excursion alone, so when I found her note in my office, I was already prepared for an argument. But when I saw her abandoned bag and computer, I panicked. It was cold and I had no idea how long she'd been gone. At least she was in a public place, I told myself by way of reassurance, and I was just about to phone Rachel to see if she would help me start searching when Claire returned with that dazed look on her face. She actually seemed annoyed with me for my concern. When I asked her why she had abandoned her things, she merely shrugged and said that something had caught her eye. When I asked her why she'd left my office when we had agreed she would stay put, she didn't answer me at all. I had no idea why she was so cross with me.

When we returned to the house, she immediately climbed the stairs to her office and left me to tend to my frustration and confusion alone. This had become typical. Later, when she got sleepy, I'd have a chance to look through her work from the day. This had also become typical. When you're used to people keeping secrets from you, you become a good spy. However, I am not proud of my snooping.

HER COMPUTER IS filled with fragments. I don't know if they are memories or excerpts from notes and research taken from her boxes or half-formed recollections that have merged with her imagination. She has been searching for information on the Maldives, and for a moment I'm touched by her desire to remember our honeymoon.

And despite my tendency to wallow in my own frustration with Claire, I'm happy to retreat for a moment into my own memories. I remember the humidity and bright sun, our voices churned by ceiling fans. It had been Claire's idea to take our honeymoon in the Maldives. She had started gathering brochures and lining her desk with images of white-sand beaches and couples holding hands, facing the camera, their faces distorted by snorkels and overzealous smiles. The sea looked impossibly tranquil; even the reproduced images held a brightness that blinded me. I had never been anywhere tropical before. When I was a child, we always took our holidays by the North Sea. The gray ocean and its rocky shore was the antithesis of exotic, I suppose—unless, of course, you consider sunburnt Londoners a particularly unique species that come out of hiding only one fortnight a year.

Since leaving England, I have been drawn to the mountains and the thick, heavy snows of Vermont. I crave extremes in wintry weather, perhaps from growing up in a persistent, cool drizzle. Ever since I arrived in the States, I've wanted to chase blizzards and the steep descent of slopes littered with moguls and mazes of whitewashed evergreens, dipping lazily over pristine whiteness. I suppose there is an overwhelming brightness to winter mountain landscapes too, but the island was altogether different. No matter how much sunblock I applied to my skin, I baked along that sea. In all our pictures from those weeks, my smile looks more like a grimace, my forehead is stretched and leathery, a look of pinched pain in the creases of my mouth. I still blame the unbecoming freckles around my lips on that trip. But Claire is absolutely radiant in our photographs, browned to a sepia glow, sandals dangling from lazy fingers, her hair dripping from the sea.

We ate alongside the ocean every night. Fresh fish netted from the waters where we took our morning swims. Butterfish and tuna, adrift in butter and garlic and chilies, eyes peering out, surprised to be on our plates. I never got used to the intimacy that came with attacking the whole bodies of our meals, their stunned eyes looking on as we peeled away their exteriors, their scales and gills—it all felt like a science lesson.

Of course, the meals tasted brilliant. I've never again eaten fish that literally melted in my mouth like cotton candy, but it was also traumatic, really. Claire took to preparing my meal for me as if I were a toddler. "I can't bear the grimace on your face," she had said, just as she began the ritual of carving and breaking away the meat from the fish bone for me. After a few evenings, her fingers became lined with scratches from the exuberance she put into her dinner work. "Sanath showed me how," she explained one night as she savored the cheeks of her butterfish. The cheeks! "It's the best part," she said sheepishly when she saw my skepticism.

CLAIRE HAD BEFRIENDED a young boy who fished for our hotel. Sanath was a Tamil boy whose mother worked as a maid at the Bayside View, a flashier resort up the coast. Claire followed him around in the early mornings while I slept in or sipped lime juice on our veranda in the shade, preparing for the heat of the day. She took photos of him in his snorkel, throwing his net, displaying his catch. And he taught her how to throw the net, a graceful, arcing motion that almost sent his slim frame flying into the sea.

Claire got the hang of it after a few tries, and they both beamed back at me as I waved and gave them a thumbs-up. I felt ridiculous up there in my wicker rocker, useless and fussy. Claire and I were the same age—twenty-six at the time—and yet I was always feeling older than she was, less energetic, stodgier. She called my reticence my "lingering Englishness." But I imagine I would have been the same kind of person even if I had been born in the States. If only this boy could see me on skis, I thought to myself, while I secretly hoped his net might come up empty and give me a respite from fish for at least one night. If there's no catch, I continued thinking, then Claire might not look at me disapprovingly when I suggest I might just order the spaghetti Bolognese.

WHEN I THINK of Claire, upstairs in her study with her fragments, I feel guilty. She had always wanted to go back to the Maldives, but we never did. We took our holidays in closer places because time never quite seemed generous enough to us and because I think Claire knew I was resistant to the idea. She was kind enough to avoid the topic, though I realize now how disappointed she must have felt over the years. I had been an absolute failure at honeymooning. A sunburnt whiner who couldn't even muster the expertise to eat his dinner without her help. She had sent copies of her photos back to Sanath, but he had never written back to her. She missed him in a way I never quite understood. I think he became a sort of ghost to her, reminding her of all the things we couldn't get back.

AND SUDDENLY MY mind travels back to Florida, to Claire's body in the hospital. The Keys had reminded me so much of our honeymoon. The heavy, humid air, the taste of salt from sweat and sea air. I think of Claire in her hospital bed. Her eyes are closed and her breathing looks clumsy and difficult. There is a snarl on her lips. I remember wondering if it is possible for people to feel anger when they are in a coma. The doctors have forced her into this state for her own good until they can get a handle on her seizures. They tell me to talk to her, to hold her hand, but when I do, all I can see is that grimace on her face. Who knows if she even wanted me there. It has been so long since we've actually had any kind of real communication. I have lost track of who is more angry at who. When she opens her eyes again, I want her to see me here and be glad, be relieved. I want her to know that she is not alone and that she is going to be all right because she is a fighter and she never gives up on things, with the exception perhaps of us.

CLAIRE WAS PLANNING to return to the Maldives before she got sick. I found notes from travel agents and hotel rate quotes in her inbox when I was called to the hospital and ended up staying in her hotel room. I wondered who she was planning to go with—the rates were for double rooms. This was when my snooping started. It was a relief, even a revenge of sorts, to click on each and every one of those messages. Delete. Delete. Delete. I certainly haven't mentioned any of this to Claire, and I haven't even brought it up with Rachel. Claire would feel betrayed and Rachel would be disappointed. Whereas I make excuses for myself. I wouldn't have to snoop if Claire didn't have so many secrets. Originally I had been trying to help the doctors locate some information that might help with their diagnosis. I was trying to help us make a fresh start, all the while failing miserably, of course.

When I feel that seething, relentless anger growing in my gut, I try to remember our courtship, if one can even call it that. I force myself back to a time when we were happy in each other's company. When we first moved to this house, for example, Claire brushed her hand across every surface. She told me she wanted her fingerprints to start marking the house as ours. I want to fill it with our smells, Charlie, she said. The house creaked with her every footstep and I felt so incredibly lucky to be making the house groan with our shared company.

She chose the paints just as she had at Rachel's house, and soon our downstairs burst with vibrant greens and blues and yellows. Claire was never one for subtlety, and even then she was insistent on turning the old, muted house into something fresh and vital. She unpacked our pots and pans with a clanking intensity while I moved the larger furniture into the bedrooms, kitchen, and study with the help of our neighbors' teenage sons. Our things were shabby back then, everything a hand-me-down or something purchased on a whim from the Goodwill. Our closets were half-empty and we didn't even have a television. We spent the evenings picnicking on the living room floor, a blanket spread out, illuminated with candles. We drank wine and played Scrabble and made love right there on the floor. Afterward she would laze about, naked, in front of the fireplace and tease me for scrambling back into my trousers. "Such a prude," she taunted. "When will the

rugged Vermonter replace the modest Englishman?" Perhaps
even then I was starting to disappoint her.

She seemed truly happy when we were first settling in.
Though it was my job that had brought us up to Burlington,
she was able to work from home for the most part. She had
access to the university library and she would phone in for
editorial chats with her boss in Boston and later New York.
She had started doing freelance long-form journalism, which
allowed her to be home for long stretches in between assignments, researching and editing and scribbling out plans for a
new story. She would go away on occasional assignments that
took her far from Burlington—an investigation into the toll
quinoa demand was taking on local communities in Bolivia,
a piece on the abandoned military bases of Micronesia, the
environmental threat damaging the preservation efforts of the
"floating gardens" of Xochimilco, Mexico—but she would
always come back after a few weeks, refreshed and reinvig-
orated, and it never occurred to me that she could be or was
unhappy here.

Upon her return she was always eager to get back to her
rhythms of "rural life," as she called it. She would insist on
taking a hike up Camel's Hump or going to UVM's dairy
farm for an ice cream sampler or riding our bikes across the
Lake Champlain Islands, our passports tucked away just in
case we wanted to cross the border into Quebec. It was often
hard for me to get away from work; I was in a new job and
the reporting and editorial staff was small and we all worked
long hours. Even as I cling to the happier memories of bike

rides and autumn strolls, I wonder if Claire, even then, saw our life—my life—as too small. I really don't recall the moment when her assignments started taking her away for longer stretches of time or when she started making excuses for stopovers in Boston or New York rather than traveling "all the way" up north. By that time, most of our relationship was happening over the static connections of long-distance phone calls. Perhaps if I had made more time away from work. Perhaps if I hadn't grown defensive when she mocked me about what was keeping me so late at the office—another article about a hunting accident or perhaps the annual festival of trees, she'd tease. Perhaps if I had seen that the silence of our little forest didn't charm her as much as it charmed me. Perhaps then we wouldn't be in this stifling predicament where Claire is upstairs and I am downstairs and one of us, at any given moment, is uncertain about why the other seems so full of anger and impatience and disappointment.

Rachel

When I returned from the library, it was clear that the day hadn't gone all that well for Claire and Charlie. Charlie was sulking in the living room when I got home, his face buried in a book, a fire dying out in the fireplace. When I asked where Claire was, he pointed upstairs and up I went. It had felt good to be out and about for the day, so returning to such a forlorn quiet made me feel already nostalgic for the day's ease.

I found Claire in front of her laptop, highlighting passages from her Cauvery River notes. She looked determined but a little hazy, and I wondered if she had had another seizure or if the day had just been exhausting for other reasons.

She looked up at me and smiled. "Charlie is angry with me again. I did something stupid and now he won't let it go."

"He'll be fine in another hour or so, after some wine and brooding," I said. "What happened?

"Oh, the usual," Claire answered. "I didn't stay put." She laughed, but I could tell she was angry too. She clicked the laptop shut and wrapped a shawl tightly around her shoulders. "Have you met Charlie's coworkers yet?" she asked. "Henry? Emile? Sophie?"

I hadn't been to Charlie's office in over ten years. I had no idea who these people were. I was impressed, though, that Claire had remembered all their names. "Not a one," I answered.

"I met them all today," Claire said. "Or remet them, I guess. I brought a cheat sheet with me in case I forgot their names, but I got every one of them right except for Sophie. I'm not sure I've met Sophie before."

"How was the office?" I asked.

"Fine until I got bored. It looked so nice outside, I decided to take a walk and sit in a café. Charlie was rather displeased by my decisions."

"Ah, I see," I answered. I was sure there was more to the story than Claire was telling me, but I knew how hard it must be for her to have all these rules and restrictions limiting her every movement.

"Would you do me a favor, Rach? Do you mind spending a couple of hours with me tomorrow if you don't have too much work to do?"

I still wasn't used to this new side of Claire. The uncertain, hesitant, slightly needy version of my best friend, who I had always known as the one who took charge and made decisions and rescued everybody else. "Of course! I can take the day off. What did you want to do?" My voice, too, had started to surprise me when I was with Claire. Too chipper. Too patronizing, even. Charlie, perhaps, was rubbing off on me.

"I want to go shopping for some new clothes. I was so embarrassed showing up at Charlie's office today. I mean, I'm basically wearing his clothes because I'm too skeletal to fit into any of my old stuff. And then I had to run into Sophie, who was this lovely creature with everything she wore just so. Next to her, I looked like a hobbit or some kind of shut-in. Even if I never leave the house, it will feel good to look like a sane person."

I laughed. "You look nothing like a hobbit, but sure, let's go shopping. I could use some new clothes too."

IT HAD BEEN almost a month since Claire and Charlie had picked me up at the Burlington airport, and more than two since I'd left them in Florida. Before I arrived, Claire insisted that she was desperate for company other than Charlie, and she joked that she needed a chauffeur too. Charlie also phoned to explain that Claire needed to be seizure-free for three months before she'd be allowed to drive a car again, and according to his updates, her seizures were still erupting every few days. The doctors were mystified by these little "break-throughs," as they called them, and Charlie was terrified that she might have one of her "spells" (Charlie's word for it) while he was at work. I'm not sure if Claire knew about those late-night calls I received from Charlie, if she realized the image of her that had taken shape in my mind—bruised and cloudy, blurry in her gaze and unsteady on her feet. If I were to be-lieve Charlie, she had become a walking accident, clumsy and shaky and out of focus.

It was selfish of me, but at first I didn't want to come. I had finally got myself back into some semblance of a routine. My plants had only just begun to forgive me for their yellowed leaves and drooping stems. I had been feeling tired from lack of sleep for days, and my back was aching from too many late hours cramming edits onto a glowing computer screen. When I looked in the mirror, I saw that shadows had crept under my eyes, and my skin seemed dusty—the effects of that unplanned-for Florida sun. All of these were, of course, merely excuses. Mostly I was afraid—afraid of what I'd find in Claire, afraid that what Charlie had said was true. I was also afraid of the three of us navigating this new territory where Claire had suddenly become the vulnerable one. I'd grown used to protecting Charlie from Claire, but I was wor-ried that Claire might be the one needing protection these days. I knew that Charlie had been angry for a long time. I could imagine his need for revenge, or his longing for a sort of punishment at least, even if he wasn't conscious of it him-self. I've felt it too, over the years, a need for revenge, against Claire or perhaps both of them, which was another reason I was frightened to come.

But despite it all, there was a part of me that was hopeful that whatever had gone on inside Claire's brain was provid-ing an opening, a clearing away of old clutter, a chance to answer some old and aching questions. After I hung up the phone with Claire those weeks ago, I thought about Charlie standing by the window at that Key West hospital with Claire beeping a few feet away, and how he had leaned into my body and wrapped his long, skinny arms around me. It had been a long time since we'd been so close. There was a comfort in feeling his weight again, even in the midst of all that worry and uncertainty. As I said, maybe I was being selfish.

WHEN CHARLIE AND Claire picked me up at the lo-cal airport, Claire would have run into my arms if Charlie hadn't restrained her. She pushed and pulled out of his grasp until he let go in exasperation. "Careful, Claire," he urged as she caught me up in one of her enormous hugs.

"You smell delicious!" Claire grabbed me by the hand and led me away from Charlie. "Did you check bags? Tell Charlie what to look for and then he can meet us outside. I want to have you all to myself for the first few minutes at least."

The force of Claire's energy surprised me initially. If it hadn't been for Charlie's words of warning over the phone, this is just what I would have expected from Claire—the bear hug and the demand for undivided attention. But under the surface of things, I could see that Claire seemed unsure of herself. Despite the largeness of her gestures, she kept looking to Charlie for his okay.

"My suitcase is green and duffel-shaped. It's got a little piece of yellow yarn attached to the handle." I smiled at Charlie. "We'll meet you outside."

"All right, then, I'll go fetch the bag, but at least give me a hug first, Rach." Charlie pressed me into a careful hug and whispered into my hair. "Keep a close eye on her. When she gets too excited, she can totally lose it, and then the next thing you know, she'll be on the ground."

Before I could respond, Claire was tugging on my arm. "Leave her be, Charlie." With Charlie searching out my eyes and Claire locking her elbow in mine, I began to wonder if this was what the next weeks were going to be like, this push and pull of competing loyalties.

It was Charlie who released me first and made his way toward baggage claim. "We'll see if he brings back the right bag," Claire called out after him. "He gets his greens mixed up with his reds," she added more quietly.

Now this was unlike Claire. Sure, she could push and poke and tease—we all expect that of her—but it was rarer for her to be so clumsy with her teasing. If Charlie had heard, his swift gait didn't show it. I must have looked confused, because Claire felt the need to explain. "Charlie is color blind. That's what I was giving him a hard time about."

"Claire," I said, "I know Charlie's color blind. I've known

him even longer than you have, remember?" And before the words were out of my mouth, I realized that I had come here in part to test her in some way, to search out her willingness to return to the past, to find out what we might be allowed to say to one another now.

But all Claire said was, "Of course you did," and there was nothing in her expression that registered more than this fact.

Yes, I wanted to say. Of course I did. And I met his parents before you did. And I knew that he got motion sickness before you did. And I slept with him before you did too. Instead we sat down on a bench next to the taxi stand, feeling the cold breath of late autumn as we waited for Charlie.

"I'm so glad to see you, Rach." Claire rested her head on my shoulder and I watched her breath puff out in little bursts of mist. She smelled different to me, piney, with traces of woodsmoke. Over the years, Claire had developed an appreciation for exotic scents; you could smell her as soon as she entered a room, sandalwood or bergamot or jasmine drifting in ahead of her. Now she smelled a whole lot like Charlie.

Charlie had always smelled clean to me. He packs satchels of lavender in his suitcases—he is the first and only man I have ever known who does this—and his closets are lined with cedar blocks. There were times in the past when I tried to smell his skin, to get a little closer to the human presence in him, the vulnerable, sweaty earthiness that we all must carry around with us, but Charlie never seemed to have that. I had been doing a lot of this kind of thinking lately, imagining and remembering a Charlie apart from Claire, my first impressions of him, how much I trusted the solid consistency of him before I had learned to doubt him.

Claire kissed the bottom of my jaw quickly as she raised her head and smiled. It was an awkward gesture.

"It's really good to see you too," I whispered back, not certain if I was quite telling her the truth. What did Claire look like to me? I searched for traces of my best friend framed between her oversize woolen hat and the scarf wound round her neck. Her eyes looked tired and they couldn't seem to settle on anything for more than a few seconds. She had hardly kept eye contact with me since our initial hug. She didn't seem to want to be looked at.

Claire talked to the wall behind me. "I think I might be going a little crazy, Rach. It's like I've become Charlie's clumsy shadow, following him wherever he goes, being still when he chooses to be still, walking when he feels like some fresh air. Sometimes I catch myself asking him permission to go to the bathroom. We've really become quite ridiculous." Claire lifted her head and smiled in the direction of the taxis. "I don't blame either of us, really, for this stupidity. We have no idea what to do with me."

Even in a weakened state, Claire could still pull me to her. The force of her will, the texture of her familiar voice—I could feel Claire tugging me into her orbit. I wanted to help her; I wanted to help Charlie too, just as they had helped me all those years ago. And I was starting to understand that I enjoyed how much they both seemed to need me. I was being made important again, just as I had been when I opened up my home to them and arranged family dinners and built bookshelves for all of us and gave us a place to celebrate the holidays. Our self-made orphanage. Of course I wanted Claire to get strong again and I wanted Charlie to have his life back, but selfishly I also wanted to go back to whatever moment it was when we all still loved each other equally and hadn't started lying yet. "What should we do with you, Claire? What do you want to do this week? I'm all yours."

Claire turned her focus back to me and smiled. "Well, I want to walk alongside Lake Champlain. The whole bike path. I've been working on my endurance. I think we can do it." Claire took out a notebook and started making a list. "If I don't write all this down, I'll forget it by the time we get home."

"Charlie told me about the notebooks. They seem like a good idea."

"They were Charlie's idea. I'm not sure if they're really working, but they help cut away some of the boredom at least. I want to go to the grocery store too and fill the cart with my choices, my cereal, my fruit, my brand of coffee . . . whatever those might be. I have the hardest time deciding what I like."

As Claire continued her list, Charlie rounded the corner, rolling my suitcase behind him. He waved once and I waved back.

"Charlie got the right bag after all," I whispered to Claire, but she was busy with her writing and didn't seem to hear me or notice Charlie's return, so Charlie and I watched her in silence, exchanging amused smiles over her head as we waited for her to finish. Perhaps I was already choosing sides.

THIS MORNING, CHARLIE and I had breakfast at the kitchen counter as he got ready for work and I waited for Claire to wake up, a routine we had fallen into during the weeks I had been there. Charlie spread some butter on a slice of toast and handed it to me. "She's been getting tired more quickly lately, don't you think?" he asked between sips of tea.

As he drooped his long frame against the counter, he pressed his shoulder against mine. He was doing it again, placing his body next to me in ways he hadn't done for years now. Once he had chosen Claire and the two of them moved into the same room, he was careful around me. He made sure that he and I were never in the same place alone for any length of time. He became even more polite, asking me permission to use things in the house, though up until then, I had made it clear that everything we had was shared. All this propriety, all these evasions, were the only acknowledgments that anything had ever passed between us. I used to try to touch him, just to be certain that he would pull away and it wasn't just my imagination. I liked his discomfort; it was the only source of power I still had over him.

"You know, Charlie, you speak about her like she's a toddler. She must hate it when you do that." I hadn't meant to scold him, but I could imagine Claire's outrage if she had heard herself discussed like this.

"You're right. It's a horrible habit. It's just that I've been put in charge of everything—organizing her medications, making her doctor's appointments, urging her toward naps, reminding her to take the clothes out of the dryer. And she relies on me to do all of this. It's not like I want to parent her, for God's sake, but then she does something idiotic like she did yesterday, and I want to lock her up in her room like a child."

"I didn't mean to say that you're enjoying any of this, Charlie. I'm sorry I said anything."

"Oh, Rachel, please. You can say whatever you like. And you're absolutely right, of course. I nag her and she resents me. Perhaps we're being punished for never having any children." Charlie attempted a smile, but it traveled over his face more like a grimace.

I'm sure I must have frowned too, because Charlie kissed me quickly on the forehead. "You're good to take her shopping, Rachel. Don't let any of my whining bother you. I'm just exhausted and grumpy and I don't like to have to think about the way I've been behaving lately."

Charlie had always been so proper and polite, and easily the most graceful person I know at changing the subject. But lately he'd been nervous and fluttering and offering dry kisses. He was a mess. "I thought we might go down to Church Street and wander around the stores there for a bit."

"That sounds perfect." Charlie took one last sip of his tea. "Just be careful on the cobblestones down there and try to have her home by three so she can rest up before dinner."

I raised my eyebrows at him and shook my head. "You're unbelievable. You're forgetting that I've been here for over three weeks."

"You're right! I am! I am! It's shameful, isn't it? All right, then I'm off. Ignore me and have a fantastic day. I'll see you both for supper."

Even though Charlie was occasionally driving me nuts, I was sad to see him go. I could still feel his kiss on my forehead as I listened to his car pull away. I realized that this had become our new rhythm. When Claire was tucked away for her naps or her long sleep into the morning, Charlie and I would have our moments in the kitchen, on the couch, where he would reveal things to me. I suppose it was up to me to reveal things too, including the lingering questions and not quite forgotten anger. There have always been those questions I could never ask him, such as, how easy had it been for him to leave me behind? Did he ever think about the hurt he caused when he chose my best friend over me? These questions are unfair, especially now. I kept far too many things from him too. I imagine that to Charlie we have always been only friends, good friends, of course, who had slept together, but nothing more. And I never contradicted him. So how could he have known?

I HAVE BEEN in this house so infrequently over the years but watched as Claire's presence diminished over time, until she seemed to exist only in the frames of old photographs. She was overseas on assignment so frequently that more and more of her things must have been packed away or stored in her New York apartment. On the rare occasion when we were all here together, Claire often forgot where things were kept—the bottle opener, her raincoat, her photo albums. Perhaps Charlie had rearranged things while she traveled, or perhaps her mind was someplace else. There was not much more evidence of her being here even now. It was easy to forget that she was upstairs, sleeping in the master bedroom, surrounded by Charlie's things.

Claire took her time getting ready, but we managed to get into the rental car by eleven. It was a cold day, but bright, and the leafless trees looked apologetic in the late-morning light. Claire was wearing one of my sweaters, a speckled orange bundle of wool, shapeless over her leggings. And on her feet, she wore some clunky Wellies. I laughed at her as she approached the car.

"What's so funny?" She looked suddenly uncertain and I felt bad about making her question herself at all.

"It's just that you look like such a Vermonter! And it's not even that cold outside."

She laughed and I knew right away that everything was all right again. "I know! It's awful, isn't it? I never feel warm here." She climbed into the car and I followed, taking my place at the wheel. As I started the engine, she turned to me and punched me in the shoulder. "I'm so excited for a clothing overhaul. I want some skirts and some pretty blouses, and some new shoes. That'll be a good start."

BUT WHEN WE eventually entered the first boutique, Claire had lost some of her enthusiasm. She looked overwhelmed by the racks of clothes as she clinked through the hangers and layers of sweaters and shirts and trousers. She'd grab a shirt, hold it up to her chest, then squish up her face.

I had no idea what this expression meant—it was not one I was used to seeing. "What do you think of this?" she asked me with each new item. This was something else I wasn't used to. I don't think Claire had ever asked me for fashion advice in all the time we'd known each other. "Do I even like purple?"

"You like green more," I answered, handing her a blouse with scalloped cuffs and some black embroidery. "And this seems like you." I offered her a flouncy little 1950s-style skirt littered with pansies. I wrapped my hands around Claire's waist, surprised by how little of her I felt there. "My God, Claire. What are you, a size four these days?"

"I have absolutely no idea. Grab a couple of each one and we'll figure it out in the dressing room."

The sales clerk took our expanding piles into the dressing room as Claire riffled through the sale rack. I was already exhausted and the day had barely gotten started. I'd grown so used to making decisions only for myself; I was out of practice at having these kinds of discussions.

Claire asked me to come into the dressing room with her as she sorted through the mounds of clothes we had amassed for her to try on. I watched her as she slowly and carefully stepped out of her leggings, all the while balancing against the wall. Every one of her actions was studied and deliberate, and I couldn't match this slowness with the Claire I used to know—always in a hurry, always impatient, always waiting for others to catch up.

As she took off her sweater and stood in the severe light of the changing room, she suddenly appeared so worn out, so gray and mottled, that I almost couldn't look at her. Her skin was still marked with blue-and-purple bruises, some even black, from IVs and the ghosts of blood draws and other injections. At the hospital the nurses had complained again and again that Claire had terrible veins, blaming her for their missed pricks and "traumatic" draws. And here she was, all these weeks later, still splotched with the aftermath of those invasions.

But the worst thing for me was the pink-white scar puckered into her neck. A slit where the intubation tube had connected her to the respirator. I remembered too clearly the gurgles and sucking noises that had emanated from her neck, the thick sounds of near suffocation. This tiny scar, no more than an inch long, wrinkled into her neck, brought back the memory of all these sounds and struggles, and I felt something shudder in me. To disguise my reaction to Claire's body, I pressed my palms against my eyes.

"Am I that bad to look at these days, Rach?" Claire laughed at her reflection.

"It's not you." I tried to meet her gaze. "Just some bad memories came out of nowhere."

Claire was standing in front of me, the green blouse buttoned high up her chest and the billowy skirt swishing against her legs. Covered, she looked lovely. She still looked tired around her eyes, and that scar still peeked out between her clavicles, but she was smiling and the green lit up her face and she started to sense that she looked good, that she looked better than she had in weeks, and suddenly I could see that a part of her was returning.

"I love it," I said. "You look really beautiful."

"The green is nice, isn't it? You were right about the color. And the skirt makes me feel flirty."

"You look flirty," I teased. "I recognize that look on your face."

"Hmmmm . . . if only there was someone to flirt with."

"What about Charlie?" I was prodding and I knew it.

"Oh, poor Charlie. If I tried to flirt with him, he'd probably tell me not to excite myself."

"You never know; he might appreciate it." I felt a sudden need to defend Charlie. I kept thinking of the way he'd scolded himself earlier that morning. He needs to feel like a husband again, I thought. I wondered how they were approaching each other, now that Claire was out of the hospital. In the months leading up to her illness, Claire had confided to me that she and Charlie hadn't slept together in months. He was angry with her and wouldn't say anything about it, she explained, and Claire had been too busy to care. And of course there were other reasons too.

But what about now? It was easy to see that Charlie seemed fully conscious of Claire's health, her medications, her sleep, her seizures, but at the same time so unaware of the person that was suddenly in such close proximity to him again. He hadn't touched her once since I arrived, except for one of his quick kisses on the forehead before we all retreated to bed.

He sat across the living room from her, watching her from a distance after we had returned from the airport. I wondered if Claire had been keeping her distance too.

What I saw, I suppose, were the effects of a distance that had been growing for years, outside my own understanding and sight except for occasional glimpses during rushed visits. And what did I feel about all of this—the careful but cool interactions, the controlling politeness, all these tentative gestures? I wondered if it was possible to feel sadness and satisfaction at the same time. Was there a word for this kind of feeling? Was it a kind of revenge? I wondered.

"I doubt it. Charlie spends most of his time on the sofa, reading, and scribbling notes. He pretends that he's going to come to bed 'in just a bit,' but the next morning he'll explain that he slept on the couch because he didn't want to disturb my sleep." Claire let the skirt drop to her feet and grabbed a pair of cropped jeans from the pile. I looked away from her. Even if I had been the one to start it, I wasn't sure I wanted to have this conversation with Claire; it felt disloyal to Charlie somehow. "He doesn't look at me, except when he's frustrated or angry, and even then he tends to look above one of my shoulders rather than at me directly." Claire's hair brushed against my arm as she reached for a sweater. "Kind of like you were doing just a minute ago."

I met her gaze in the mirror. The red turtleneck sweater she had put on covered her scar and rested just above the belt loops of her jeans.

"Don't look so guilty, Rach. I didn't mean to make you feel bad. I don't always like looking at myself these days either."

"I swear, Claire. It's not you. You look good; you look beautiful, really. It's just that sometimes I can't get the image out of my head—you attached to all those machines, and the doctors looking helpless and without any answers, and all the blood taken out of your veins as they tried to figure out how to make you better again. I try, but I can't stop remembering it."

Claire smiled at me in the mirror. "You look at me and can't get away from those memories of Florida. You wish you could forget. But for me, I look for the clues on my body to tell me what happened to me in that hospital, to fill in the missing spaces of my memory. Isn't that strange?"

I tried to smile back at her. "It is strange, Claire. I can't even imagine what that unknowing must feel like for you. But if you have any questions, if there's anything I can tell you, you only have to ask me."

Claire looked at herself in the mirror. She wiggled her butt and then she grinned at me. She was trying to make us both feel better, but I couldn't match her efforts. I was irritated with her suddenly and I wasn't even sure why. "Ah, Rach. I know I can ask you anything. It's one of the reasons I wanted you to come. Sometimes I think Charlie is too frightened to tell me the truth."

I wanted to be generous, I really did. And I meant what I said to Claire. I was willing to answer her questions, but I wanted her to answer mine too. It couldn't be only me providing the answers; I'm not that selfless. Before I knew what I was doing, I asked her, "Have you spoken with Michael?"

Claire turned away from our reflections and looked at me directly. "Michael who? What Michael?"

I examined her face, the way I imagined Charlie must have been doing for weeks now, looking for a glimmer of recognition, some small sign of memory. Charlie and I were both very aware of Claire's black hole, the joking name they had given to her memory loss, but I needed to be sure. However, there was nothing in her face that betrayed any kind of recognition. There was only a lopsided look of confusion, and I immediately regretted my question.

"Oh, Michael was the photographer you were on assignment with when you got sick."

Claire rubbed at her eyes. "I don't remember any Michael." She spoke at the floor.

"Please don't worry about it, Claire. It's nothing important." I took her hands away from her eyes. "Let's look at you." I turned her to face the mirror again. "The jeans look great, but I think you need a smaller size in the sweater. How about I run and get it for you? I'll be right back."

As I left the room, I felt a sickness in my throat. It was so easy to lie to her, as I just had. I promised myself I would make it up to her as I sifted through the sweater sizes. I would help her sort through the boxes piled high in the garage, just as she had asked me to do, the boxes Claire was sure Charlie didn't want her to open. She had told me that every time she mentioned sorting through some of her things, the boxes from New York specifically, he would make excuses that it was too late, that she had had a strenuous day, that he was too tired now but would make time over the weekend. I wondered what the boxes held—perhaps her work files or her old correspondence. I wondered if they held any of the photos she had kept in her studio or on her desk, or if Charlie had thrown most of these memories away. It was hard for me to imagine him doing that; he was far too ethical and too kind. But I could imagine the temptation he must have felt, the desire to discard all the evidence that reminded him just how far away from him Claire had traveled. I'm not sure I would have been strong enough to let the clues remain, clues that maybe, one day, would lure her away again. Like me, Charlie wanted his second chance. I wondered how much of ourselves we'd be willing to sacrifice to bring it about.

WHEN I GOT back to the dressing room, Claire was on the floor, thrashing and spitting, and her lip was turned up in a snarl. I straddled her legs. Charlie had told me to keep her as still as possible if this happened, and to talk to her so she could hear my voice as she came to, so that she would be less disoriented, less scared. Her breast had fallen out of her bra and I was crying. "Come back, Claire. Come back," I was pleading with her. "I am so sorry, Claire. I didn't mean to upset you. Please, Claire. Stop it. Come back."

And then it was over, so suddenly. Claire's eyes regained their focus, but she couldn't talk yet. There was a line of drool running from her chin to her cheek. She had bitten her lip and her mouth was bloody. I took my sweater and pressed it to her lip. "You're okay now, Claire. You're okay. We're in Burlington, and you've been trying on some lovely clothes."

Claire smiled and brushed the hair out of my eyes. "Hi, Rachel," she said. "It's all right. I'm all right." She had found her voice again. "Please don't cry. It makes me feel too guilty."

We sat on the floor together, holding hands, our legs entangled and our backs resting up against the wall. The sales clerk approached and knocked on the door. "Is everything okay in there?" she asked.

"We're fine." Claire answered for us both. She was suddenly ready to take charge again, while I was willing to sit, waiting, on the floor—waiting, I realized, for Claire to tell me what to do next.

Claire

Burlington's Fletcher Allen hospital is not very far from Charlie's work, so on the days that I have appointments, Charlie will drop me off at the hospital in the morning, then fetch me for lunch later in the day. He makes sure I bring my notebook, the charts the doctors have asked me to keep, and a checklist of all the recommendations the occupational therapist left with me the previous month. This is my current checklist:

- Use labels to indicate where things go (like which cupboards are for food, baking pans, aluminum foil, etc.).

- Put signs in places where I might forget to take something, like a sign by the door reminding me to remember my keys (not that I'm ever allowed out of the house by myself anymore).

- Hang an oversize wall calendar in a prominent spot to remind me of the date and any events that are taking place. (For me, events = doctors' appointments or a library book coming overdue. I have been told that this calendar will lessen the times I need to ask Charlie or Rachel for help remembering things and make me feel more "self-reliant." Instead the calendar only reminds me just how reliant I am on others—to drive me to the library to return my book, to take me to the pharmacy to refill my prescriptions, to bring quizzes to the doctor's office to remind me just how useless my brain has become.)

- Keep a journal and write notes. (I have added: Keep my camera with me at all times and upload the images every night onto my computer. Write notes alongside the images while the information is fresh in my mind.)

- Try to stick to a regular routine. (What other kind of routine would I have around here anyway? But yes, wake up, have breakfast, take meds, get some fresh air, maybe some exercise, lunch, meds, nap, rummage through notes/boxes and/or read, dinner, meds, Scrabble, TV, meds, sleep.)

- Prominently display photographs of family and friends and label them with their names. (I have taken the labels off. I don't need them. I don't want them. If Charlie has to deal with an occasional question, so be it.)

TODAY, CHARLIE HAS put together a little quiz that he has been very secretive about, and he'll be keeping me company during whatever the game is that he and Dr. Stuart have planned for me.

I meet with Dr. Stuart, my neurologist, once a month. The tests are always the same: He has me walk in a straight line, touching the heel of my right foot to the tips of the toes of my left foot and so on, as if I've been arrested for drunk driving. I am terrible at this. Usually he has to catch me before I fall. He asks me who the president is today, who it was eight years ago, who it was in 1988. He'll say a list of words in a row that I have to repeat back to him. I am usually miserable at this test too. I throw up my hands and he laughs with me and always says, "At least you haven't lost your sense of humor." He looks over my chart and lists my medications and I nod and he asks me, "Who is in charge of your meds, you or Charlie?" And I always give him the same answer. I'm in charge, but Charlie double-checks my pillbox every evening to make sure I haven't skipped a dose. Dr. Stuart usually nods at the chart, saying, "Good, good," and I find myself nodding enthusiastically alongside him. We are quite a pair.

He asks me about headaches, and I tell him they are not a problem.

Dizziness?

Yes, sometimes in the morning when I first wake up.

Loss of balance, any recent falls?

Not this week, luckily.

Sometimes he'll ask me a trick question. He'll behave as if we're just having a normal conversation, as friends might be having. Just last week he asked me, "Have you seen any movies lately?"

"Charlie and I just watched *The Bourne Identity*. We thought it might be educational."

Dr. Stuart crinkled his eyes. "I haven't seen it yet. Tell me about it."

"It's about a spy who doesn't remember he's a spy, until he starts speaking other languages, finds a bunch of passports with his identification, and realizes he's a really good fighter."

"Sounds intriguing. Does he ever remember how he came to lose his memory? Who he really is?"

And then I realize Dr. Stuart's caught me. I think back to the film. I remember a scene on a boat, but the image quickly fades. I really don't remember the movie at all. I know the bare facts of it, but nothing particular about it takes shape in my mind. I shrug my shoulders; I'm hesitant to give anything away. "You never know for sure." Maybe I'm wrong; maybe I'm right. Dr. Stuart doesn't betray much.

• • •

TODAY, DR. STUART welcomes Charlie with a warm handshake and offers me a quick hug. We have become friends of a sort. I see Dr. Stuart more than I see anyone else besides Charlie and Rachel. He is married, has grown children, has lived in Vermont for most of his life, and loves peppermint patties (the miniature ones are always in a jar on his desk), but other than that, I know very little about him. I will say, though, that he is always a kind and encouraging presence in my life. He is patient, and that is really all I can ask of anybody these days.

We start off with the usual series of questions and tests. Dr. Stuart asks me, "What is the date?" Then, "Could you please draw a picture of a clock on this piece of paper? Now draw twenty past two o'clock on its face." I pass with flying colors! We are all smiling in this very small and overheated office. There is a picture of a snow-covered mountaintop with a minuscule figure silhouetted at the summit. I would give anything to be that person, alone, and far away from here.

Dr. Stuart asks us to sit down around his desk. He smiles at me. "Charlie has brought a small photo album for us to look at together, Claire. Charlie tells me your friend Rachel brought it from Boston, so you probably haven't seen these pictures in a very long time. Don't be concerned if you can't remember them. We're just treating this as a little puzzle to see how your long-term memory stacks up against the shorter term. We're just mapping the geography of your black hole." I'm getting tired of this metaphor.

Charlie is all smiles as he pulls out the album. We are always on our best behavior in front of Dr. Stuart. Charlie brushes his hand against my forearm and nods a quick encouragement, and then I settle in to look at my past.

What Charlie doesn't realize, or perhaps doesn't accept, is that it is easy for me to drift into the distant past, when my mother was still alive, when she told me stories of my eccentric relatives and her childhood adventures. Or when my father told me stories about battles between his father and uncle over a claim to him. I remember their stories as if I had experienced them myself. Their past is often more available to me than my own. I miss them more than I miss myself.

When Charlie brought me back to Vermont from the hospital in Florida, Rachel unearthed some old photo albums that Charlie and I had apparently forgotten to pack when we moved away. She apologized for never having sent them to us, and explained that over time she had forgotten about them. It was only when we were leaving the hospital, and the doctor had suggested that photos might help unleash some memories, that Rachel had remembered the albums. One of them had actually belonged to my parents and was filled with images from their childhood, and seeing them, I remember the stories they told me about growing up. This is the album that Charlie has chosen to bring to Dr. Stuart's office.

My mother told me stories about her grandmother Viv, who was an avid fisher. Before her family left Latvia and moved to Queens, she had kept her brothers company in the early-morning hours as they fished the local lakes for pike. Viv was in charge of curing the fish once they got home, and my mother told me that Viv's hands had been hardened with salt and cold air and had been pricked by too many fish bones and that she had taken to wearing gloves even when she was inside. I remember her touching my skin only once with her bare hands, my mother told me, and it was like being touched by granite. My mother told me that when she was a small girl, Viv would take her fishing at Howard Beach in Queens. They would stand together on the pier, her grandmother sturdy and stoic, while my mother grew bored and entertained herself by watching the planes take off from and land at Idlewild Airport, just on the other side of the beach.

Here is a picture of my great-grandmother Viv, bundled up in her black winter coat, perpetually in mourning for her first child, a son lost on the crossing between the old country and the new. She carried a simple fishing pole and a tackle box of fresh worms and, on occasion, a shucked clam, and she planted herself on the pier, where she would stand, patiently, for hours at a time. My mother told me that she had never known anyone with the patience of her grandmother. Even on the murky, bleak days of late winter, she would tromp out to that pier, a beaten slab of concrete jutting out into the bay, and claim her favorite spot.

She hated the local herring in the New York delis, Viv used to tell my mother. So instead she would fish for her own catch on the piers near her home. She complained that the fish weren't the happy fish of her childhood, that the striped bass and occasional flounder she was lucky enough to catch were "sad city fish." She would bring the fish home to my grandfather, who humored her and ate the smoked city fish without complaint. My mother was absolutely forbidden to eat the fish, though. When her mother would drop her off with Viv for the day, she would make my mother promise not to eat anything her mother had hauled out of that disgusting water. Complain that you have a stomachache or just tell them you aren't hungry, she was advised. That water is filthy, her mother warned, and filled with pollution. You'll spring a third eye if you eat her fish.

My mother told me that she was ashamed whenever she had to turn down her grandmother's fish. She would have to sit at the table, stomach churning with hunger, and pretend she didn't want any of the fish or bagels or potato salad or pastries that her grandparents gobbled up in front of her. She felt terrible for lying to her grandmother, and as far as she could tell, her grandparents were still healthy, a bit hunched and wrinkled like all the old people she knew, but neither of them had a third eye or glowed green, and they weren't losing their hair any more than normal. But whenever she complained to her mother, she was warned: Who knows what's happening on the inside. You might not sprout a third eye, but perhaps your children will. That was all it took, my mother told me, adding "And you should be pleased, Claire, that I followed my mother's advice. Your two eyes are perfectly placed in the middle of your lovely face."

Now, telling this story to Dr. Stuart, I can hear my mother's voice more clearly than my own. I know her grandmother's story with more certainty than I know what I ate for dinner two nights ago. I know that I have mourned my mother for over twenty years, but telling these stories makes the loss feel all too immediate. I try not to cry in front of Dr. Stuart or in front of Charlie. If I do, Charlie will start to get worried, thinking I'm overdoing it, and Dr. Stuart will tell me to take a break, which is exactly what I don't want to do. When I tell these stories, I finally feel as if it's my own voice coming out, alongside my mother's and father's. I take a deep breath and Dr. Stuart tells me to go on.

WHEN MY MOTHER and her parents moved away
from the city to Massachusetts, she was given a pig to raise.
Her family had relocated to a small town outside Springfield,
where her father found work at Hasbro and would often bring
home sample board games for his family to try out. Even
though their evenings were filled with games and the buzz of
a new job, my mother missed the city and was having trouble making friends, so her mother signed her up for 4-H. My
mother told me that the day she knew she was going to be
okay was the day she was introduced to Sunshine, her very
own pig.

Sunshine had to be fed twice a day. I think my mother
thought of Sunshine more as a pet dog than a pig. She had
been told that pigs need to exercise to produce lean muscle,
so my mother had made a special leash for her new ward and,

much to the farmer's amusement, took Sunshine on walks through the fields and even sometimes along the dirt road that wound toward town. My mother used to hide her head in her hands when she told me these stories about Sunshine and the walks the two of them would take. "I don't know what I was thinking," she told me. "I'm sure I hadn't really let it sink in that, at some point, Sunshine was heading to a fate of bacon and pork loin. And I sure don't know what my parents were thinking," she added. "They had given me my first new friend in Springfield, and one day in the not too distant future I was going to have to murder him. If I ever do something so dumb to you," she would say to me midstory, "you have to tell me. And then give me a quick, swift kick in the backside."

The pig had done the trick: my mom had started to make friends through the 4-H club; she was less sullen and mopey around the house; she took more interest in the games her father brought home for the family to play. But when my mom learned that Sunshine was scheduled to be slaughtered about six months after they had met, she ran away from home. To be more precise, she kidnapped her pig, and the two of them set off on the road to who knows where. My mom confessed to me that she had no idea what she was doing—she was only ten years old—but she knew she had to protect her best friend. She had packed a backpack and filled it with apples and bread and cereal and carrots, an extra sweatshirt, her pajamas, a toothbrush, and a Nancy Drew book. She broke into a shed, tied Sunshine up in one corner, fed him some apples, and settled in for the night. It was the flashlight she was using to read her book that revealed her location the following night. "The policeman was quite nice to me," my mother said. "He put Sunshine and me in the backseat of his patrol car and dropped us both off at my parents' house. My mother wouldn't speak to me for about two weeks, but my dad bought Sunshine from the farmer and helped me build an enclosure for him in our backyard. The pig died during my first week of college."

I tell this story to Charlie and Dr. Stuart and explain that my mother used to bring out the Sunshine narrative whenever I was feeling low or lonely. As I explain all of this, Charlie looks at me like I'm crazy. "Did all of this really happen, Claire?" he asks. I know it's impossible for him to understand how I can't remember our honeymoon but I can remember the intricacies of my mother's childhood stories. I don't know how to explain it to him or to myself. When I look at these photographs, I can hear my mother's voice. Her memories are clearer than my own. Even if I couldn't find most of my own memories in my misfiring brain, my parents' stories seemed perpetually available.

Dr. Stuart jumps in. "This is one of the mysteries of brain damage and memory loss," he explains. "Certain moments can be recalled as clearly as if you were watching a movie, but another year might be irretrievable." He smiles and Charlie frowns. I choose to ignore them both and continue with the next photographs. I feel in control when I look at my old photo albums. Charlie can't tell me I'm wrong; he never knew my parents. I don't even know if he's ever heard these stories

before. I think that, maybe, being forced to listen to me will do us both good. And so I turn to my father.

MY FATHER'S PARENTS pursued their courtship in Atlantic City. Rose and Harry, and Harry's cousin Lenny and his wife, Mildred, would leave the city once every couple of months for a journey to New Jersey, to the boardwalks and the fancy restaurants. Lenny and Mildred had a lot more money than my grandfather ever did, but they saw themselves as not only the young couple's chaperones but also their cultural guides to all things cosmopolitan and snazzy. Even after Rose and Harry were married, the two couples made a habit of traveling to Atlantic City a few times every year. In these photos, Rose and Mildred pose in front of their favorite restaurant, Captain Starn's.

My father loved these photos of his mother. He told me that it had driven his father crazy, the fact that Rose was exposing so much of her leg for all the world to see. My grandmother was always very proud of her legs, my father told me, and Harry was a very jealous man. After my father was born, his parents used to take him to Captain Starn's. "Sometimes I thought their greatest pleasure was watching me eat," he told me. "And this place was all about abundance. The restaurant was a very grand place with a raw bar that extended the length of an enormous banquet hall. My mother would fill my plate with clams and mussels and shrimp and oysters, and then, once we were seated, in would come the lobsters. The waiter would pop the cork of some expensive champagne and Lenny would toast the table and claim my father as a shared son. Lenny and Mildred never had any children of their own.

"I think my mother hated the way Lenny and Mildred would ply me with gifts that she and my father couldn't afford. She worried that they were claiming me, that I was somehow owed to them since Lenny and Mildred had facilitated my parents' courtship. They had paid for their wedding, or most of it, I think," my father continued. "My father's father had been dead for years, and he was the youngest of five siblings. Lenny had taken him under his wing. It took me a long time to realize that my mother hated them. I was more preoccupied by the lazy sea lions that glided along in their pens outside the restaurant. While my parents and cousins finished their champagne, I was allowed to walk the boardwalk and visit the sea lions and porpoises or gawk at the seaplanes that would come in for a landing right outside the restaurant."

My father was also a dislocated New Yorker when he met my mother in Springfield. They met in ninth grade, four years after my mother had run away with her pet pig, and one year after my father left Brooklyn. Their fathers worked together and liked to sing the praises of a nice, robust lawn, quiet streets where the kids could play, and space, lots of space. But there were grandparents to visit, and after my father and mother's parents became friends, they decided it would be safer for their children to travel to New York on the bus together, when their parents couldn't join them for the journey, and so my parents fell in love on the Greyhound buses between Springfield and New York City. They were only fourteen years old. This still seems impossible to me.

My father loved to take me to the aquarium. Perhaps it was all those days spent out on the boardwalk of Atlantic City, the playful porpoises and sea lions of his youth. Every now and then, he would pack me up in the car, we'd wave to my mother, who hated zoos of any kind, and head off to Boston, where we'd stare at the harbor seals, swimming in the entrance-area tanks, for so long that sometimes we'd forget to buy our tickets into the main part of the aquarium. "The only thing I wish we had out in Springfield, Claire, is the ocean. You should always try to live near the ocean, if you can," my father said.

As I LOOK at these images, I think about our house here in Vermont. I know it is beautiful here. From the little shards of memory I have, I know I love the lushness of the forests that surround our home, and I love the gentle landscape that rolls and meanders as you travel south from Burlington. But the sea isn't close by, and I wonder if my father would be disappointed to find me living here. I wonder what he'd make of Charlie, who admits to being frightened of the ocean and prefers to keep his feet on solid, earthly ground.

I look now at Charlie, who is fidgeting in his chair. I know he doubts all of what I'm saying, which gives me all the more reason to keep turning these pages. If he would only listen

closely, he might learn a little something more about me too. When I encounter these pictures, it's not only my parents' stories I'm remembering; it's how they told me to live my life.

THIS IS MY father and his best friend, Robbie. Their mothers took them one summer to the Adirondacks, where they visited a historic site that reenacted scenes of life in the French settlements of colonial Canada and northern New York and Vermont. It was one of those places where you might duck into a shed and meet a blacksmith, who, dressed in colonial garb, would lecture you on the art of crafting horseshoes in the early eighteenth century. Or perhaps a milkmaid might greet you at the stable and lead you in an awkward demonstration where she would milk a cow and then churn the milk into butter and cream. Or perhaps, if you were really lucky, you'd show up on a day when there was a reenactment of one of the battles of the French and Indian War. I often look at this picture and wonder who the man standing to the right of Robbie is. What sort of colonial was he? I feel sorry for my father because I can't imagine this visit coincided with any sort of exciting battle reenactments. I think he must have stood and listened to this costumed man ramble on and on about the fur trade or fishing in nearby Lake Champlain.

In this photo, my father wouldn't have known that in another few years' time he'd be moving away from the city, that he'd have to say good-bye to Robbie and his other friends. His new home would resemble the woodsy landscape of the Adirondacks, and perhaps his new neighborhood would feel just as removed from his previous life as the colonial reenactments had seemed during his visits to Fort Ticonderoga.

I used to wonder why my parents never wanted to move back to the city. It's possible that they settled into the peaceful life and slower pace of our little town, that they wanted me to feel safe and protected and have woods to explore and nature trails to wander and apples to pick during the autumn. But I remember the excitement that would gather in the house when my father was taking me to the aquarium or my mother was taking me into Boston for a shopping adventure. At those times, I always sensed a longing in them to be someplace else. Somewhere bigger and filled with surprises.

My father loved walking through the city. He would grab my hand when we left the aquarium, and we would spend the rest of the day wandering. Through the North End into Chinatown, across the Common and the Public Garden, down Commonwealth Avenue, across the bridge into Cambridge. He would point out MIT and then Harvard, where we might finally sit and eat some ice cream at Brigham's. Coffee ice cream for my dad, strawberry for me. My mother liked the subway. She loved studying a map, figuring out where we would have to exit a trolley and enter a new train car, heading off in a different direction. "I know it's strange and a little, well, gross," she said to me once, "but I love the smell of the subway. I like that warm air that puffs out of the grates and reminds you that you're in the city."

After my mother died, my father stopped traveling. He never wanted to be far from our house because I think he still sensed my mother's presence there. We had boxed up most of her belongings, donating the clothes that I wasn't keeping to the Salvation Army, but my father insisted on keeping a few of her things on the bathroom counter (her perfume, her contact lens case), on the nightstand (the book she hadn't finished reading—Margaret Atwood's *The Handmaid's Tale*), in the garage (a pair of hiking boots). When I left for college, my father promised to come visit, but it was always me returning to him. And I returned to a diminished version of my father. He was shrinking by the month as I found myself wanting to take up more and more space.

As I'm telling the stories behind the photos, I'm also trying to remember my own. I think I moved to the city to get closer to my parents' memories and stories, and I couldn't get enough of the busy streets, the honking traffic, and the anonymity of the bustle around me. I remember fragments— taking long walks from Brookline to Chinatown and hunting for bargains in the overflowing bins of Filene's Basement. I imagine that I worked hard at school and got good at listening to other people's stories. I wrote for the student paper, I went to football games, I drank beer with arrogant boys, and I must have wished I could tell my mother and father about all these things. Eventually I would have Rachel, and later Charlie, to share my stories with. There are so many memories in my addled brain; they're just not the ones that Charlie is particularly interested in hearing anymore.

When I look up, Dr. Stuart is scribbling notes into my chart and Charlie is staring down at his hands. He won't look at me. Apparently I have made him angry, and again, I have no idea why. Did I speak out my thoughts in the midst of my narrations? I suddenly can't remember.

Dr. Stuart glances at Charlie, then at me, and must sense that something is wrong. "Charlie," he says, "why don't you get some air? Maybe a coffee? It's hot in here, isn't it? I'll crack a window and have a little chat with Claire."

Charlie follows Dr. Stuart's orders (and for a moment, I'm pleased to see him having to do what I do every day) and leaves us.

"He is angry with me because I can remember all these things from my childhood, but I don't remember the things that are important to him," I tell Dr. Stuart.

"Perhaps not angry, Claire. Maybe frustrated or sad. It's understandable, don't you think?"

Dr. Stuart is just as much a referee for us as he is a doctor to me. "Of course it's understandable. I'm angry with myself too."

"Try to be patient, Claire. With yourself and with Charlie." Dr. Stuart offers his benign and, right now, infuriating smile. "We need each other's memories as much as our own to understand our shared history. If you can't corroborate Charlie's version of your past, then that past starts to feel less stable, you know what I mean?"

Of course I know what he means. I'm not an idiot, I want to yell at him. I'm in the middle of all this too, I want to scream. We can add to the adjectives Charlie and I are supposed to be feeling. In addition to *angry*, *frustrated*, *sad*, and *confused*, I get to add *guilty*. I'm tired of feeling guilty all the time. So I try to change the subject. I ask Dr. Stuart if he'd be able to write my prescriptions so that I don't need to refill them as often. He looks surprised, then concerned, so I quickly add, "In case I want to travel, say, with my friend Rachel."

"We could always call in a refill for you, if you planned to be away from Vermont. I'd just call a Walgreens or a Rite Aid or any other drugstore in California or Colorado or wherever you want to be."

"But what if we wanted to travel outside the country, to France or Canada or Mexico or some other place?" The more I've been studying my half-complete articles, the more my mind has been traveling toward India. I want to finish what I started there. Most of me understands that this is an impossible fantasy, but the other part is rebelling against this knowledge. I have a feeling I am a person who has often made impetuous decisions.

Dr. Stuart removes his glasses. "Claire, we've talked about how travel might be off limits for a while. It's important for you not to put too much strain on your body. Routine is important. Small trips are okay, preferably by car, but nothing too far afield. Does Charlie know you're thinking about traveling?"

I suddenly feel I'm being accused of something. I realize I can get paranoid sometimes, but there are moments when I really believe that everyone is acting as one of Charlie's spies. "I'm not planning on going anywhere. I'm asking more theoretically."

"I see." Dr. Stuart rubs his eyes and sighs. "Your antiseizure meds are barbiturates, Claire, so we're not really permitted to prescribe them beyond the stretch of a month or two. Plus, you've only been on this combination of drugs for a few months now. It'll take some time before we know how you're really progressing and when we might be able to reduce some of the steroids and benzos. Brain trauma is tricky, Claire."

How many times in a given week do I want to shout: I know all this! I have done my research; I am not an imbecile. For instance, I know there are places in the world where it's much easier to get medicine over the counter, without a prescription. I know, too, that conversations between patients and their doctors are confidential. And so I say to Dr. Stuart, "I'd prefer if you didn't mention any of this to Charlie."

"Of course, Claire." And here is where he starts to lecture me. "You owe it to yourself to take it easy, give yourself time, allow your body to rehabilitate itself. The brain is a fragile thing. The smallest stress can trigger enormous and damaging reactions."

Every time I am in Dr. Stuart's room, I feel my world shrinking. I leave his office with all the reminders of what is forbidden: drinking, traveling, becoming overheated, driving, becoming overtired, running, swimming, being alone for an extended period of time. Where am I, Claire, the actual person, in any of this? I feel as though I have to ask permission even to go to my next appointment with my internist, who will draw blood and ask me the same questions as she shines a light into my eyes. "Good, good," is all everyone says around here, while all the while I just want to run away.

Soon, there is a gentle tapping at the door. Charlie has returned. I could identify his polite, hesitant intrusion anywhere. Now it is time for Dr. Stuart to pull Charlie aside for "a little chat." This is typical too. I sit just outside in the waiting area, but I can hear them discussing me through the door. I listen for the betrayals. Dr. Stuart asks Charlie many of the same questions he's asked me. Dizziness? Falls? Seizures? While I downplayed the situation in my answers—I really do feel much better—Charlie highlights and exaggerates each small mishap.

Dr. Stuart: Has Claire's balance and equilibrium been improving?

Charlie: She is still quite unsteady in the mornings. If she doesn't take a nap, a fall or a seizure is guaranteed by the end of the evening.

I imagine Dr. Stuart taking notes.

Dr. Stuart: Have the seizures been longer? Shorter? Has she started to anticipate them?

Charlie: Claire can be stubborn. Even when she senses them coming, she'd rather keep to the task at hand than have a pause and take care of herself.

Dr. Stuart: On average, how many seizures do you think Claire has in a given week?

Charlie: I'd say four, maybe five.

This is a lie. I document all my seizures in my notebooks.

Over the past weeks, I am down to two a week, I'm sure of it. So what is Charlie's purpose in upping these numbers and making my health and recovery look more precarious? I am baffled. Most of the time, Charlie seems exasperated with me, impatient and snippy, even if he tries to disguise his impatience with his everyday politeness. We are tiptoeing around each other like boxers in a ring. You'd think he'd want me out of the house more, capable of doing more things on my own, but the things he says to Dr. Stuart serve only to contain me within his walls and routine.

As I gaze at celebrities' dresses versus the images of movie stars captured in their shopping clothes in this month's *People*, I fantasize about my escape. What would it take to burn Dr. Stuart's files, to replace them with a more optimistic prognosis, to chart all my accomplishments rather than my ongoing failures? Even without setting fire to the evidence of my helplessness, how many weeks will it take to persuade Dr. Stuart to give me permission to go about my life on my own terms? I have showed him how orderly my notes are, how conscientiously I keep track of my medicine, my seizures, my sleep, the little sparks of my memory. I would like to convince him that I can get on a plane again, that I can map a new story to research, that I can be the person captured in the image of my now useless driver's license and passport, and remind him that a passport cannot be revoked in the same way my driving privileges have been.

When I really want to torture myself, I flip through my passport's pages and marvel at the distances I've traveled.

How can someone with a passport like mine be expected to haunt the creaking floors of an old farmhouse or her husband's little office overlooking a quiet park in a quiet little city? My passport makes me feel like a much smaller version of myself, even if I am not entirely sure of who I used to be. What I do know is that Charlie's new version of me is not the self I would ever choose to claim. Seizures or not, I am not helpless, diseased, failing. I have evidence that I am capable of traveling great distances. One day both Charlie and Dr. Stuart may be surprised at just how far I have come.

Charlie

After we returned from the hospital, Claire went up to take a nap and I joined Rachel in the living room, music from the stereo barely humming in the background. Rachel was sitting cross-legged on the floor, balancing a mug on her inner thigh. Her toenails were painted pink, which surprised me. She still drank coffee late into the day and bragged that she never had problems falling asleep. She didn't look as though she'd have any trouble tonight either. She looked rattled, and I wondered if she was still a bit shaken from her shopping trip with Claire a few days earlier.

It took me a moment or two before I saw one of Claire's boxes half-unpacked beneath the coffee table. It took me another moment still to realize that Rachel had been crying.

"Rach? What have you been up to all day here by yourself? Are you all right?" I tried to meet her gaze. There were times when she was impossibly difficult to talk to, and I feared that I might be up against one of them now.

Rachel fixed her eyes on the box. She seemed angry—with me or with Claire or just generally, it was impossible to say. "Rach?" I asked again. "What's wrong?"

"Have you been through her things?" Rachel finally looked up. "Have you let her go through all of them?"

Her tone stung me a little. "I'm not a prison warden, Rach." I tried to laugh; I tried to get her to laugh with me, but she was making me unsure of myself and she refused to look up from the box.

"Sure you're not. No one is accusing you of any such thing, Charlie." She was trying to smile as she kicked the box away. "I'm going to help Claire sort through some more of these tomorrow if she's feeling up to it."

"Of course," I answered. "I'm sure she'll be up for it."

Rachel raised her eyebrows; her look was almost teasing, but I was still sensing some hostility in her gaze. "It's all right with you, then? There's a lot of her work things here. Her stuff from New York, her correspondence." Rachel paused.

"I know what's here, Rachel. I moved it myself." I was becoming irritated. After our visit to the hospital, my patience

was already worn thin. There were things Rachel wasn't saying, and she seemed to be savoring the process of leaving me
in the dark.

"If she asks me about things, I'll have to tell her the truth."

I squatted down beside Rachel and picked up a photograph she had taken out of one of the boxes. It showed the
three of us perched on a wall on Charles Street. Rachel was
licking an ice cream cone and Claire was wearing a Red Sox
jersey. I remembered the day the shot was taken. We had just
been to Fenway Park. It was August, just before school was
about to start up again. I had a mustard stain on my shirt
and Claire was staring directly into the camera, her gaze not
entirely friendly. Who had the photographer been? One of
Rachel's short-lived suitors perhaps. Her classmate from Magazine Editing or the bartender from the local pub. I couldn't
remember.

"Of course you will. I haven't been hiding anything from
her, if that's what you're getting at. If she bothers to ask me
things, I tell her the things I remember."

"And if she doesn't know what questions to ask?" Rachel
leaned closer to me to take another look at the photo. "You
have a stain on your shirt. It's very unlike you."

"What's with all this hostility, Rach? I'm not a mind
reader and I refuse to do all the work for her. I think you're
asking for too much."

Rachel took the photo from me and slipped it into her
pocket. There again was the half-attempted smile. It looked
as though the gesture was causing her some sort of pain. It

shouldn't cost her such an effort just to smile at me. "I'm sorry," she said. "I'm not being fair. It's been a tough couple of days, Charlie. I haven't been able to sleep since Claire's seizure in town. It was a bad one. I was terrified. I felt helpless—you know how much I hate that." She tried to smile again and, this time, took my hand in hers. "As usual, Claire ended up reassuring me when it was all over."

"Yes, she'll do that." I squeezed Rachel's hand. "I'm sorry you had to see her like that. It is rather traumatic, though she assures me that she doesn't feel any pain. She's convinced, actually, that the whole thing is harder on me than it is on her, but it's a difficult thing to believe."

Rachel dropped my hand. "She doesn't remember India, Charlie. She doesn't remember her research or her articles. She barely remembers our time in the house or when she moved in. And what she remembers sounds like regurgitated facts that she's memorized. There's no feeling to her memories, if they are, in fact, her memories."

"It unsettles me too."

"She sounds like you, Charlie." Rachel laughed. "It's funny to hear your descriptions come out of her mouth. No one describes things like you do." She paused again. I wondered if she meant that as a compliment. "This morning, she asked me when the two of you had your first kiss. I told her I thought it was the day we were painting the bedrooms upstairs. She asked me if the paint was blue and I told her no, it was yellow, and her face completely changed, Charlie, she looked at me as if I were lying to her. It all felt very strange."

"Oh, I'm quite familiar with that look." It felt good to have some of my experiences confirmed by Rachel. These small accusations that showed themselves on Claire's face, the coy smile that suggested she had caught me in a lie. It was maddening.

"And then you start second-guessing the truth of your own memories. I sat there for a second, thinking maybe it was blue paint, maybe I don't have it right." Rachel laughed again. "I live in that house every day, Charlie! Of course the master bedroom is painted yellow, not blue! She has me tied up in knots." Rachel played with an edge of packing tape on one of the boxes. She had stopped laughing. "I was right, though, wasn't I? That was your first kiss? In my parents' bedroom with paint all over the place?"

It was difficult for me to look at Rachel. Even all these years later, it still feels like a breach. We were the three of us, the closest of friends, and I knew I was upsetting the balance even if Rachel no longer had feelings for me. I had sensed her presence that afternoon when I had leaned in to kiss Claire. In my nervousness, I had missed her lips entirely and knocked my mouth somewhere against her chest. "It wasn't really a kiss that day."

Rachel wasn't looking at me either, which was making the conversation rather unbearable. "Well, maybe I'm remembering it wrong, then. Maybe you should tell her when it was. She seems eager to remember." She was growing distant again, the tension creeping back into her voice.

And there was that familiar anger growing in me. It wasn't Rachel's fault, but I felt like slapping her. As if all of this should be my job, this remembering for the two of us. I have my memories; Claire has hers. They are in there, somewhere; I know they are. And she has to do some of the work to get them back. It isn't for me to tell her how or what to remember. "What good would it do for me to tell her, then, Rach? If she doesn't remember, it doesn't exist for her. I can't tell her that she loved me, that she kissed me first. I can't force her to remember these things—they're just words to her. Like you said, regurgitated nonsense out of my mouth. Who is even to say that I've got it right? Maybe I imagined the whole thing the first time around, and she never loved me at all. Maybe I kissed her first. There's no one else who can confirm it for me."

Rachel raised her hand to cut me off. I realized just then that I had been yelling. "I'm not exactly sure why you're angry with me. I can understand, Charlie, how hard this is for you. I can even understand you feeling sorry for yourself from time to time, or even taking things out on me if it helps." She looked up at me. "I came here to help. I love you both. But I think you're being a bit ridiculous—being jealous, or maybe *protective* is the better word, of your own past." Rachel straightened her skirt. She reached out to touch my arm. "It's not only you, Charlie. I still drift back to that time. I want her to remember those years too. Without her memories, it's hard to be certain that we all loved each other; it's hard to believe that those moments ever existed. And of course, it's impossible to lay blame, isn't it? When the other person can't confirm the past. It must be really frustrating for you, Charlie." Rachel took her hand away.

"Which part, exactly?" I tried to laugh, but when I looked up at her, she wasn't smiling back at me. I moved to the couch.

"That she doesn't seem to remember him."

Now it was my turn to try to change the subject. I didn't trust myself to continue without becoming angry. Rachel had no right to try to rattle me just because she herself was feeling unsettled. "When did you start painting your toenails? It seems out of character somehow."

Rachel seemed embarrassed and her mug almost spilled over as she shifted her feet under her. "I started painting them out of boredom, and now I'm hooked." She grinned. "I'm a sucker for fuchsia."

"I would have pegged you for something more vampish— Red Diva or Glammed Out Garnet or Razz Berry." It was a clunky attempt at teasing. I was trying, perhaps too hard, to put things right between us.

Rachel wasn't playing along. "My goodness, Charlie. Who knew you were such a nail polish expert? Very mysterious, I'd say. After all, Claire has never worn nail polish." Rachel gave me a mischievous grin, but there was a hardness to it. She was fishing for something and I suddenly wondered if she and Claire had made some kind of pact. Rachel would get answers out of me for Claire without Claire's having to muster the effort to ask questions herself. I was tired from all our bickering, the half-spoken accusations, the old hurts pushing to the surface.

I thought about Claire's questions coming out of Rachel's mouth. It made me drift back to the earliest days of our friendship, when I was so very convinced of our shared loyalties and trust. I wondered now if there hadn't been something competitive brewing all along, jealousies developing alongside the devotion to one another. How could there not have been? I am certain that we all loved each other, but of course, we were all capable of being brutal in our own ways. Rachel, though, was surprising me now. Perhaps it was the trauma of the past days or the fact that we'd plucked her from her routine again, but she had seemed so short fused with me. And prying too. She had me on edge. But just as I was about to leave the room to make some tea, she scooted over to me and reached up to grab my hands.

"I'm so sorry. I've been feeling cranky all day. I'm being unkind." She rested her head on my knee. "I think those boxes triggered something in me and then you walked in, just at the moment I was feeling most frustrated."

"There's really no need to apologize, Rach. None of us are at our best right now, obviously."

She lifted her head and smiled a bit sadly at me. "You don't want to talk about it. That's okay, Charlie. Mostly I just wanted to say I was sorry."

She was right; I didn't really want to talk anymore. I was still cross with her for her earlier comments and I was tired and worried that at any moment the conversation might take a nasty turn again. But instead of heading toward the kitchen, I pulled Rachel next to me on the couch and said, "I do want to talk. There's not much of that going on around here these days."

Rachel smiled. "The photo made me mad—isn't that stupid of me?"

"The one in your pocket? Whatever for? I remember that being a good day. The Sox beat the Blue Jays, didn't they? We were stuffed full of hot dogs and beer. Claire had gotten her hat signed by—who was it?—Gedman, the catcher, I think?"

Rachel laughed. "It was a good day. Of course it was. But I was sulking. Do you remember? Looking back now, it might have all been in my head."

"What do you mean?"

"This is stupid. This is—what, now, fifteen years ago?"

"Go on, then." I tapped Rachel on her knee.

She rolled her eyes. "I was convinced that Claire had been flirting with Ben—the guy from my class that I had been dating for something like three weeks. I knew the relationship wasn't going anywhere, but still, I was furious with her."

"Ben! That was his name! I had forgotten. I was trying to remember if it was your classmate we had gone with, or if was that chap from the bar who you used to see from time to time."

"Frank? Are you kidding? I never went out in public with that guy!"

"Surely not. My mistake, Ben it was, then." We were both laughing now.

"Ben it was, indeed, Charlie. Anyway, he kept maneuvering closer to Claire every chance he got, and I thought, out of loyalty to me—and to you, for that matter!—she should be moving away, but I was convinced, absolutely convinced, that she was encouraging him."

"I wouldn't put it past her. She liked to make us both jealous, I think." I laughed as I said it, but there was a catch of meanness in my tone. I heard it and Rachel certainly did too. Rachel dropped the back of her hand on my thigh.

"I guess I wouldn't either." Rachel sipped from her mug. She had grown quiet. I had made things awkward again. "I wonder if you should bring it up, Charlie. I tried to at the store, but she had no reaction to his name."

So this is what she had been wanting to tell me all along. I was suddenly furious with her all over again. "I wish you wouldn't do that, Rachel." I pushed her hand away. "I am trying to hold things together here. Can't you respect that even a little bit? It's tricky enough as it is. Why should I bring him up? He's actually had the decency to stay away. Why is it my responsibility? I am taking care of her. I have opened my house—our house—back up to her. I am not asking questions; I am not making accusations; I am not—"

"Of course you're not, Charlie! You never do." Rachel was shouting now. "It's easier for you this way."

"Easier for me? You must be joking."

"Yes, easier. This way, everyone looks at you as if you were the saint. Stoic, kind, generous Charlie. How does he do it? Such patience. Such selflessness."

"You are not being fair, Rachel."

"And all the while, you get to keep holding in this anger, this blame. You keep judging her, and she doesn't even know anything about it. You keep her in the dark so you can remain good and she can remain bad. She knows you are angry; she's not stupid, Charlie. But she doesn't know why. It's not so different from lying."

We looked at each other in surprise. I had lost track of who I was angry with, and I feared Rachel had done the same. She had started to cry. I was unwilling to admit the truth in what she had said.

"We have never confronted her. Not once over the years." Rachel directed her words into her own lap. "Why didn't we ever ask her to explain herself? We never held her accountable for anything. We let her be. I wonder all the time why we always did that." Rachel put down her mug and stretched her legs out over the edge of the couch. She rested her head on my lap and I didn't know where to put my hands.

"It's a simple answer for me, Rach. You already know it. I am a coward. I was afraid of losing her entirely, so I thought I was willing to pretend. I thought I'd be able to share her, rather than let her go completely. She must have taken me for an idiot. I think back and I wonder if all that time she was just waiting for me to finally stand up to her. But I was a coward. I was going to make her do the leaving—I wasn't about to do it for her. I couldn't bear the idea of it." I paused. "She talked to you about him, of course. About our separate bedrooms. How infrequently she came back home."

"Yes, she did." Rachel wiped at her nose. "I'm sorry. I figured you were too perceptive not to know, so I imagined you had somehow given your okay to the whole thing. I have to say I was a bit furious with you."

"With me?"

"Yes, with you, Charlie." She reached up to pat my cheek. "I suppose I wanted you to make her suffer, even just a little bit. I wanted her to have to lose you. Maybe I was hoping you'd act out my revenge for me or something. It wasn't fair, but I wanted you both to hurt, and then maybe there'd be some kind of balance again. It was an awful way to think, I know, Charlie. And I'm sorry for it."

"I'm not sure I'm completely following you, Rach. What sort of revenge do you mean?"

"I know you don't understand, Charlie. How could you? I've been a coward too. I never said a word when you left. We're all perfect for one another." Rachel laughed but there was no joy in it. She got up from the couch and kissed me on the forehead. "I'm going to head out for a walk," she said. "Maybe I'll be better company when I come back."

AFTER HER NAP and while Rachel was still out for a walk, Claire approached me in my study. She held out a photograph and asked me to look at it. Claire told me she had found it with the pictures from her time in India, amid the articles and notes and crumpled rupees. "It's the only one of you I could find. Were we there together? How often did you come?"

Despite my attempts at pleasant conversation on our drive home, I hadn't done a very good job concealing my frustration. I know it's not Claire's fault—rationally I understand this—that she remembers her parents and grandparents more than she seems to remember me, but at my most impatient, I want to accuse her of picking and choosing from among her memories. Selfishly I want to be there in her mind alongside the stories of her mother's pig. I don't know if this was Claire's attempt at assuaging me, this picture from my only visit to India. And after my conversation with Rachel, I wasn't sure I was willing to have this one. "I came whenever you invited me." I watched her for a reaction. When she didn't offer one, I added, "I joined you once."

Claire studied the picture. "I'm sure we were both busy with our work. It's not as if you could leave the office for too long at a time, I imagine. India is a long way away."

It had come to this: the two of us talking to one another carefully, as if it were a conversation between a parent and a child. "Yes, Claire, that was part of it, certainly. India is very far away and you were quite busy and never in one place for very long. And like you say, I had the office to run and the local politics to cover and the Take Back Vermont chants to record."

"I wasn't making fun of your work, Charlie." Claire looked injured.

"I know you weren't." I examined the photo. There was

a coastline in the background and a baguette sticking out of Claire's purse. It was taken during the few days we spent in Pondicherry, a brief respite from the stifling heat and chaos of the inland cities. We had watched with some fascination as foreigners, mostly Europeans and Americans, dressed all in white, marched to and from the ashram of the Mother, an aging French woman, the local guru. There was a commune not too far out of the city, modeled on a local, sustainable agrarian society. Supposedly, there were members from every continent there, tending their own patch of land, sharing their goods with their neighbors. No money changed hands. Claire wanted to do a story there, but she was coming up against quite a bit of resistance. She was in a grouchy mood because of it. You can see a slight scowl in her expression. Or perhaps she was cross with me. I was rather unhappy too, as I recall, and a few hours before this picture was snapped, we had been discussing whether I'd stay for the full three weeks we had planned for or perhaps head home a week or so early.

The picture is quite beautiful. Claire is lovely. She is wearing a straw hat, and beads of sunlight are filtering through the hat's gaps, casting bright speckles across her already freckled face. Her skin is glowing, and all the hiking around in the villages and riverbeds have made her strong and fit. She is wearing a modest sundress that matches the muted pastels of the French colonial buildings behind us. I am looking away from the camera. I am squinting out toward the unswimmable sea and refusing to meet the gaze of the camera. It is a very professional-looking picture, the depth of field elongated to keep us in focus while showing off the UNESCO-protected architecture lining our route. Of course, it is clear who has taken this picture. It is why I won't meet the viewfinder directly on. I wonder what Claire sees when she looks at this picture and whether she notices that I am looking away, refusing to confront the reality of our situation.

"Why did I choose India?" she asked me. "Was I there long?"

"Off and on for two years. You had done some pieces for the *Globe* on ecological sustainability, overpopulation, land rights. You had been down to Ecuador a few times, and Brazil. The science editor from the *Times* liked what you were doing. He got the travel editor on board; they thought you could tackle two birds with one stone. 'Thirty-Six Hours in Chennai.' 'The Cauvery River Shrinks.' 'Shantytowns and Nightclubs in Bangalore.' They hired you on a freelance basis, but you always seemed to have work. We were very proud of you."

"Did you think about coming with me?" Claire was still eyeing the picture skeptically. "Did I like the food there? I'm annoyed the doctors won't let me eat spicy foods these days."

This was how our conversations had been going lately. Claire would ask me something seemingly (at least to me) quite important, but then she would shift to some mundane question about food or her medications or why we never had a dog, and I would lose my focus too. "Which question do you want an answer to first?" I asked. I have always thought of myself as a patient person, but I was failing miserably at keeping my composure during these wandering chats. At this point I wanted to shake her and shout: Think! What is it that you really want to know? Do you really not remember?

She sensed I was getting exasperated. "Whichever one you want. I've forgotten where I started. Remind me." Claire walked into the kitchen, leaving me with the photo in my hands. She called to me from the stove: "Should I make some tea? Or we still have that hot chocolate that Nancy gave us."

"Whatever you like, Claire. I'm happy with either," I shouted back. This was also something Claire continued to do. If she sensed a conversation growing difficult between us, she'd simply move away. To the kitchen. To the garage. To the computer to look over her ever-increasing folders of notes and pictures. I brought a scanner home from work a week ago, and now I had begun to regret it. The hard drive was getting overloaded with all of Claire's archives of the past. I was going to need to buy us—me—a new laptop. I could no longer even find most of my work on the old computer. And here I went again, finding ways to be annoyed that had nothing to do with the topic at hand. What did our computer have to do with Claire's work in India, her increasing distance and time away from home? Her new group of friends, expats and foreign correspondents and NGO workers and local activists and the photographer?

I walked into the kitchen. "The doctors won't let you eat spicy food because of your throat spasms. They expect all of that to improve once they get the seizures under control and your coordination starts to get better. And yes, you loved the food in India, though it often made you sick as a dog. You insisted on eating all the street foods—the sugarcane juice and the fried lentil patties, the rotis and the horrendous sweets. You'd send me e-mails whose entire subject was the food you had discovered that particular week. You were lucky I visited only once. I tried one street samosa, and I was laid out for two days."

Claire grinned. "Maybe we should try to make some version of all those things here. We could make them milder. Maybe eating something from the past could jog my memories from that time. The doctors say that sensory stimuli are sometimes the best way to access memories—smell, in particular, I think it was they said. Or taste? I can't remember. Anyway, it might be worth a try." Claire handed me a cup of steaming chocolate. It seemed she was going to ignore my last comments.

I couldn't shake Rachel's voice from my head, her accusations about my silences, my confessions of cowardice. Was this a moment in which I should confront Claire with the past? Should I mention the photographer's name, explain whose eyes were gazing at the two of us through the viewfinder? Should I describe my sense of embarrassment, shame even, at letting him look at me, at the two of us together, and click the shutter in his own version of judgment? What could I say? What would I ask? How could you have put me through that, Claire? Instead I said, "You didn't want me to come with you, Claire. Or rather, you knew I wouldn't come: I hate the heat, I hate crowds, I hate untidiness and unpleasant smells. I would have ruined India for you. We both knew that."

Claire sniffed and scratched at the nape of her neck, where her hair was slowly returning.

If she wasn't going to say anything, I figured I'd just follow her lead, though I could feel my stomach shriveling up inside me. I had been angry for so long that I didn't know how to start talking about any of this. "It was clear that you had made up your mind, and we both used my work as the reason for my not coming. My job wouldn't be waiting for me upon my return after two years away. I had worked too long and too hard to just give it up. We both agreed." I looked up at Claire, who was gazing at the floor. "It was a convenient lie for both of us."

"Do you still blame me for going away?" Claire kicked at the bottom of the cupboards. She smiled at me. "I mean, it's obvious that you're still angry."

"I'm beginning to understand my own complicity in all of it, Claire. I never asked you to stay."

"That's not entirely answering the question, Charlie." Claire approached me and rested her elbow on my shoulder. "Why are you so angry with me?"

I pinched the end of her index finger. "It wasn't the first time you had gone away. You had already rented your flat in Boston, and then you had moved on to New York. First we would take turns on the train, you traveling north, me traveling south, but then you started coming here less and less, and I thought I could match your stubbornness, so I stopped taking the trains too. You barely seemed to notice. You had already left; India was just a bit farther away. I knew things wouldn't change much."

"I didn't like it here." Claire flicked my finger away.

Her words struck me, and anger must have flashed across my face.

"I'm sorry; I meant it as a question, Charlie. Why didn't I like it here?"

"How am I to say, Claire, for God's sake? Only you can know that. You pretended to like it here, but I always thought you found it provincial and claustrophobic. You complained that there were no good pubs and the place was overrun with students. It was cold all the time, and then suddenly too hot with too many mosquitoes. The only time you could bear it was during the autumn. You were restless; you took long walks by yourself. You tell me, Claire—why didn't you like it here?"

"I'm sorry." Claire offered me a sad smile.

I really couldn't stomach her feeling sorry for me. I wanted to push her elbow away, do something dramatic like throw my mug against the wall, and shout, Why would you make hot chocolate, when after all these years you should know I prefer tea? Really what I wanted to do was simply push her, push her away from my chest, out the front door, hand her my car keys, and keep pushing. Instead I pushed her the only way I knew how these days, by tapping ever so slightly at her guilt and her faulty brain. "How can you be sorry for things you don't even remember? You can't apologize without knowing what you're apologizing for."

Claire took my head in her hands. "I'm sorry I can't answer your questions, Charlie. I would tell you why I didn't like it here if I could." She tugged on my ears, just like she used to, and pulled me to her. "I like it now. It's peaceful." She pressed her nose against my neck. "And you smell good, always like the outside." And then she kissed me in our kitchen, our hips leaning against the stove, a simple kiss, as if she were testing how it might feel to her. We stared at each other, her thumbs tucked into my belt, kissing with our eyes open. We were watching each other for a reaction, neither of us pulling away.

Rachel

While I'm out for my walk and debating whether I even want to return to Charlie and Claire's house, I think how easy it is, how easy it's always been, to simply blame Claire for my losing Charlie. It is true that I had to sit back and watch them fall in love—watch her drape her legs over his lap as we watched movies in the living room, and ask him his advice on her latest story (he was always a sucker for flattery)—and once everything started, I of course had to watch them exchange quick kisses in the kitchen over tea before they both headed out to start their day. Perhaps that was the hardest thing—to see their easy familiarity with one another, as if this part of their relationship had been there all along. All those weeks of Charlie in my bed, passing me the newspaper and asking me if he should bring home dinner or if we were planning to cook at home, had just been a placeholder for him and Claire. It was impossible to deny that there was an easiness between them that had never been there between Charlie and me. We had always been rather careful with one another, asking before doing, watchful of the other's expression. Or perhaps I should speak only for myself. I was always watching Charlie for signs of really being in love with me, and it's true that I was never certain how he felt about me, which made my decision slightly easier when Claire helped me make it. I certainly wasn't going to make Charlie love me because of a child.

I was terrible to Charlie when he came back from his conference. My body was wracked with cramps and I couldn't find the energy to leave my bed, and I was terrified that he would be able to read the truth of what I had done in the awkwardness of my movements, in the dark circles under my eyes. I didn't leave my room much for a week or more, and every time Charlie tapped on the door so very lightly, so very politely, I urged him away. Claire had told him that I had the stomach flu, and when he brought me tea, oversweetened with honey the way I like it, I shooed him away and refused to meet his kiss. I remember him leaning in, telling me he had missed me, and my turning my face away from him so that his lips brushed my ear awkwardly. Later in the week, he brought me the newspaper and began to tell me about the conference and how he had met an editor up in Vermont who was planning on retiring soon and how one day there might be a job in it for him. But I heard few of the details because my insides were screaming and I felt so damn guilty, listening to him chatter away when my silence then, and my silence from that point on, would unspool a continuous lie between us. I knew for the first time with complete clarity that I loved him and I also knew that I had ruined everything. When he sat on the corner of my bed, an electric jolt of pain shot through me, from my pelvis to my brain, and I yelled at him. "Damn it, Charlie," I think I said, "can't you see that I just want to be left alone?" I don't remember exactly what I shouted, but I do remember the hurt in his face as he told me to rest up and said he'd be back to check on me a bit later, but either he didn't return or I slept right through his visit, and he was careful with me from that point on.

I avoided him for days. I listened for his voice in the kitchen, calling out a good-bye to Claire and perhaps to the absent me, and then finally I would drag myself out of bed. Claire was good to me. She skipped a few classes or went to campus late so that we could have breakfast together. She didn't say much, but she would brush out my hair and look over the writing assignments I was trying to keep up with and make me feel as if I wasn't alone. "I can't look at him," I remember telling Claire one of those mornings.

"It'll get better." She smiled at me. She tried very hard to make me feel like myself again. Maybe she was feeling guilty too. I'm sure she hadn't anticipated my sluggish sadness, my sleeplessness, the anger that was so quick to spill over into our conversations.

"No. I don't think it will." It was hard for me to look at Claire. I suppose it was hard for her to look at me too. She avoided any direct eye contact with me during our halting breakfast conversations. I remember her constant movements, clanging about in the kitchen, offering to make me some eggs or oatmeal, or taking my work and bending over it at the kitchen table, scribbling notes and edits, and avoiding me while simultaneously trying to keep me company, trying to look after me. I knew it wasn't her fault, all this hurt and anger and fear welling up inside me. I was the one who went to the appointment, folded my clothes into a bundle, and shut my eyes when the doctor and nurse came in, willing time to push forward so that the whole ordeal would already be in the past and I could open my eyes and be a normal person again.

Because I didn't let myself talk to Charlie, it was easy for me to turn my anger toward him. I reasoned that if he loved me, he would see how much pain I was in. If he loved me, he would know that something was deeply, deeply wrong. If he loved me, he would have barged into my room and shaken my shoulders and forced me to open my mouth and just tell him what the hell was going on with me. But that wasn't Charlie. Charlie doesn't yell and Charlie doesn't barge in and demand things. Charlie is polite and careful and kind. But Charlie is also weak and easily frightened, which may have been what drew me to him in the first place. It's funny how the people you think are incapable of hurting anyone can cause the most hurt.

Eventually, Charlie and I settled into an uneasy peace. I came out of my room and we ate breakfast together and sometimes walked to the T together, shopped for groceries, went to the movies. We did these things sometimes with Claire, sometimes just the two of us. We had never talked about any of it—my shouting at him, my avoiding him for weeks, or the fact that we had stopped holding hands or kissing one another or falling into bed, wine drunk and shy and giddy. Some agreement had been made in our mutual silence. We were finding our way back into a friendship, me subtly apologetic, Charlie slightly befuddled. We smiled at each other and complimented one another on silly things and bought each other small gifts (a scarf from the secondhand store, a used copy of a Wallace Stevens poetry collection, an ugly watercolor of a brook and a bird that reminded us both of East Anglia)—something we had never done before—and grew at the same time more comfortable with one another and more distant.

I think about this awkward courtship back into friendship and I blame a lot of things for the damage done. I blame how young we were, twenty-three and clumsy with our emotions. I blame Charlie for not being braver and I blame myself for agreeing to a silence. It seemed too easy to blame Claire, when really it was me I was most disgusted with. She had been a good friend who had taken my words and transformed them into the advice she thought I needed to hear. Just as she had started to put order into my parents' house after their death, she had been trying to restore order to my life.

Weeks went by and eventually we all settled back into the rhythms of our house. As I relaxed, Claire relaxed too, and then came the decision to paint and clean and make the house truly ours. I don't remember the exact moment I started noticing the changes between Claire and Charlie, when it became the two of them sitting on the couch, entangled, while I sat on my dad's corduroy recliner, in front of a rented movie, or when they would meet up for a drink after classes while I stayed in the library working on my thesis, or when I would go to sleep, listening to their chatter carrying up from downstairs, a record hissing from the living room. Instead I remember only the ladder and the kiss and the paint-spattered room and all that anger, deep and weeks old, groaning in my body. I hated them both in that instant, but not nearly as much as I hated myself. I have always thought that it was I who let that kiss happen. I hadn't been strong enough to make my own demands, and it would always be my fault if I ended up alone. More than the kiss or the fact that Claire and Charlie were falling in love with one another, what made me angry was that they were going to leave me. The two people who had become my family, the only two people in the world who I loved and who loved me back, were one day going to leave me behind.

Of course, that was still a few years away. We would

continue living in my parents' house, we would finish our degrees, and Charlie would find work with the *Worcester Telegram and Gazette* while Claire covered local stories for the AP, and eventually that editor who had been planning to retire actually retired and remembered Charlie and called him one evening and put him in touch with his managing editor up in Burlington.

CLAIRE WAS RELENTLESS in her search for a boy-friend for me. "What is with you?" she used to tease me. "I know you have a vagina. I know you have feelings." It seemed like every weekend Claire would organize some kind of evening for us—some live music at the Paradise followed by cocktails, dinner out in the South End, after-hours "cool tea" in Chinatown, long after the bars had stopped serving. And at each of these outings, a man would show up, saying that Claire had invited him. I don't know where or how she met so many people. My life, at that time, consisted mainly of showing up at work in Copley Square, sitting in a cubi-cle for eight hours, editing textbook copy, and then heading home or to some destination Claire had suggested for the evening. I was lucky if I met up for lunch with a cubicle mate or was called into my boss's office for a planning session. Otherwise it was pretty much me, a stack of papers, worn pencils, and my computer keeping me company throughout the day.

Claire's job with the AP sent her all over the city, covering stories as disparate as school zoning and Red Sox recruitment scouting. Wherever she went, she seemed to pick up a new friend, and if that new friend was a guy, she'd invite him along to our next outing. If she found him particularly promising, she'd recommend a specific outfit for me to wear. Sometimes she'd tell me to meet her somewhere an hour before she actually arrived, so I'd be forced to chat with David or Henry or Max at a dimly lit bar until she and Charlie showed up. I'm not sure who would be more disappointed in these moments, me for being set up, yet again, with a dude wearing a Celtics T-shirt, or the dude who was hoping to meet another Claire and instead got stuck with me.

I can admit that I started behaving badly. I drank too much and I flirted with these poor guys even when I wasn't remotely interested in them or even attracted to them. I let them buy me drinks and then I let them take me home, long after Charlie and Claire had left the bar, and we stumbled into the house, loud and drunk, and were noisy in our clumsy and ugly sex. By the time Charlie and Claire and I were having our morning tea, I had already kicked David or Henry or Max out, and when Claire would ask if I planned to call him later, maybe invite him over to dinner some night later in the week, I'd tell her that I had forgotten to get his number or that he had a girlfriend who was just out of town for the week or that he was a Republican and that it would never work. I figured Claire would eventually get tired of fixing me up on these hopeless not-quite-dates, but she'd always just snort and roll her eyes at me. "You're terrible, Rach," she would say to me. Or "Well, there's always next time."

"Who asked you to become my matchmaker?" I asked her more than once. Or if I was feeling more mean spirited, I'd accuse her of being conservative and judgmental. "Not every date has to lead to another one," I'd say.

"No. That's true. But maybe one date could."

"That never used to be your attitude."

"Fine. Forget it. You're on your own," she'd threaten, but then the next weekend would come around and there would be Jonathan sitting at the table.

Charlie usually kept his mouth shut during these interactions. Whether he was amused or embarrassed, it was impossible to say. Sometimes he'd just offer some innocuous comment like, "I thought Max was a nice bloke. Maybe I'll call him some time if you don't."

And then I would sigh and pour myself a drink. I'm embarrassed, thinking back on this time. I was young and didn't realize how angry I was. I had just lost my parents and I was terrified I was losing my best friends too. I was trying on a version of meanness I had never embraced, and thought it was making me tough and resilient and independent, but in the end I think it was just turning me into an ass.

ON ONE OF these nights, I met Bernard. His name was so old-fashioned sounding that I was ready to write him off immediately. Bernard in his self-consciously unhip James Joyce glasses, his sagging brown corduroys, his curly hair, which would spike up in certain spots, coiled and unpredictable. Bernard, to use Charlie's phrase, was "a lovely bloke." He was smart and funny, and he would dance if he had enough beers in him, and he liked to cook adventurous foods and surprise us with unexpected plans. Bernard was an obsessive contest enterer. He insisted that if you make a point of entering drawings in supermarkets, buying raffle tickets from the local Boy Scouts, purchasing an occasional lottery ticket, chances were you'd win something great every once in a while. Claire teased him, called him a gambler, but she didn't really mean it. In the end we had to agree that Bernard was right. Because of him we ate a lovely meal at the top of the Hancock Tower; we got free admission to Canobie Lake Park, where we got sick on fried dough and roller coasters; we won a shopping spree—EVERYTHING YOU CAN THROW IN YOUR SHOPPING CART IN 4½ MINUTES!!!—at the local Market Basket.

Bernard lived in a tiny studio in Allston, so we stored most of his winnings at our house: In the living room, an antique poster for *Broken Blossoms* that featured Lillian Gish eyeing a crystal ball. In the guest room, a replica of the fortune-telling machine from the movie *Big* that made us all a little nervous. On our bookshelves, commemorative snow globes for every month of the year. Until Bernard won this dubious prize from a local antique store, we had all thought snow globes contained only winter scenes. How wrong we were. Instead of snow, July rained butterflies, September rained orange and yellow leaves, April rained rain.

Bernard was a photographer Claire had worked with on a story. They met on a ferry that was taking them to the Boston

Harbor Islands for some investigation of a former mental institution that had been built out there a century ago, on one of the spits of land jutting out into the bay. "He's shy," Claire had whispered to me that first time, when we all met at an oyster bar after the shoot. "It took a lot of persuading to get him to come out tonight, so be nice to him." It wasn't hard to be nice to Bernard. He was sweet and quietly sarcastic and easily embarrassed. He had grown up in Maine in a family of boys, who had always teased him for being arty and sensitive when most of them chose to head toward the ocean and work on fishing boats.

I think what I appreciated about him the most that night, though, was that he watched Claire with a bemused expression much like the one I had tried to master over the past months. He gave her the space to tell her stories of the day. They had arrived on Long Island, one of the harbor islands, early in the morning, the fog still layered over the landscape. It was misty and cold, and little drops of moisture hung from the trees and the abandoned buildings. They visited a shelter on the island where homeless people, picked up in the South End mostly, were transported each evening to a warmish bed and some hot food, much of which was grown at an organic farm neighboring the shelter. "It's a weirdly self-sufficient community out there," Claire explained while Charlie replaced her empty Guinness with another. I had been noticing the way Charlie always had his hand on Claire, a gentle but persistent presence. He might graze her shoulder on the way to the bar or touch her forearm as he replaced her drink. I suppose it was his way of telling Claire that he was listening, that he was always near, but without making any kind of fuss. They had entered an easy sort of rhythm over the past months, and as I listened to Claire's recap of the day, I was taken aback all over again by their—at least it felt this way to me—sudden intimacy.

I liked that Bernard interjected, quietly, when he felt Claire had gotten a detail wrong. When she complained that the shelter smelled of urine and was an oppressive place, he suggested that it was actually pretty humane, comparatively speaking. He turned to me at one point and explained that the food co-op was run like a kibbutz, that the volunteers lived out there all year round, gardening and canning and maintaining a greenhouse. It was an extraordinary little world, he said. And then Claire explained how she had talked Bernard into climbing into an old, abandoned building that had once been some sort of hotel and an almshouse and a dormitory for wayward boys. "And then he just disappeared, chasing photographs, and left me in an old kitchen." Claire took a sip of her beer and paused. "It's a place where you can hear the past," she said, and Bernard smirked at me across the table. He was amused by Claire but wasn't completely charmed by her, and I found myself drawn to him and his skepticism.

Bernard wasn't much of a drinker, and my boozy antics and aggressive flirtations hadn't seemed to affect him much, so I was a little surprised that he mustered the energy to ask me out. He had just graduated from MassArt and invited me to the opening of a show of some of his recent work. We were just saying good night, so I suggested he might as well come home with us, but instead he wrote the name of the gallery and the address on a napkin, underlined "Thursday" three times, and gave it to me without even a kiss on the cheek or a quick hug. He shook Charlie's hand and told Claire he'd send her some of the extra prints that didn't get used in the story, and then he strolled out of the restaurant. He had a bounce to his gait, a tendency to walk on his toes, that I found a little silly. I certainly had no initial plans to go to his show, but when Thursday rolled around, I headed out alone to the gallery, leaving Claire and Charlie on the couch in front of an old Polanski movie that I had picked out much to Claire's dismay. Not another Polanski, she had whined earlier. I had been finding small ways of punishing her.

The gallery was in the South End, and it had started snowing by the time I got there. My feet were wet and cold and I can only imagine the scowl I was wearing as I entered the room. Bernard was standing toward the back of the space, surrounded by a few friends, mostly women. I wasn't quite sure if I was jealous, but I certainly wasn't going to approach him. I slowly meandered around the exhibit, refusing to make eye contact with Bernard. If he wanted to talk to me, he could come up to me, thank me for coming out on this stupid, wintery night.

I had to admit that his work was good. He shot in black and white, focusing on the meeting of light and shadows. His subject was the city itself, anonymous blocks that suddenly made Boston seem strange and unfamiliar to me. I'm not sure how he managed it, but he seemed to snatch portraits accidently, the shutter pausing just long enough to catch the eye of a woman burdened by grocery bags or a garbage collector caught in the act of window shopping. I remember thinking that Bernard would make a great spy. All his subjects seemed oblivious to his presence, and yet his camera caught them in these intimate acts, their expressions revealing their fatigue, their desires, the transitory thoughts that were marked, so very briefly, on their faces.

The images were lonely and lovely and I think I was a little angry with him for being talented and for capturing my interest. I didn't want him to have the upper hand, and at the same time I suddenly very much wanted him to like me. I had been keeping my eye on him surreptitiously. He had moved to the corner of the room, sipping his wine, looking a bit uncomfortable. Eventually I raised my hand to him and he nodded and smiled and took a sip of wine. I was afraid he wasn't going to come over to me and I was too stubborn to go to him, so I turned back to a photo of a young woman who was crouched on the sidewalk, tying the shoe of a toddler with tears streaming down his face. She looked too young to be the child's mother, but the way he rested his hand on her shoulder suggested that she probably was. Perhaps she had sensed Bernard, because she had looked up from her task, her expression accusatory. She had a small scar running down the side of her cheek, and a rhinestone earring had caught the light, shimmering in the late-afternoon sun. It was the only bright thing about the picture, and its sparkle made the rest of the scene sink into even greater shadow. The photo made you want to apologize for looking.

"Thanks for coming, Rachel." Bernard stood next to me, straightening his glasses on his nose. "How are you?"

"Wet and cold and now a little bit sad too, after looking at this photograph, but you're welcome." I knew I should be saying something nice about his work, but there was something in me that refused. I didn't want to repeat something that the gaggle of art-school girls had probably said to him just a few moments ago.

"It was nice of you to come." He handed me a plastic cup of white wine. "We're all out of red."

"I'm too cold for white wine. I'd rather go find some hot chocolate." I took the wine anyway. I was nervous and drank it too quickly.

"I don't think I can leave yet."

I hadn't meant to ask Bernard out, and for a moment I was irritated that he took my comment as an invitation, but his obvious discomfort calmed me. I looked around the room. It was a good crowd for such a miserable night. Bernard explained that he was supposed to be interviewed by someone from the *Phoenix*. The way he told me this sounded both anxious and apologetic.

"Maybe some other time, then." I felt foolish for saying it. I was embarrassed that I wanted to spend time with him. I was humiliated for admiring him and I worried that my neediness was written across my face. I was not acting like the person I had worked so hard to become over the past several months. Ferociously self-reliant. That had been my goal.

"Or you could wait around for a little bit. There's a café a few doors down if you don't want to stay here."

"I'll stay."

Bernard nodded and gave me a half smile. "Good."

"I like your photographs, Bernard." I hated myself for the bland compliment, so I tried for something more intelligent. "It takes a while to see everything that's in them."

Bernard shrugged his shoulders and straightened his glasses again. I had made us both embarrassed. "Okay, well, I'll find you in a bit." Bernard walked away and I turned back to the scolding face of the young woman. I wondered what my own face might reveal if it were caught unprepared.

IT IS DIFFICULT to date a photographer. Or at least it was difficult for me to date a photographer at that time, particularly one like Bernard, who had this uncanny ability to see secrets in people's faces. Whenever he raised his camera to snap a shot of me, I brought my hand to my face or to his lens and shooed him away. I certainly didn't want any of my secrets revealed, but even in those images of me turning away, my hand extended in protest, he caught a piece of me, one of those fleeting thoughts, and I was scared of him a little bit.

Of course Bernard the person was much easier to deal with than Bernard the photographer. He was about as private and reserved as I was, and it was easy to be silent around him. He never pressed me to offer details about my past or explain my moodiness or occasional bouts of anger. There are days when I still feel guilty for being terribly unkind to him. I tried to make him feel stupid for liking a book I might have found vapid. I canceled plans on him at the last minute, trying to make him feel less important than other parts of my life. And then I would just sit home by myself, order a pizza, and watch made-for-TV movies as punishment. I told him I needed space, then pestered him about his art-school girlfriends. I don't know why he stayed with me as long as he did.

He knew about my parents' death and he knew that I had dated Charlie briefly before he and Claire became a couple. He knew that Charlie and Claire always came first, that they were my family. He knew that I wanted to be a writer more than an editor but that I was becoming a good editor and suddenly making a grown-up salary. I think I tried to embarrass him; I insisted on paying for dinner, or I would show up at his place with a present—a new sweater or some records or tickets to a music show. I pushed and pulled, and still he wouldn't go away. He told me that I thought about things more than most people he knew. He liked that I wouldn't let him get away with things, that there was nothing easy about me, that he had to work for a smile and so he knew when to trust it. He told me that mean was better than dishonest. He had to deal with insincere people every day, he said. I was refreshing, he said.

Both Charlie and Claire loved Bernard, which probably doomed the relationship from the start. Claire was basking in her success; she had finally found me the perfect man, while Charlie had a new cooking mate in the kitchen. I'm sure they were both relieved by the sudden balance in our dynamic. Four is easier than three, and whatever guilt they had been feeling seemed to evaporate with the presence of Bernard. Perhaps I didn't want to let them off that easy or perhaps I liked the difficulty of three more than the harmony of four or maybe I simply didn't really love Bernard, even if I loved his photographs and his raffle-ticket habit and easy silences.

I don't know if I meant to sabotage our relationship; what I mean is, I don't really know if I had planned out the destruction or if it had always been there, dormant, throughout the months we were in each other's company. Eventually I ran into a guy on my way home from work; we had slept together once or twice and I'm embarrassed that I don't even remember his name. He handed me a cupcake on the T; he had an extra one, he said. It was pink with spicy cinnamon crunchies on the top of it. I bit into the cupcake, and this man licked the frosting off my upper lip. And then I took him home.

I don't know if I deliberately didn't call Bernard to cancel our plans for the evening, if I wanted him to catch me and the cupcake guy when he showed up later to take me to the movies. But when the doorbell rang, the cupcake guy was in the kitchen, barefoot, drinking a beer as if he owned the place, and my hair must have been sticking up and out every which way, and there was Bernard in the doorway, confused and hurt and silent as ever. When he walked away, I realized what a dangerous person I'd become. I made some kind of decision there and then. I kicked the cupcake guy out of the house and took a long shower and I cried a little bit and then I felt calm. Charlie and Claire would be home in a little while and I would tell them that Bernard and I had broken up and we'd all go out for a sloppy, greasy meal at Chef Chang's and find our way back to the house, sluggish and full bellied. And the next day would start again and we'd find our way back into the rhythm of three.

How could I not see that one day they would leave? They would move on with their lives and get married, of course they would. And I would be alone with the decisions I had made in that shower. I could have called Bernard and tried to win him back. I could have made all sorts of decisions differently. But I thought that—and I admit that I might have been lying to myself—I'd rather be alone. Perhaps Bernard was right that it's better to be mean than dishonest.

And here I was, returning to Claire and Charlie's house so many years later, still wondering what kind of person I was. Which would win out? My love and loyalty for my best friends or my lingering resentment? I had already unfairly unleashed my venom on poor Charlie earlier that day. I had to work harder to be a kinder person. I wanted to believe I had it in me as I entered their house, long after the sun had set and I had probably begun causing them some worry.

Claire

It is true that I've been scheming. I'm enlisting Rachel's help for one of my plans—it is Charlie's birthday in a few days. The sneakiness around another scheme has been much more covert. No one should be terribly surprised. My confinement within these walls—kitchen, garage, bedroom, study, stairs—and within these woods, where even a short walk requires a chaperone, is making me restless.

Rachel and Charlie have bundled me up with wool sweaters and scarves and fleece slippers. They tell me that it's drafty in the house and I have to be wary of catching a cold. But I

itch under these layers and overheat, scratching at the surface
of my mottled skin. When I'm in my study, I pull off the layers
and read my words on the computer screen. I see the pictures
and I trace the stories and notes I wrote in Tamil Nadu. The
earth is sun scorched there, and the sunlight casts deep shadows onto the landscape. I look out my own window and force
myself to believe that I was once so far away. In Tamil Nadu,
there was a drought so destructive that people were killing
one another for water. Here, outside my window, a dusting of
snow coats the dirt road, but I can still hear the current of the
nearby stream when I lift the windows. The cold, penetrating
air is a relief. It is impossible to trace the distance between
where I sit and where I wrote the words illuminated on the
screen in front of me. I want to find my way back to the person who traveled freely, who saw a world beyond the confines
of this room, this season.

I want to go back there, to the town where I had been
staying in India, an industrial center that, based on my photographs, was dusty and dry and filled with activity. I can hear
the noise of this place through my pictures. Salem was my
home base when I wasn't in Mysore or Pondicherry. It gave
me good access to the Cauvery River, the Stanley Reservoir,
and the politicians in Karnataka and Tamil Nadu who were
battling one another over rights to the river's diminishing re-
sources. I know how selfish this makes me sound. Here I am,
overheated in early winter, in a house where I can take all the
baths I want, and all I want to do is run away to a home not

my own to write notes about others' struggles with drought
and famine. It is an ugliness inside me, but it is what I want.

I know the desire is also rooted in a larger sense of purpose. Before I got sick, I was investigating drought, waterway disputes, and environmental conflicts around the world.
I was supposed to stay in India for only a month, according
to my correspondence with my editor, but I had asked for an
extension before heading to Pakistan. I don't know what was
keeping me in Tamil Nadu beyond the month. I had already
interviewed the family of a man who had thrown himself into
the Kabini Reservoir. He had been a farmer who believed his
family's life was in peril if Karnataka continued to release
water to Tamil Nadu at such a meager rate. He had drowned
in the shallow waters of the reservoir, unable to swim. I had
interviewed Tamil Nadu chief minister Jayalalithaa, who had
gone on a three-day fast in protest of Karnataka's refusal
to release more water to her state. The debates were over a
hundred years old, and both sides of the state borders were
suffering from a dismal monsoon season, perpetual drought,
and a failing crop. Everyone was angry. The Water Disputes
Tribunal had allocated water distribution at a rate lower than
either state had requested, but the farmers on the Tamil Nadu
side of the border felt like their land and their livelihood were
being threatened by their neighbors to the north. People had
taken to the streets on both sides of the debate. A few pro-
testers had been injured; no one seemed to be backing down.

I study these images and interviews: members of the

Handicrafts Manufacturers Association forming human chains along the streets of Mysore toward the Palace and legislative offices; Tamil Nadu farmers shouting slogans at their regional ministers, pushing their children into the faces of the tribunal officials; Karnataka ministers returning, slightly hobbled and stoic, after a long pilgrimage between Bangalore and Mandya in an attempt to placate their constituents. Because I can't remember, I force myself to imagine the dryness in the air, the relentless heat of the summer months, the slogans shouted from the riverbanks, the shriveled tapioca harvest.

The drought in Tamil Nadu had entered its eighth month when I arrived there. I followed the depleted river south and east until it trickled into the Bay of Bengal. The Cauvery used to pour out into the ocean in southeast Tamil Nadu, but it doesn't make its way to the coast anymore. Women wash their clothes in the salty ocean water because there is so little fresh water.

I study my notes. Mass migration, malnourishment, and dengue fever carried by the mosquitoes in the still waters were threatening the population of farmers all along the river's path. I think about those mosquitoes now and wonder where, along that route, I received my near-deadly bite. I was closing in on the end of my story. I was planning to take a break and head back to the States for a while, perhaps to rest and take long, decadent showers without guilt. And now, here I am, desperate to get back there.

When I start to feel guilty for my imagined escape plans, I think of my other scheme. Charlie and Rachel are downstairs, and they are my home again. At least I can make some kind of attempt to brighten all our moods. Planning a little party must be easier than traveling across several oceans. I can enlist Rachel's help, and together perhaps we can wash away at least a little of Charlie's bitterness.

Charlie

The three of us here gathered around the kitchen table, sprawled out in the living room, taking trips into town, has got me dwelling on the Orphanage. Neither Rachel nor I challenged the name of our home once Claire had decided on it. Claire buoyed us up with promises of adventure and freedom and fresh starts in a genuine attempt to ease Rachel's loss and my everyday discombobulation. I suppose neither of us wondered about Claire's own needs to be cheery in the face of loss, to erase bad memories with newer, happier ones.

Claire had lost her parents early, and obviously Rachel

suffered her loss soon after we first met, but I chose to lose my parents. This minor detail never fazed Claire or Rachel when they took me into their home and accepted me as another orphan. Perhaps it should have bothered me more than it did, but I was charmed by the idea of reinvention and clean slates and a past made up of little more than blurry memories. I already had a good deal of practice at trying on new selves. In the end I was probably better equipped for it than Rachel, whose memories were happier ones than mine.

My parents are still alive and as well as they can be, tucked into a little cottage in Eriswell between Cambridge and Norwich in Norfolk. They haven't always lived there. When I was born, we lived in London. My father was a lecturer at King's College and my mother worked for a lawyer who had become famous for advising several members of Parliament. We lived on a busy street and my parents left in a hurry each morning, entrusting me to the care of a nanny who insisted on fresh air every day even when it was drizzly and severe outside. These are some of my earliest memories, being pushed around in a pram through various parks, my wool blanket growing damp and smelly. My nanny had soft folds in her skin and carried her weight around with a sense of dignity. "C'mon, little man," I think she used to say. "If I'm not cold, you're not cold."

But we were forced to leave the city after some sort of scandal involving my father. It may have been an affair with a colleague or a student. It may have been stolen grant money. My parents never talked about it. It's amazing how private people can be, even those you should know best. I've never gotten very far with my own research into the past, into whatever it was that forced my parents out of their London life, and for all intents and purposes out of their marriage, and certainly out of love with one another. They stayed together because, I suppose, that was what was expected of them. And they had lost almost everyone else in their lives. My father's family kept a cold distance, getting in touch every now and then with a postcard announcing a death in the family, though my father never seemed to hear when there was a birth. As far as I know, the cards were merely sent to inform, never to invite. And because my mother carried my father's shame on her shoulders, she distanced herself from everyone she had once cared about too. I've never been able to make it all out with her, whether it's a sense of pride or stubbornness or denial that has kept her with my dad all these years, but they seemed to enter into some sort of agreement that the past would never be discussed and that an agreed-upon silence would fill their days.

My father spent his time in his "library," which was really just a small room filled with piles of books. Our house was small and this room should have been my bedroom, but instead I slept on a foldaway bed separated from the rest of the living room with a lacquer partition that matched nothing else in that house. My father claimed to be doing research on his book projects, which had suddenly shifted to Norse legends and fairytales. When he had been a lecturer, he had focused on the modernists. He had published pretty successfully on Wyndham Lewis and Ezra Pound and he had stacks of old journals gathering dust on his floor. After his dismissal, he spent his time drifting further and further into a past that had no obvious connection to him. Perhaps he believed he could be swallowed up by a Norse god who might direct him toward a life that was very different from the one he presently suffered through. He grew a long beard and took to wearing spectacles at the end of his nose. If he went out, he took the bus to Cambridge or Norwich, where I imagined him trolling the antiquarian bookstores, having an anonymous cup of tea, and then returning to his study.

My mother continued to work because someone had to. She bustled about the house in the mornings, fixed her hair in the mirror, and shouted out that there were muffins warming in the oven and some tea on the stove and that she'd be home before six. She worked as a legal assistant in a dreary little town called Thetford, commuting every morning with a neighbor named Mrs. Crawford, who announced herself with a beep from the car's horn and, as far as I can remember, never set foot in our house. I never knew if my mother became friends with this woman or if my mother was even capable of being friends with anyone anymore. She protected her privacy and her solitude like no one I've ever known.

My parents treated me like an inconvenient ghost in their house. Perhaps I reminded them of a happier time that they had both managed to ruin, or perhaps they simply forgot about me in their shared quest to erase the past from their lives. My father took his meals in his library and my mother would take hers in front of the TV. Sometimes I would join her in front of the news or *Warship*, a sort of claustrophobic series that documented the lives of Royal Navy officers. My mother watched her series, rapt. Like my father with his books, my mother dug herself as deep as she could into fictions far removed from her own life. Usually I ate my dinner alone in the kitchen, going over my lessons and listening to the radio. I became a very good student and joined every club I could think of at secondary school so that I could be at home as little as possible. My mother came to my graduation, and when it was time for me to leave for UEA, I awoke to find two neatly packed suitcases leaning against the couch and a bagged lunch. My mother and Mrs. Crawford took me to the train station, where my mother handed me an envelope of money and didn't bother to get out of the car.

My marks on the A levels had earned me a small scholarship, which must have been a quiet relief to everyone because I wouldn't even need to be in touch over expenses. I would return to Eriswell for Christmas each year but quickly learned to find work over the summers so I could remain in Norwich. The school was rather ugly and new, built in the 1960s, and I think I rather liked its lack of history and the traditions that go with it. I convinced myself that the university was forward looking, since it had no past, and that it would encourage me to start looking forward and away. I built myself a new identity in Norwich; there were no secrets to keep and no house to hide from my schoolmates. I could say that my parents traveled a lot, so that it was difficult to arrange trips home. Once or twice I actually told a friend that my parents had moved abroad, and the kind soul invited me home to Lowestoft for the Easter recess. It was a lovely feeling, to be in another family's home, everyone sharing their meals together, going to the cinema, talking to one another. There were snapshots all over my friend's house, awkward family photos framed proudly and unembarrassedly on the walls alongside the staircase. The parlor sofa was worn but welcoming. We sat there in the evenings, playing cribbage, and I laughed often and kept my head down so that I wouldn't be asked too many questions.

I think I always wanted a house like my school friend's, filled with memories and worn things that embraced you. Rachel's house was like that. Her parents had filled it with their lives; it was big and inviting and just cluttered enough that it felt quite lived in. She brought me there when her parents were still alive, during our first year of graduate school. Her mother kissed my cheek when I first walked in the door, and she smelled of cooking, and I truly wanted to stay there forever. I didn't know what it meant to feel homesick, but I understood how one could forever miss a place like this, once one had experienced it. Rachel was embarrassed by her parents, as I suppose most children are, but I think I would have been quick to love them. Her father actually offered me a pipe after dinner, and we sat on the back porch, quiet, listening to the rustling of fall. Perhaps I should have felt nervous; I was dating this man's daughter, after all. But he never interrogated me beyond an easy interest in my coursework, my articles, how I was settling into Boston life. I remember thinking then how many forms of quietness there could be. I was used to my own parents' version, and this was nothing like it.

I had several meals there, including some Sunday brunches; at one of these, I met Claire, who had obviously been there several times as well. When I came in that late morning, Claire was in the kitchen with Rachel's mom, whisking some eggs and calling out to Rachel to bring her some basil and the cherry tomatoes. "Hi, Charlie!" she called to me from the kitchen. We had never met, so it was strange to hear my name come out of her mouth, but I was slowly getting used to the particular brand of American friendliness that had greeted me in Boston. Everyone seemed bemused by my Englishness, my accent, my tidy shirts and tennis shoes. Nothing about any of these things had ever seemed remarkable to me, but I had suddenly become more noticeable in my new surroundings.

Rachel's father and I sat on barstools, looking into the kitchen while we sipped our coffee. Claire teased us for being men who sat on our asses while the women slaved away in the kitchen, and she handed me two baguettes and a knife. "Why don't you at least slice these and put some butter and jam out on the table?" I remember that Rachel's father raised his eyes at me and shrugged. "I'll get the table set," he said. "You deal with the bread."

It was a shock to all of us when they died. I think both Claire and I had been using them as surrogate parents in our own ways, and I certainly didn't have the words for the kind of loss Rachel was experiencing. For Claire, I think their death must have brought up too many memories of her own. Once Claire had gotten Rachel out of her room, I held Rachel's hands and took her for long walks in the cold fall air and waited for her to say something. I made her hot chocolate and rented her stupid comedy films to take her mind off things. I am sure I was clumsy and rather useless at helping her navigate those early days of grief. Claire was the one who eventually helped Rachel with all the practical things and told her that it was fine if she didn't want to go through a formal kind of funeral. We would just have people over to the house for an evening, her parents' closest friends, some nearby relatives. Claire arranged everything, occasionally sending me off to a florist or to the catering place around the corner to order more pasta salad or to change the cake order to a collection of pies and tarts. She took Rachel out to find a new dress and encouraged her to get her hair cut. I was relieved. It was easy to let Claire be in charge.

After the dinner gathering, after the guests had finally left and Claire had sent Rachel off to bed with some kind of sleeping pill and a glass of milk, we set about cleaning up. We stuffed garbage bags full of wine-stained plastic cups, crumpled napkins, the remains of all those pretty pies. Claire wanted nothing of the dinner gathering to remain the next day, so we threw out all the extra food and sparkling water and paper plates. It was when I was emptying the last boxes of tarts that I saw Claire crumpled against the wall, her head in her hands. Claire had put an extraordinary effort into the past week and a half. I hadn't even thought about the strain on her because all my attention had been on Rachel and my own feelings of helplessness. I crouched down next to Claire and gently touched her shoulder. She grabbed my hand and used it to wipe away some of her tears. She smiled up at me. "I think I should move in, Charlie. I think it would be the right thing to do."

And just like that, it had been decided. Claire broke her lease, and after only two months, I had broken mine too. Claire took Rachel's parents' bedroom and I eventually took the guest room and Rachel moved back down to the room she'd had as a child. Slowly, Rachel returned to us. We made ourselves into a new family. I couldn't believe it—how quickly our lives had been transformed. We had let Claire be our guide through all of it, and for a very long time she navigated all of us successfully. She seemed incredible to me—her strength, her loyalty, her resilience.

Even when I am angry with her now or when I grow impatient, I am still in awe of Claire. She survived something none of the doctors expected her to survive. She takes risks that she shouldn't because she doesn't know how not to. Even if she doesn't remember her willfulness, her confidence, her courage and sharpness, I absolutely do. I feel myself, and Rachel too, watching her, hopeful (and, yes, perhaps a little bit fearful too) that the old and new in Claire will merge, and she will find her way back.

Rachel

In Charlie and Claire's guest room, I am surrounded by framed photographs of memories I have worked hard at forgetting. For some reason, this room seems to be a shrine to Charlie's youth. On my nightstand is an image of a twenty-year-old Charlie who must be on vacation with a friend. They are framed by the edge of the North Sea and a quaint little seaside village that I recognize as Lowestoft. Charlie and I first kissed in a rented boat in Great Yarmouth, a much less picturesque place alongside the same sea. Great Yarmouth was such an ugly town that Charlie had been embarrassed to bring me there. It was the kind of place where automated clowns threw up water into rusted garbage cans, where the fish-and-chips were too greasy even by East Anglian standards. You could tell that it had once been a beautiful place, with Victorian summer cottages lining the once quaint streets, bathing shacks along the coast painted in pretty pastels. Most of the cafés had black-and-white pictures framed on the walls, reminding everyone of more glamorous times—ladies holding parasols on sunny summer days, their men in high-waisted swim trunks skipping toward the sea. Those old pictures only made the town seem more ragged and neglected in its current state.

We had taken the train out there from Norwich, had skipped out on our modernist poets class, looking at the sky, hoping the sun would last. It was spring and still cold, but it was bright and we were eager to have an adventure. Charlie had taken my hand on the train; his was softer than I was expecting it to be. Neither of us was any good at flirting, and it had taken me a long while even to imagine that Charlie might be interested in me. He had organized study sessions for our cohort three times a week, and we had packed into a back corner of a nondescript pub. Charlie and I often stayed late, after the others had left. He had started inviting me to his flat for tea and a chat, but our conversations always drifted back to our studies, how he'd like to visit Worcester because that's where Elizabeth Bishop had lived for a time and because it would give him a chance to leave England. I told him that it would be nice to have him in Boston, that maybe he could try applying to postgraduate programs there, and he seemed happy with the suggestion. I was trying to tell him more than that, of course. I was trying to tell him that I would miss him, that I liked him, that I wanted to have him in my life after this spring semester ended. But I could never be sure if he was trying to tell me the same thing, so I would get shy and pack up my things and give him a kiss on the cheek.

When we got to Great Yarmouth, Charlie hooked his arm in mine and took me toward the water. He bought us a Dixie cup each of cockles drenched in vinegar as we walked past the busy arcades and the ice cream vendors and chip shops. The cockles were chewy little blobs and the vinegar made my mouth feel sour. I had eaten them because I wanted to be polite and because Charlie was putting forth a real effort as tour guide, but I'm sure I was worrying that my breath was growing hostile, and really, more than anything, I was hoping Charlie might kiss me as the afternoon wore on.

"I never come here," Charlie admitted as we neared the gray and churning sea. There was nothing welcoming about this ocean; it was hard to imagine anyone, ever, being able to swim here. "My parents always found it charmless, so we'd take our weeklong seaside vacations up north in Cromer or down in Southwold. But we could never afford to stay close to the water, where the posh B and Bs were, so we'd end up packing these overflowing bags and walking several blocks to claim our space in the sand."

I nodded, having no idea where or what he was describing. "I suppose it's a bit like vacationing at the Cape if you're from Boston. All the fancy people get to be close to the sea, and all the other folks have to make due with overpriced motels while they fight off horseflies."

"And which type was your family?" Charlie brought me in close to his chest as he pointed out the Ferris wheel in the distance.

I hoped that Charlie couldn't tell that my neck was growing blotchy—I always got a rash when I was nervous, meaning it was close to impossible for me to keep a secret. "We vacationed in the mountains; my father didn't like going to the beach."

"I think I might prefer the mountains too. We don't have many of them here. At least we have some hills in Norwich."

THIS IS HOW I remember our conversations going. Polite and timid, we'd talked about the different geographies of our childhoods, waiting for the other person to give some sign of interest. In the end I had suggested that we walk away from the town center and toward the Broads. We found an old dock and persuaded the owner of a rowboat to let us borrow it for a while. Charlie took the wooden oars and coaxed them through their rusty oarlocks, and the boat groaned with every pull. Charlie wasn't much of a rower, and we zigzagged that poor boat through the narrow passages, so intent on the effort that we hardly spoke to one another. I remember thinking that this was, or at least should be, one of the most romantic moments of my life. I was twenty-one years old and a nervous English boy was rowing me through the Broads on an early-spring day. He loved poetry and wanted to be a writer and told me that he liked my American accent and called me Rach from almost our first introduction. But he wasn't going to kiss me on his own—even I could tell that—so I grabbed the edges of the boat and shifted my weight toward Charlie. I balanced myself in front of him, letting my hair slap him in the breeze. Still, I wasn't going to do everything. I needed to know that he wanted to kiss me too, so I crouched there, suspended, half standing in that small boat, and waited for him to make a decision. It took three long breaths before I felt the press of his lips against mine. And then he kissed my forehead and my nose and said, "Rach, come sit here beside me for a while." And the boat rocked and got tangled in the weeds as we stretched out under the sky and I finally knew that Charlie liked me.

PERHAPS BECAUSE I am masochistic or because I continue to be overwhelmed with missing them, my house is filled with pictures of Charlie and Claire. Of course there are photos of my parents—their wedding day, and a trip we all took to Quebec, and one of my mom holding me when I was probably only three days old. But other than that, there is only Charlie and Claire. No cousins or aunts and uncles. No other friends or their babies. On my fridge I have Claire's postcards from Quito and Rio and Pondicherry and Mysore. And front and center, there is a picture of the three of us, sitting on the front stoop, Claire in the middle, her legs thrown out straight into the sidewalk. We are twenty-three years old, and Charlie has moved in with us, and my parents have been dead for two months. I am trying to smile, my chin resting on Claire's shoulder, but it is hard to read the expression on my face. It was a sunny day, and I am squinting in the glare.

It is difficult for me to remember the person I was in this picture. Too many things had happened all at once, and I know that I was desperate for some kind of tethering. Claire gave me advice and I listened to everything she told me. She had been through this before. She kept me distracted and my days full. She got me through our graduate courses and edited my articles and pretended she needed help from me too. She brought home cookbooks from the Brattle Book Shop by the Common and we learned how to debone fish and how to make our own curry paste and a perfect pie crust and baked stuffed cabbage because Claire insisted I embrace some of my "culture's cooking." "If I had any cultural history, you know I'd be digging into it, so let's use yours."

"But my parents didn't even cook this food, and cabbage makes the house smell awful," I remember saying to her. But Claire wasn't going to accept that. By the end of our first two months of cooking adventures, we had learned to make kugel and brisket and blintzes. Poor Charlie was forced to eat all our experiments. Once, when he finally found something to praise in the apple blintzes we presented him with on Sunday morning, Claire warned, "Don't think you're getting off easy, Charlie. You're up next—shepherd's pie, pasties, Yorkshire pudding."

"Holy Christ, Claire, you mustn't joke about these things. There was a reason I left England for America."

But Claire was relentless. She made a ritual out of our dinner preparations. She did finally back off the English cuisine when we all began complaining that our clothes were no longer fitting. I know there were other friends who came by during these months, people we knew from grad school, a couple of British expats Charlie had met at the Gardner Museum one day, some of Claire's old acquaintances from childhood who had left western Mass for the city too. But the memories of these guests feel like flashes to me; they were brief companions who never stayed long, who shared some wine with us and told me how lucky we were to have this big, fancy house to ourselves. We loved to share our annoyance at these interlopers, Charlie, Claire, and me. After they left, we'd trade observations and criticisms and feel closer because of it. There are moments when I like to convince myself that it was all Claire's doing—that she would do the inviting and then the dismissing. That she trained us somehow to ward off the threat of other friendships. But it is too easy to put all the blame entirely on her shoulders. If people are wary of my friendship now, it is my own doing. I could have invited people back into our house for a second or third visit, could have made them feel more welcomed than judged, could have invited a man to stay in my room for more than a night or two. But I loved us too much, and I didn't want there to be more than the three of us, who seemed to occupy this house so perfectly. Claire upstairs, Charlie sleeping in the converted study downstairs, me in the attic. Our books and notes and mail spread throughout the house in overlapping piles.

Charlie's tea and Claire's coffee and my hot chocolate in the cupboards.

It was perfect until it wasn't anymore, when I came to realize, far too late, that I was suddenly the outsider looking in on a relationship that had changed. Claire and Charlie lingered late on the couch downstairs, the stereo turned low, telling me that they'd get off to bed soon enough, that I should go on ahead. And then there were evenings when they wouldn't be home for dinner and I would make up a quick salad or some pasta before drifting upstairs, waiting for the sounds of their return as the night wore on. But there we'd be in the morning again, the sounds of all our chatter filling the kitchen. Charlie would often walk me to the T stop before continuing on to his internship. Claire and I would sit over glasses of wine after class, ogling the South End waiters, as we anticipated Charlie's arrival, followed by a shared stroll home. Claire introduced me to a part-time professor in the Communications Department—Linus was his name—who I later found out had hit on her at the gym, and for several weeks he joined us for dinner or for our wine hours or for Sunday journeys up to the North Shore. He would stay late at our house, and because Charlie and Claire seemed to so want me to have company, to restore some balance to the evenings in our house, I would ask him to stay some nights.

But he disappeared after a while in the wake of my disinterest, and he was replaced with temporary others. Some Charlie would bring home, singing the praises of my cooking; others Claire wooed on my behalf, and I would watch them shrug off their disappointment as they turned to me and realized the alignments for the evening. I played my part as gamely as I could for a week or two, or sometimes even for a couple of months at a stretch, but I eventually let my apathy send them on their way, and Claire, Charlie, and I would settle back into the routine of us three. I couldn't bring myself to admit the truth of our situation—that I was in love with two people who were my only family, and that they were in love with each other. And when I wasn't feeling like a fool who couldn't trace the moment when things had shifted, I started to resent my best friends. And I hated myself for my jealousy. It had been I, after all, who had broken things off with Charlie. But it had been Claire, of course, who had guided me toward that decision, and I had let her, just as I had let her make the other choices that, ultimately, freed Charlie up for her taking. I loved them and I hated them and they were my family. And their pictures are still the only photos, the only traces of my past and present, decorating my refrigerator.

NOW CLAIRE WANTS me to help her plan a surprise party for Charlie's birthday. I know that Charlie hates surprise parties, but Claire is determined, and it's good to see her so animated and driven to be in charge of something. We have been making plans while Charlie is at work. Who should we invite? Claire asks me. Who are Charlie's friends? We both have very little idea, so we decide to include Charlie's coworkers, a few neighbors, and us. Claire is particularly insistent that we invite Sophie. "I've got my eye on that one," she said earlier tonight with a little mischief in her eyes. Claire seems strangely delighted that she might catch Charlie out on some illicit flirtation. As for me, I have my doubts that Charlie would be capable of any real kind of deceit. It's against everything he values in himself, and it would even the score between him and Claire, and I suspect he wouldn't be willing to sacrifice his moral high ground.

So Sophie is invited and Claire has laid out her plan for her own private investigation. I have agreed to help. Claire is still extremely skilled at devising plans and encouraging those around her to join in her orchestrations. My job is merely to lure Charlie out of the house; the rest of the plan is up to Claire.

Claire

Out of one of my "India/Articles" boxes, there is a man who looks up at me from several pictures. He smiles from the photographs with a straightforward gaze, or sometimes his profile is cast in twilight or he holds up a palm to block the glare of the sun. He flirts with the camera or the person holding it, and there is intimacy and trust in his gaze. I think this man is speaking to me in the way that he is looking at the camera, but I couldn't tell you his name, even though Rachel has planted a name in my mind. I call him Michael, and his image seems to respond. He looks like a Michael—sturdy, reliable, easy in himself. He was paper-clipped to my India notes and he is suntanned and a bit travel worn. Perhaps we traveled together. Without really knowing why, I hide his face from Charlie. I have tucked him into the folds of my books, which are still boxed up in the garage. There is one that I keep out, though. I stuff it into the pockets of my jeans. We are conspirators in this place of restrictions, and the photo is starting to bend from even my limited movement.

This photograph suggests all the ways I don't trust my own memory. I know this person; I feel it under the surface of my skin. But when I go looking for him in my memories, my brain jumps to an image of my uncle and the pair of roller skates he bought me for my eighth birthday. They were metal and they clanked along the sidewalk, their straps awkward over my green sneakers. Or I skip to a day when my mother taught me how to crochet a little blue dress for my favorite doll. Or to the day my father took me up on a chairlift for the very first time. This is what happens when I try to remember one particular thing. My mind suddenly becomes a kaleido-scope of fragmented memories, and I lose track of the original path that brought me there. And so I try to focus again. I look at the picture and I stare at Michael's expression. I listen for his voice in my head, an escaped snippet of dialogue that we might have spoken, something mumbled over a shared curry at the snack shop I can see in the corner of this photograph. I can almost hear him. I can almost see him popping a piece of chapati into his mouth. He is wearing a camera around his neck and he is asking me a question, and then he vanishes again. In his place is the owner of the diner at the center of my hometown. He pushes a plate of pie and french fries across the counter at me and winks. We are sharing a secret in the late afternoon of a wintery day. These memories exhaust me.

WHEN I'M ALONE I breathe in the insides of these boxes and wonder if there is a trace of Tamil Nadu in them, a trace of New York City. I sniff around a lot, craving a sensory trigger or two, an opening up of my mind where suddenly the past will spring to life. The doctors tell me that smells and sounds are just as good starting places for memory as sights or stories that other people tell. Perhaps Michael might begin to speak to me, fill in the gaps of silence that Charlie is so eager to protect.

I kissed Charlie two nights ago, or perhaps it was he who kissed me, in our kitchen, which still smelled of burnt onions and garlic. Rachel had already gone upstairs with her book and a final glass of wine, or perhaps she had taken a walk. I don't remember. Who knows whether I've ever been a good cook, but I'm as absentminded in the kitchen as I am on my wanderings. I get to thinking about something, searching my memory, or feeling the tug of an image that is almost taking shape, and suddenly the smoke alarm shrieks and I'm holding a smoking pan. We salvaged dinner—a stir-fry, not too spicy, with rice on the side, and a rather sad-looking salad. I have no interest in eating meat these days, so Rachel helped me stock the fridge with peppers and eggplant and zucchini and cheese. Fortunately, Charlie doesn't complain. This house makes me think that Charlie is a kind of aesthete anyway, and there's something in his carriage, or perhaps it's just a romanticized notion of his Englishness, but I think he enjoys deprivations. I think I may have kissed him just to see how his body would respond. Would it surprise me, or would I recognize the feeling of his lips, the press of his hips, the smell of his neck? How can I describe it now? Can something be expected without being familiar?

Charlie's lips are dry and soft. His neck smells like his sweaters, which I often wear around the house—a bit of fireplace, a bit of neutral soap, a bit of piney sweat. His hips are bony and hesitant, his body keeps the same distance and control as his words. He kissed me with his eyes open, so I know he was looking for my response to him, just as I was hoping for his mysteries to be revealed. I smiled in order to reassure us both and I rested my hand in the small of his back. Was I a changed Claire to him? I wondered. Was the taste of my mouth familiar to him, or has it become more metallic from all these stupid pills? Perhaps it felt strange to him that my hair didn't fall across his shoulders. He couldn't brush it away playfully, because, of course, I don't have my hair anymore. Was this still a shock to him? Did I ever wear perfume or use lavender soap or taste like the wine I'm now forbidden to drink? Was he disappointed? Was I?

It is a strange feeling—this guilt at not being the right person. It would be kinder to myself to say that I raised his sweater over his head and unbuckled his belt because I wanted to help him, to ease the disastrous unfamiliarity of me, but I

was being selfish. Curious, pure and simple. I needed to know
how our skin felt pressed together, how his hands felt on my
breasts, what sounds he might make as I climbed on top of
him. I needed him to reveal some secrets and I thought my
body might make his face show something to me. So I did it
for myself, not for Charlie. I coaxed him to the couch and
I smiled and I said, "I miss you," and here he stopped and
clutched my wrist and stared into my face and I realized he
was looking for a secret too.

I wanted him to know that I would tell him the answers
he was looking for, but I didn't even know his questions, so I
couldn't possibly have the answers. So I said it again. "I miss
you, Charlie." His expression should have stopped me—is it
possible for a face to hold disgust and grief and desire simultaneously? But I was too curious, and so I used my free hand
to tug at his trousers and to unzip my skirt. He kicked his
legs out of his pants and he looked so very exposed to me.
Such skinny legs, with their coils of black hair. Two argyle
socks, one halfway up his calf, the other scrunched down
by his ankle. All the while he was staring into my face and
I was smiling without really meeting his eyes. I did not have
the things in my mind that he needed, but I was happy to feel
him kiss my shoulder blade, to move his warm, callused hand
between my legs. I was glad to hear him sigh and finally close
his eyes and let himself be laid out on the carpet, socked toes
pointing up at the ceiling. I traced my fingers across his eyebrows and pressed them into the crinkles of his forehead. He
pushed my hands away and opened up his eyes, and again,

that stare, that mix of anger and sadness and pleasure. "What is it, Charlie?" I asked.

"I just can't be sure, Claire," he shook his head so gently and rested his hands on my hips, "if you're really back here with me."

And then I had to close my eyes because I still didn't have his answer and because his body didn't feel familiar to me as I had hoped it would. Charlie is being greedy, I thought, he's asking for too much. How can he expect his body, his house, his smells, to feel like home to me, when he gets to keep his silences? Even his body is silent; it reveals nothing. Why this disgust in your eyes, Charlie? My bruises are healing, my scars less jarring. It is something deeper than what is marked on the surface of my skin.

And so I grew angry at Charlie for not providing any more answers than I could, and I punished him without his even knowing it. I closed my eyes and I replaced Charlie with Michael. I rocked my hips and I listened for a camera clicking. I saw desert and roaming water buffalo, pink saris pulsing in the wind. I saw the faces of vibrantly painted gods stacked up on temple roofs. I heard the camera clicking and I saw Michael's eyes grinning back at me. He was my secret to keep.

To make up for my guilt over ghostly Michael as well as my escape fantasies, I arranged a surprise party for Charlie's birthday. Rachel was in on it, of course. Our plan was that she would bring him into the office for a couple of hours while I arranged the house and got some food together. The day before, Rachel and I had gone on a shopping excursion and hidden our surprise in the garage. Later that night, she had made some excuse to Charlie about needing to fax some documents to Boston, to get some editing work off before the end of the weekend. Charlie was easy to convince—he had some paperwork to catch up on too, he said, and perhaps he was just happy for the excuse to get out of the house and away from me for a few hours. I wanted to laugh at him, for his eagerness to go into work on his birthday, and on a Saturday, no less!

Rachel helped me shop for his favorite foods (she had to remind me of some of them): samosas with peas and potatoes, salmon with just a touch of lemon and dill, aged gouda with those little specks of salt, southern Italian wine, fig spread. None of the ingredients seemed to go together, but Rachel assured me that I'd make it work somehow, and regardless of how it all came out, Charlie would appreciate the effort. I had wanted to do something nice for him, and at the same time I wasn't sad to have the house to myself for the afternoon. To be honest, I had some ulterior motives of my own, even as I wanted him to enjoy his birthday. I had invited his work friends over for the evening, emphasizing the surprise, and Nancy, Henry, and Emile were due to arrive at 6 p.m., but I had asked Sophie to come early to help me with some of the preparations. She had been eager to keep me company, even offered to make a lemon curd cake; she thought Charlie had once mentioned its being his favorite dessert. She asked me if she was right, but I told her that her guess was as good as mine. I seem to remember Charlie loving his chocolate cakes—chocolate everything, really—but perhaps lemon curd cake was his favorite after all.

I suppose that I wanted to balance out my feelings of guilt with the possibility that Charlie might be guilty of something too. Maybe this combination of wanting to do something good for someone else while simultaneously sleuthing a little bit would bring me even closer to Charlie. After all, him bringing me home to this house seemed more and more like his attempt to both rescue me and punish me for some past misdeed.

Rachel had arranged to grab lunch with Charlie in town before they headed to the office, so I was counting on at least five hours before they'd return, so that I could get the meal together and have some time with Sophie. As soon as they left, I printed out the recipes and ingredients and charted the schedule for prepping and cooking. I find that lists help me keep my head on straight these days, but even after all my efforts, I kept forgetting where I had unpacked the peas or the baking soda or the lemons. More often than not, the thing I was looking for was only two inches away from my nose, and I would blush, locating it, embarrassed in front of an invisible audience. I always hear Charlie's voice in my head these days: For God's sake, Claire, the book is right where you left it. Just lift up the damn magazine." I would lose patience with me too; in fact I am always losing patience with my unreliable brain, and trust me, it doesn't feel good to misplace one's entire life. But I've learned to keep my questions to a minimum, write them down, and save them for later or at least for when Charlie or Rachel are in better moods.

When Sophie knocked on the door in the middle of the afternoon, my hands were covered in mashed potatoes, so I just waved her in from the window. She was dressed as if she had come from the office, a straight tweed skirt and a perfect little blouse with capped sleeves and those same pretty shoes with her pretty toes peeking out of them. Despite all the images and memories and questions that flash and disappear through my brain, I always remember Sophie's pretty, painted toes. I can conjure them up in a moment, and here they were in the entranceway to our house. This was how my misfiring brain worked. Years retreated into a fog, and yet an image could appear to me so clearly, so precisely, it was as if a glossy picture from a magazine had been tacked onto my mind's eye. I wished these isolated, precise memory snapshots could add up to something, but instead they appeared unpredictably and without a workable map to get me out of the maze of my brain.

Sophie carefully hung her coat and purse on our coat rack, stepped out of her heels, and shook her hair out from under her hat. She smiled as she approached me, arms outstretched, ready for a hug, and I was pleased to notice a run forming on the heel of her stockings.

"You smell delicious," Sophie said as she pulled away from me. "What are you making?"

"Come on into the kitchen," I told her. "I'm wrangling with some samosas, but the dough for the wrappers is doing me in." I reached out to help her with her grocery bags, but she waved me off.

I took a step back to watch her. How well did she know this house? I wondered. How many times had she been here before? It was easy to find one's way to the kitchen, so that would tell me nothing. I followed her through the living room and watched her unpack a bundle of lemons, sugar, and flour onto the kitchen counter.

"Would you like a drink?" I walked over to the stereo. "Help yourself to wine or water, or I think we have a few beers and ginger ale in the fridge."

I turned the stereo on. Charlie's CD started playing— something Scandinavian and electronic. It sounded like static bubbles to me. "Do you like this all right?" I asked Sophie.

"It sounds a bit futuristic. I kind of like it." Sophie smiled at me from the kitchen. I watched her reach toward the cabinet to the right of the sink and grab a drinking glass. First try, I thought to myself. Could be a lucky guess.

Of course I had invited Sophie over so I could observe her in our house. I figured her presence here would offer up some clues: How comfortable was she in this space? Would she know where the measuring cups were? Had she baked Charlie his favorite cake before? I don't like feeling suspicious, having a gut sense about something with no tangible proof, so I hoped Sophie might reveal what Charlie was so good at hiding.

Sophie smiled again. "I might get started with the cake unless you needed help with the appetizers."

Despite my best efforts, I had left the kitchen in a fair bit of chaos. Most of the counter was dusted with flour, there were onion skins lacing the floor, a few peas had scattered here and there. "You should get started. Despite what it looks like, I'm almost done with these creatures." I looked at my misbegotten samosas, pinched and mangled on the baking sheets.

"All right then," she said. "Do you have an apron I can wear?"

"I have no idea, actually." I laughed. And then I looked at myself: my pants were patterned with my handprints, and my fingernails caked with dough. "I'm a mess," I said mostly to myself.

"You look like you've been cooking." Sophie was now standing next to me. She smelled minty and I admired how pretty her skin was up close. She had a delicate spattering of freckles over her eyebrows—something I didn't think I'd ever noticed before. "Something tells me that Charlie would have an apron," she said, beginning to rummage. From a low drawer, she pulled out a Colman's mustard apron, bright yellow with red lettering. And in a strange, almost hallucinatory image, I saw Charlie in our old kitchen in Rachel's house, a spatula in hand and a ski hat lopsided on his head. He had a ritual of making Sunday brunch for us every weekend. He loved pancakes, which he claimed were rare in England, and he made all different kinds—oatmeal apple, blueberry cranberry, honey buckwheat, pumpkin cinnamon. I could smell our old kitchen suddenly, bacon frying on the stovetop. Charlie in his Colman's apron from the mustard shop in Norwich, one of the few things he had brought from home. In fact, Rachel might have had a matching one. Rachel and Charlie always appreciated breakfast more than I did. At least I think that's true. Another half-formed memory of me nibbling on a banana while Rachel and Charlie feasted on syrup-drenched pancakes. How is it that I can remember this when I can't keep track of the movie Charlie and I went to see last week, or what my computer password is, or what my apartment in Mumbai looked like?

"Found one!" Sophie laughed, and I was transported back to our kitchen, and Sophie, now wearing Charlie's apron and standing next to me, looking quite pleased with herself. "What a flattering shade of yellow, don't you think?"

"You wear it well, Sophie." I smiled at her, but I couldn't shake the image of Charlie and Rachel from my mind. I must have hurt his feelings even back then, not eating his decadent breakfasts. I opened the refrigerator to see if we had any maple syrup or extra eggs in the fridge. Maybe tomorrow morning, I could surprise him with a postbirthday brunch.

Sophie was opening another drawer, and as I returned to the present again, I saw her grabbing a stack of measuring cups and laying them out on the counter. There—she had known exactly where they were without having to look. Unless, of course, she had opened the drawer earlier in her search for the apron. I am, it turns out, an absolute failure at detective work. Even when I've drawn out my master plan, my brain gets the better of me. I wonder about these sudden flashes of memory, these vivid daydreams that erupt unexpectedly. Was I always like this? Scatterbrained and so easily distracted?

Well, whether or not Sophie had known where the measuring cups were, it was obvious that she was comfortable in this kitchen. But perhaps this was just Sophie—comfortable in her freckled skin in every possible surroundings, taking up so very little space and smiling those helpful, reassuring smiles. I had to admit that she brought a brightness into our wintery house, and for that I was grateful. Did it even matter to me if she had been sleeping with Charlie?

"You look like you want to ask me a question." Sophie was gazing at me, lemon in her hand, with a slightly confused expression, and I realized I must have been staring at her for some time.

"I'm so sorry, Sophie." I put my hand on her shoulder and then immediately took it away as I saw my dingy fingers against her lovely blouse. "I have this tendency to get stuck in a thought these days without realizing it. I was just remembering an old kitchen Charlie and Rachel and I used to share. I didn't mean to make you uncomfortable."

"Oh, I'm fine, really. You just looked like you wanted to ask me something." She put her hand over mine and put the lemon back on the counter. She smiled and waited.

I looked her directly in the eye. Could she really be this friendly? This helpful? This trusting and open? It seemed impossible. There was no coating of guilt in any expression, no carefulness in her approach to me. She didn't treat me like a sick person, and for that I wanted to hug her. "I was just wondering if you'd ever been here before. You look so familiar in this house or maybe it's that this house seems so familiar to you, and to be honest, it's hard for me to remember if I've ever seen you in this kitchen before. I have to admit that most of my life lately feels like déjà vu."

Sophie squeezed my wrist. "It must be so strange, Claire. Not quite remembering things. I actually have a terrible memory myself. My mom gets so frustrated with me when she wants to reminisce about a moment from my childhood and there's nothing there for me, just a blank. Or if not a blank, just the thinnest of images and a sort of feeling. My brother is much better at remembering than I am. He also knows baseball statistics like a computerized robot and can tell you each of the members of Congress, state by state. I feel rather humiliated when I'm around him, especially when I see what a relief it is to my mother that he can really go there with her, you know? Anyway, I can't imagine how hard it must be—all that you've been through recently."

I don't know why Sophie's hand on my wrist created such a stirring in me. Her hand was so cool and so light and so unfamiliar. Her easy kindness made me want to cry, and I think it was the first time I've wanted to cry since Charlie brought me home. Mostly I've been feeling so much anger and frustration and confusion that, yes, I've wanted to throw things or pack up my bags and run away in the middle of the night like a teenager, but I don't think I've come close to crying. I've got too much to prove to myself and Rachel and Charlie—that I'm strong and that we'll all get through this bad stretch.

The kitchen—my kitchen—smelled of Sophie's presence and lemons, and I felt so unsure of myself standing there, a stranger in this house that is supposed to be my home, and here was Sophie, looking so at home and trying to comfort me, and I wanted to ask her what it felt like to be at home, in her body, in her brain, in a living room or kitchen, or in a neighborhood, or in a family.

I lifted Sophie's hand from my wrist, and without really thinking about it, I kissed the inside of her palm, which made her blush. She turned back to zesting her lemons and I worried that I had upset her, but she just continued on with our conversation. "I've been here twice before. Once, you were supposed to be here, home from an assignment, but your flight had been delayed or canceled, so we had to have the dinner party without you. This was maybe a year and a half ago. And then there was last year's office Christmas party, which Charlie ended up hosting after Nancy came down with a bad flu. So, yes, twice. I've been here twice before."

I watched Sophie. It would be impossible for me to tell if she was lying. I have no ability to read people anymore, a skill I think I must have possessed at some point, after so many years of searching out stories and talking to so many strangers. "So Charlie organized a party for me that I never showed up to? How awful of me." My lumpy samosas were almost finished and I turned on the oven, listening to the pilot light clank and shudder. It was an old stove, and Charlie had shown me over and over again how to make sure the pilot lights caught and to listen to the clicks—one, two, three—that indicated the gas had come on.

"Oh, not at all! I don't think it was your fault. Something happened with your flight. A missed connection in London, maybe."

"Of course that's what Charlie would have told you."

Sophie interrupted her measuring to glance up at me. "I don't think you would have deliberately missed the party."

"Of course not." Now I was trying to reassure her. "Maybe I didn't even know about the party and delayed my return or something like that. I'm sure it wasn't on purpose, though." I don't know why I felt so certain that I had disappointed Charlie, thwarted his welcome-home party for me, but it somehow seemed likely. There must be too many reasons to count for Charlie's anger with me, his perpetual coldness. I must have hurt him quite badly and I must have been careless with my travel plans and embarrassed him in front of his friends, who must already have been wondering about me, where I disappeared to, why I never came home to be with Charlie in his life.

"I'm sure," Sophie said after a while.

I was probably exasperating this poor girl with all my mental wanderings. There was so much I wanted to ask her: Did Charlie ever talk about me when I was away? Was he angry with me before I got sick? Did he confide in you, did he invite you over for wine and a chat, did you put your soft, slightly cool hand against his face and listen to him? Did he say that he missed me or that he didn't feel like he knew me anymore or that he worried that I'd never return home? Did he show you photographs of the old brownstone in Brookline, of our wedding, of his family, who he no longer talks to? Did he run his fingers over your freckles and down the side of your neck and tuck a piece of your hair behind your ear? Did he bring you upstairs or did you lie down on the rug in front of the fireplace and did you make him feel wanted? Did you leave your scarf or your smell of mint or an eyelash that made him feel less alone? Did Rachel know about you? But instead, I just said, "Please don't mind me, Sophie. I can't keep a thought straight in my head these days. I'm sure you're right about the party and I'm sorry I missed it and missed the chance to meet you sooner."

Sophie smiled at me again with a look of relief. It is not so hard for me to make an effort, to be charming in my way. And it was surprisingly easy to make Sophie feel welcomed. "Thanks for inviting me over to help, Claire. It's nice being here with you."

And so she zested and I chopped dill and we filled the kitchen with sweet and warm smells and spent the afternoon together waiting for Charlie's return.

Charlie

When Rachel and I walked in the door, there was a sort of forced, hushed silence, and for a moment I was sure that Claire had had another fall, that she was sprawled and bleeding on the kitchen floor or in the upstairs bathroom or in the garage, or that she had managed to contact a neighbor and they had rushed her off to the ER and the house was still holding on to the tumult of sudden panic and then quick departure. I had turned off my phone while Rachel and I ate lunch and had forgotten to turn it back on again, and when I reached for it, preparing myself for ugly news, there was a sudden cry of "Surprise!" and out popped Claire, her face flushed and grinning, and behind her, Sophie in my Colman's apron, Nancy, Emile, Henry, and Mr. and Mrs. Culver.

And then I felt Rachel pat me on the back and push me forward as she moved toward the gathering. She grinned at me, sheepish and knowing, and winked. She knew I hated surprises, and she was feeling quite proud of herself at keeping me fooled all afternoon long. Claire came up to hug me and she smelled like cinnamon and my deodorant. She was wearing an old sweater of mine. Perhaps she had forgotten to change after whatever cooking endeavor she had been up to, because the sweater didn't match the rest of her outfit, which she had obviously put some effort into: a green blouse, which Rachel had picked out for her, peeking out of my collar, and a corduroy skirt that flounced about at her knees. She had put on some makeup, lip gloss and mascara, and had pulled her short bangs off her face with a hair pin. Her hair had just started to grow back into some semblance of a style. I felt suddenly quite protective of her, and a bit embarrassed for her mismatched outfit. She looked tired but happy, and I pulled her into me because I realized I was looking a bit baffled and silly.

I kissed Claire awkwardly as she whispered, "Happy birthday," into my ear. As she pulled away, she smiled and pointed at the small gathering. "Rachel and Sophie and I had it all planned out. We managed to surprise you—I wasn't sure it'd be possible. You always know everything that's going on long before the rest of us." She tugged at my hand and brought me into the small crowd. Sophie handed me a glass of wine, and Emile gave me a half hug and patted me on the back. Nancy kissed me on the cheek, and the Culvers murmured their greetings, looking slightly out of place but good natured about the whole thing.

"Sophie and I have been cooking and baking all your favorites this afternoon, so I hope you're still a bit hungry after your lunch with Rach. Rach—can you put some music on? I have some CDs laid out on the table over there, some of Charlie's favorites, but also some, well, more listener-friendly selections too."

Claire's speech was hurried and her manner a bit too bright and artificial, and I wondered if she had been drinking— Sophie didn't know that she wasn't supposed to—but before I could ask her, she had left for the kitchen, and Henry was guiding me to the couch, explaining that it looked like a slow weekend for local news, so I should just sit down and relax and let him pour me a real drink.

Sophie appeared at my left, her mouth already stained purple, and I imagined that she and Claire had shared some wine. What were they doing here together all afternoon anyway? I did want to ask her about the wine, but I noticed that she had taken off her shoes, and there was something so strange about seeing her feet on my living room floor, her painted toes pressing down onto the rug that Claire had sent me from Mysore during her first months away. The rug was perfect for this room, and when it had arrived, unexpectedly, on a Wednesday, a day I had happened to stay home sick, I had felt reassured that Claire was thinking about this house even though she was so far away, and she was thinking about it with such precise memory that the green threads matched the couch perfectly, and the amber weaving reflected the color of the walls so well that it was almost as if Claire could be in two places at once. She had felt closer to me when that rug arrived than she had in quite some time, and for a while I let that rug comfort me as some sort of sign that Claire would be coming home eventually, at the very least to admire her masterly selection of the most perfect rug for our living room.

Rachel came up behind me and tousled my hair, and I wondered how long I had been staring at Sophie's toes. Sophie hadn't seemed to notice; she was being her typically polite and engaged self, listening to Mr. Culver explain the best ways to insulate windows during the winter months. It wasn't enough to have storm windows; you also needed sealant and some plastic coverings; he could recommend a few things. If Sophie had a pen, he'd write it all down for her. Sophie is a kind girl; I've never seen her grow impatient with anyone.

Rachel leaned against the arm of the couch. "Surprise, Charlie." She winked and rested her hand on my shoulder. "It was Claire's idea. She even came up with the plan for how to get you out of the house and Sophie over here to help her with the prep work."

I raised my glass to Rachel's and clinked it lightly. "Sly like foxes, the three of you."

She was wearing a mischievous smile. "Oh, you don't

know the half of it." Rachel winked again. "You haven't even seen the feast these two have in store for you."

I clinked Rachel's glass a second time; I was feeling a bit drunk already. The afternoon had already been filled with too much wine and it was barely five o'clock.

Rachel was watching Claire through the kitchen's pie window. Her expression grew a bit cloudy for a moment. "I didn't know you still had that Colman's apron. I wondered if you packed mine too when you moved up here; I haven't seen it in years."

"I don't remember the last time I wore mine. I'm not even sure what drawer Claire could have pulled it out of. Do you think she's been drinking, Rach? She seems a bit overexcited, flushed, something."

"The apron couldn't have been that hidden if Claire found it today. It makes me think about that horrendous meal we tried to cook for Claire when she turned in her thesis—you insisted on making a potpie, remember? Your mother had supposedly given you the recipe when you left for university. And I decided to make my mother's recipe for stuffed cabbage. Were we trying to torture her? I think we ended up taking her out to the Indian restaurant on the corner because nothing we made was even edible. Do you remember?"

"What an absolute disaster! I had forgotten about that potpie fiasco. The crust hadn't even risen—it was like a soggy, gray lump of paste. My mother's culinary legacy. Dear God."

I realized that Sophie had turned to Rachel and me, a pleading look in her eye. She seemed to need some rescuing, so I asked Mr. Culver how the UVM hockey team was faring this season, and at the same time Sophie asked how Rachel and I had come to be friends.

I felt Rachel shift on the edge of the couch and tap her ring against her glass. A sure sign of her being uncomfortable.

She shrugged her shoulders and half laughed. "Well, actually, we dated for a little while during undergrad at University of East Anglia. I was doing an abroad program in England and we were in a modernist poetry seminar together and he became my tour guide to all the local pubs, and then I lured him to America for his grad degree and we've had him ever since."

It was a strange way for Rachel to explain our history, I thought. It would have been quite easy for her just to say that we had all been flatmates during journalism school. Rachel hardly ever mentioned those distant moments from England. Typically, when anyone asked how we had all come to know one another, we had gotten into the habit of marking the start of our friendship as when we all moved into Rachel's parents' home.

Sophie asked something about England and whether the food was really as awful as everyone said it was and whether the heath and cliffs were really so romantically tragic, and my attention was pulled back to Mr. Culver, who was explaining that they had a promising freshman forward from Montpelier, but they didn't stand a chance against Cornell.

Sophie and Rachel had begun whispering in slightly conspiratorial tones, Sophie now sitting close to Rach on the couch, and I wondered if maybe I should stroll around a bit and let them have their gossip. I hadn't seen Claire since she had slipped away into the kitchen, which had been quite some time ago. I suppose I was still concerned that she had had a bit to drink, and if she had, there was no telling how her body would react.

Rachel

I felt a little bad for Charlie. He seemed uncomfortable at his own party, just as I had suspected he would be. Claire was right; Sophie was lovely—friendly and funny and very much comfortable in her own skin. But I don't think she and Charlie were having an affair. Not that kind people don't have affairs, but I couldn't imagine either one pushing the other across some line. I think Sophie looked up to Charlie, and Charlie was most likely content to bask in her appreciation and play the mentor.

To be honest, I wasn't entirely comfortable either. I'm not used to parties anymore, and I felt like I was constantly putting my foot in my mouth. I don't know when exactly this happened to me, but my default mode is sarcasm with a little irony thrown in. I can often feel the kinder, more patient and generous person still dwelling inside me, but then I open my mouth, and the uglier version erupts. I spend too much time by myself.

But Claire had done a lovely job putting this gathering together. The food was delicious; the cheese arranged just so on the plates she had found long ago at a thrift store in Allston. She had wrangled with some samosas, and the table was filled with other hints of her travels in India—some lentil patties, spinach and potatoes, and chicken that had become perhaps just a bit too blackened. I was impressed with all she had done (with Sophie's help). When she had found some recipes tucked into one of her India journals, I had wondered if she would be able to pull all of this off. But the house smelled warm and wonderful and the food tasted even better.

The back of my throat started to tighten. I still loved her, was amazed by her. She was always pushing against her own limitations and fears. She had always been that way. And she had always tried to take Charlie and me along with her in her relentless push forward and beyond. The past was something to build on, not dwell on, and here she was, trying to start from scratch. She couldn't see it, but I could—she was still the same person she had always been. She might feel like a stranger in her own skin, but to me she was a continuation of who she'd always been—shimmering, fearless, proud, defiant Claire.

ALL THOSE YEARS ago, the week she and Charlie prepared to leave for Vermont, she was rarely in the house. She knew how miserable I was, even though I was trying to hide it, and she must have sensed that bumping into me in the kitchen or on the back porch or in the living room would be a reminder of the absence soon to come. I think she was trying to prepare me in small ways for her—their—disappearance. I woke up in the morning to find them already off on some errand, a hastily scrawled note on the countertop asking me to meet them somewhere for dinner that night. That was another thing she arranged—no shared meals at our kitchen table. I never considered that she might have been protecting herself too. I wonder now whether she was trying to keep her eyes forward out of some kind of habit. She had trained herself not to look backward, and that was what our house had suddenly become.

On a couple of these evenings, I did join them out in the city. We went to Chinatown for dumplings one night and traveled to Cambridge on another to watch *Touch of Evil* at the Brattle. But the other nights I stayed home, trying to get used to the quiet and stillness of the living room. I drank wine by myself and left for work early, only to find that Claire was already out and about, her notes left behind. Or I stayed late at work, making excuses with fictional deadlines or imaginary plans with colleagues.

When the U-Haul appeared in front of our stoop, I forced myself to stay. I helped lug boxes of books out to the sidewalk. I dragged suitcases and two plants and a rocking chair onto the curb. I handed out water to the teenage boys Claire had hired to lift the heavier things, of which there were so few. Most of our belongings we had inherited from my parents. That old rocking chair is in the guest room where I've been sleeping now.

When it came time for the truck, and with it Claire and Charlie, to pull away, Charlie grabbed both my hands and kissed me on the forehead. "You are my very best friend, Rach. You must come to visit soon because I can't imagine us being parted for more than a day." I had nothing to say, then, though my head was screaming. I didn't cry, both to prove to myself that I was strong and to try to alleviate their guilt. Claire sat in the passenger seat of the truck, refusing to look at me. She had warned me that she was terrible at good-byes, and now I saw just how true it was. When Charlie climbed into the truck, she turned to me quickly and mouthed, "I love you," behind the closed window. It was a warm day, but she had refused to open the window the whole time she sat there. I lifted my hand. I still hadn't spoken a word to either of them. And off they went.

Claire

ere is my body on the floor. I can see the traces
of dirt and crumbs wedged into the kitchen tiles.
I thought I had cleaned this floor so thoroughly
only a few hours ago. It smells of bleach and grease, and the
ceramic feels cold against my neck. It is peaceful here on the
floor, but I know I am being selfish because things are not at
all right and I will be causing others worry. I can feel a pulsing
in my neck, where my trach scar still cuts a line into my skin.
When I feel that throbbing in my scar, I know that I am about
to have a seizure or I know that I've just had one. I fear I have
ruined Charlie's birthday party again. I cannot feel the length

of myself on the floor; I don't know if my fists are clenched or if my palms are open to the ceiling. There is a faint pulsing in my knee, but I cannot tell you where my legs are in relation to the rest of me. Perhaps there is something twisted and contorted down there. I have no idea.

The cold tiles press against my skull, and I can hear my own breathing. In and out, quiet and rhythmic. And there is my heart, beating its own rhythms against my breath. I am aware of myself on this floor and in this breathing body, but the kitchen is growing fuzzy, and there is no voice pushing out through my mouth, which I sense is open and gasping, and I feel ashamed. My eyes are open, but I can't focus on anything beyond the crumbs on the floor. My eyes are open, but I can't see properly, and I can't close them, and this too must make me ugly.

There is suddenly someone holding my wrists, and it is as if my skin has caught fire. I try to throw this presence off me, but I am being held now and there are hands on my head and I can feel others' breath on my face and my body is on fire. There is a sharp sting of pain in my left knee—there is my leg!—and I kick, kick, kick, but they won't let me go. And here, then, is Charlie's voice. "Please, Claire. Come back. It's all right. We're here. You're in the kitchen. I'm here. Rachel is here. Look at me, Claire. Please. Look at me."

Charlie's voice. I hear him, but I can't see him. I want to tell him that I'm on fire, that he must let go of me. But the hands grow tighter and I fear we are all growing desperate and frightened and I can't tell them just to let me be. I'll come back; it's okay. I can hear you, just let go of me. I'm catching fire from your hands and your breath, and even your voice, Charlie, is hurting me. "Sophie, please, call an ambulance," he says.

And suddenly I can picture Sophie here beside me, her painted toes, and the dusting of flour that had speckled the hem of her skirt, and I want her to tell me the truth, to lean in close and push the others away. Sophie is cool to the touch and she is kind and she means me no harm and her voice is calling out the address to our home and she is scared; I hear it in her voice, and I want her to come to me so I can tell her not to be afraid—that I'm not frightened and she shouldn't be either. This has all happened before. There will be calm after this; it is what we can look forward to. Just leave me on this floor and my body will cool and we can bring out the cake and sing our song to Charlie and none of this will matter anymore.

Sophie, it doesn't really matter to me if you've been in my house before, or if you know where the measuring cups are. I'm glad you know what Charlie's favorite cake is. I like your ordered calm. I am jealous of it. It is easy to see why Charlie might love you. I am not angry. Just tell them to let me be. I am fine. In a few moments I will stand up and shake out my hair and we will all be a little embarrassed, but we can still salvage this party. It is still Charlie's birthday and we haven't lit the candles or eaten your delicious cake, Sophie.

A few more moments, I promise, just let me lie here on this cool tile. I will count my breaths. One. Two. Three. And then

I will be able to see all of you again. One. Two. Three. And I will gather myself up and we will all dim the lights and sing "Happy Birthday" to Charlie. One. Two. Three. Rachel on one side of me, Sophie on the other. And the three of us will sing to you, Charlie. We can salvage this party. Count with me. One. Two. Three.

THESE ARE IMPOSSIBLE things to write. I do not believe them myself. I have no real memory of being on that floor or interrupting Charlie's party, no memory of what could possibly have been going through my mind. These notes are always approximations. I have a vague feeling of embarrassment and shame, but this, of course, could just be an aftershock. I listen to Rachel tell me about Charlie finding me on the floor. She promises me that he kept the rest of the crowd at bay, that she helped him keep the guests in the living room so that they wouldn't have to see me there, twitching on the floor. I can only imagine how ugly I look in these moments. My lips are raw and sore from where I bit them, bit them right through, in fact. Where on my body won't I have stitches by the end of this year? And my tongue feels too big for my mouth, swollen and unruly, and I don't feel like talking, so I'm writing instead, and this too feels useless, because all I have in the end are Rachel's words and Charlie's barely audible sighs.

Charlie is angry because he thinks I was drinking and that's what triggered the last seizure. Rachel told me this. Were you? she asked me, and I couldn't be sure, even if I didn't think that I had been, but I promised her that, no, I hadn't had anything to drink, not even a little wine, because I knew that was what she wanted to be able to tell Charlie, and she didn't want to have to be angry with me either. But who knows? Maybe I did have a sip or two because everyone else was and I don't like the feeling of being on the outside all the time, like a child, with a glass of water in my hands, not even sparkling, because the bubbles can send me off into a coughing spasm. I am discombobulated. My throat isn't even under my control these days, and instinctively I touch the scar on my neck, the lasting impression of my trach. These bumps on my body, scars and scrapes and the remnants of stitches, map my memories for me. Rachel sits in the chair across from my bed; the TV is on mute. She is letting me be for a while. She brought some of her own work to do. Charlie has gone out for a run. The hospital smells of overcooked vegetables and antibacterial soap and I can't believe that I've dragged us all here again.

Earlier, Rachel asked me what it feels like in my brain. "Tell me again, what do you remember?" she said. "Can you see our house? Can you see our intro to graduate research class? Can you see the day that Charlie moved in?" She leaned forward in her chair.

I told her that I have a feeling for our house. I see yellows and plants and hear the sounds of an old radiator whining and clunking. The Green Line trolleys screeched periodically in front of the house. I think I remember that.

"But can you remember specific days?" she asked me.

"Conversations we had or arguments or birthday dinners?" Rachel was searching my face. She had brought her hands onto her lap, and her feet were tapping. For a moment she looked like a much younger version of herself, and I felt a quick flicker of memory. I wanted to give her something precise and concrete so that she might know how much our friendship is still embedded inside me, even if my memories are fleeting and faulty. And then a breath of memory came.

"There was a woman, an old woman, who lived in the apartment next door. She used to steal our Sunday *Times*. We used to make Charlie get up so early on Sunday mornings to try to grab it before she had the chance, but he was often too late. Am I remembering that right?"

Rachel flinched and her voice grew disappointed, even as she tried to smile at me. "Yes, I remember that. I'm sure Charlie does too. He used to be so grumpy about our ruining his Sunday laziness." Rachel stared deep into my face. It was as though she were trying to catch me in a lie of some sort, and I suddenly felt interrogated.

"Is there something you want me to remember, Rach? It seems like you're trying to get at something."

She leaned back into her chair. "I can't tell you what to remember, Claire. There is no point in that. You can't just borrow someone else's memories—they would be meaningless."

But I don't agree with her. When Charlie is in one of his more patient moods, I'll often ask him to describe things to me, and I do feel things stirring. An image forms like an old and discolored photograph. The edges are frayed and some of the details remain fuzzy, but I can see us at a table, playing Scrabble. Charlie's mouth tastes like tea, and Rachel laughs with her head tossed back, all her lovely teeth exposed. She is the only one of the three of us with no cavities.

"You don't have any cavities," I said without really knowing why.

Rachel laughed. She had momentarily forgiven me, it seemed. "It's true. I don't."

"I'm sorry I can't remember whatever it is you want me to, Rach. You could start, you know, and we can try to remember together."

Rachel smiled at me, and for a moment it looked as if she might cry. But she didn't. Instead she took a sip of water and picked up her book again. "Forget it, Claire. I'm just being stupid." And here her voice turned into forced lightness. "Maybe it'd be good for all of us if we just focus on right now and getting you out of here and home." And just like that, the room grew quiet and I felt as though I should apologize again—for what, I'm not sure. And this might be the most frustrating thing of all: sometimes you know you have hurt someone and can't even explain to yourself why or how.

RACHEL HAS GROWN still; when she works, she almost looks as if she is sleeping. What I'd like to tell her is that I do remember things. I do have memories of my mother in the hospital, dying slowly, my father graying next to her, his gaze fixed on her at all times. I can only imagine how much my mother must have hated that—watching his vigil, knowing she was the cause of his desperation and fear. I tried hard not to look at her. Like Rachel does now, I brought books and I doodled and I played solitaire on a table with wheels. I brought stuffed animals to sleep with my mother, to keep her company, after we'd leave for the house, when evening visiting hours were over. My mind is funny that way. If I go far enough into the past, everything is so clear; it's like I'm watching a movie of my former self. But if you ask me about yesterday or last year or my wedding day, I will stare at you blankly and look to Rachel or Charlie to fill in the gaps. But there is my mother being lowered into the ground on a too-bright June morning, my father's knuckles turning white in my hand. I thought he was going to break my fingers. I insisted on wearing a green dress because it was my mother's favorite color, and though my aunt Sylvia argued with my father about the inappropriate color, saying that I should be dressed in black, I got my way because my father was too tired to fight and my aunt loved her brother too much to make the day any worse for him.

I have told Charlie that if I die, I want to be cremated and no fuss is to be made. Instead everyone should just go out for a drink and tell stories and get drunk on my behalf. If I had my way, I'd ask Charlie and Rachel to bring my body up to the highest mountain here in Vermont and let the vultures eat me and scatter my remains on their flights. Just like the Zoroastrians. Charlie flinches when I mention any of this, but it seems worth talking about. He tells me that there aren't any vultures in Vermont, but I'm not sure he's right about that.

Rachel humors me. You're not going to die, she says, but if it makes you feel better, I promise we won't bury you. And she also promises that they'll get too drunk to stand and tell embarrassing stories about all three of us, because who would care about embarrassment at that point? I love Rachel. I hope she knows how much. It surprises me sometimes that she is so much stronger than Charlie. I don't know if I ever understood that before, but I see it now.

She is happy when things grow quiet. And sitting here in this room, me in a mismatched sweat suit that Charlie brought from home (I would never wear this!) and Rachel curled up, legs tucked under her, in that horrendous Naugahyde chair, I feel memories stirring in me of our old home and of slow, sluggish evenings together, our heads angled over books. There is a photograph of the two of us; it is fall and there is an orange-leaved tree you can see on the far side of the window. Rachel is looking down, pencil clenched in her mouth, and I am staring the camera full in the face, grimacing at the photographer, who I can only guess is Charlie. The image is framed in our study, and I look at it sometimes when I'm at the house, begging it to open up some of the hidden spaces of my memory. Here, in this hospital bed, am I remembering Rachel and me hunched over our books, or am I merely remembering a photograph and what I hoped it was telling me? Everything in my mind feels borrowed.

Can I explain how much guilt I feel in bringing Charlie and Rachel here, carving that worry into their faces? Those sighs of Charlie's. And that look of orderly seriousness in Rachel's expression. She writes everything down that the doctors say. She understands that they are changing my cocktail yet again. Upping this, lowering that. She helps Charlie organize my pillbox, which looks as though it should belong to a ninety-year-old who has suffered three heart attacks. I am ashamed of that box. Perhaps it is selfish of me, but if I had it my way, I would just up and leave. Take the box and my prescriptions and just go, leaving my footprints in the snow. I'd rather take the risk of travel and movement than have to stay here and watch what I'm doing to the two people I love (or loved—this, too, is hard to distinguish) the most in this, my life.

I would leave a note, begging them not to worry, telling them that I knew what I was doing, that I'd be fine no matter what happened. I would tell them that we all have too much worry in our lives right now, that they should go back to their Claireless ways, spend more time with each other, go for walks and keep alcohol in the house, and take that stupid chair out of the shower (I never use it anyway). They are the only ones left who know me as I used to be, and even if I don't entirely know who that past person is/was anymore myself, I'd rather them think of me not as a sick person but as someone smart and funny and brave. I want to be that person in the photograph, grimacing and defiant, an outsider on my own terms. I want out of this stupid bed. I want out of this life that no longer feels like my own. Charlie would find it all impossibly ungrateful and selfish. He wouldn't see that I would be trying to give us all a gift.

• • •

I FEEL LIKE a child listening to grown-ups talk about serious matters. They whisper in front of me, as if to protect me. Charlie and Rachel wear the concerned looks of parents, and for a moment I allow myself the childish pleasure of obliviousness. The doctors are baffled; they don't know why I keep having these seizures. They don't know why the adjustments to my medications aren't working. Something has been triggered, they say. Something that might always have been dormant inside me. An autoimmune disease, perhaps. All they know is that I continue to have inflammation in my brain, along my spinal cord.

Could alcohol have triggered this latest spell? Charlie asks. He calls my seizures spells and this makes me want to laugh, but I know well enough that a chuckle in the present moment would be inappropriate. Perhaps, Dr. Stuart says. But this goes well beyond a sip or two of wine. Until we figure out a better combination of meds, it's best that she remain as quiet and unstressed as possible. And I know what this means. I will be stuck in that house, even less free to move around than I have been. Perhaps while Charlie is at work, Rachel can help me dig an underground tunnel and help me plan my escape. But the look on her face tells me that she'll be following the doctor's orders too. Oh, Rachel, you might as well leave us now. There'll be no fun to be had in our house. I am not going to be pleasant company; I can tell you that right now.

ONCE I'M HOME, I'm a despondent little brat. I am giving the universe the silent treatment because I hate this feeling of looking out at the world that is moving around me while I am stuck here on a couch. I suppose I am lucky that this is such a quiet place; it's easy to forget that much is going on outside, beyond an occasional car honking or a neighbor's dog barking a hello. But as soon as I turn on the TV, I can't help being reminded of all the minute changes, all the shifts and flux that I can barely keep hold of. The news moves terribly fast. Of course I imagine I've always known this; the news has been my job. But wars are beginning and ending in places I have only the barest sense of. I can list all the US presidents in order. I can tell you the capital of every country in the world. I can narrate the history of Indian independence and partition. Go ahead and ask me. But don't ask me the name of the woman who recently became the leader of Germany. The TV reminded me just a few moments ago, but it is already lost. It is the smallest, momentary things I cannot hold. I am driving everyone crazy with my questions.

Where did I leave my book?

It's right in front of you. Under the newspaper. Look.

Do I have an appointment with Dr. what's-his-name later today?

Dr. Abramson. Not today. Wednesday. It's on the calendar. Here, on the wall.

Didn't we have fish for dinner last night?

No. We had spaghetti squash. Look at your journal. You've been writing all this down.

I have been home for two days. My journal indicates this. I get bored reading over my own notes, especially when the information doesn't stick, so I watch sports. It must be driving Rachel nuts. Over the weekend, I watched football both afternoons. It is easy to follow. The plays get called and the bodies move and crunch, and for the next several moments I watch the replays, and the commentators' voices tell me how to understand what we've just seen. I root for whatever team doesn't score first, and that is just fine with me. Occasionally, Charlie or Rachel will bring me some pills or refill my cup of tea or offer me some bland food that disappears before I even remember tasting it. There are no memories in my mouth of breakfast or lunch; everything tastes the same. I think I miss spices. Food should hold memories.

Rachel has promised that we can go for a short walk later this afternoon, after I take at least a quick nap. I am a toddler. All I do is eat and sleep and shit and breathe. I am howling on the inside. I feel a temper tantrum coming on. Give me back my life, I want to yell at Charlie. I can take a shower by my goddamned self; I want to slap away Rachel's solicitous hands. It is an impossible feeling, craving a return to something you don't even know the shape of. I look through my photos and I read my articles and I believe in the person who wrote these things. But I will never find her stuck in this house, on this couch, with a remote control fastened to my hand. It would be nice to get outside.

WHEN RACHEL EVENTUALLY took me for a walk, it was beautiful outside, at least. A mild early-winter day, bright sun shining through spindly branches. Damp fallen leaves underfoot. The air smelled earthy and musty. Charlie was unsure about a walk. The sun is too bright, he said. Oh, please, Charlie. Don't make me beg. Rachel suggested a hat and lots of sunblock and Charlie gave his okay. When I am feeling angry with Charlie, I am convinced that he gets a fair amount of pleasure from this, regulating my movements, being the permissions granter. He would have been a ruthless parent, I think. Calm and caring and even tempered for all the world to see. But underneath, controlling and despotic and ruthless. A child would be afraid of him, without ever really knowing why. I said this to Rachel—that Charlie would make an oppressive parent—and she looked at me as if I'd struck her in the face. "Why would you say that?" she asked me.

"I think he's enjoying himself. Telling me what I can and can't do."

She relaxed a little and covered her eyes with sunglasses. It is hard to know what she is thinking half the time, but she wasn't going to argue with me. "You're probably right about that," she said. "Which way should we go?"

"How about toward the village center? Is the ice cream shop still open?"

Rachel looked at me with a bemused smile. "Leave it to you to remember the ice cream shop if nothing else."

I felt sheepish. "Mrs. Gunderson's grandkid walked by the house earlier. Strawberry ice cream cone. I've had a craving ever since." Please don't make me do it, Rach. Please don't make me plead like a child for a treat.

"All right, ice cream it is. Let's just not tell Charlie we walked so far."

And I thought, There you go, Rach. You're looking after

me in your own way. You'll have to remember to keep the secret from Charlie because I'll probably forget all about it. It's
no fun keeping secrets when you have no idea you're doing it.
My brain is a maze of secrets, I'm sure of it, but I don't get to
pick and choose what to reveal anymore. I don't even get the
pleasure of knowing them.

Rachel urged me to stop and rest often and she didn't
mind that I took the time to scribble mundane details in my
book or take a quick photo. She was happy to crouch alongside the creek, tossing pebbles or scratching drawings into
the dirt with a stick. We must have looked like two slightly
bored children, but happy in each other's company, doing
our own thing. I wondered if we would have been friends as
eight-year-olds.

THERE WERE VERY few people at the ice cream stand, which, it turned out, was open only for this unexpectedly warm weekend. I don't really feel like talking to anyone lately. I tried not to let it bother me at first, not knowing if I should recognize a neighbor, if I had met this grandfatherly-looking man before. I was happy to stand back and smile and wait for Charlie or Rachel's cues or the stranger's first words. My goodness, Claire. It's so good to see you out and about.

It's great to be out and about!

How have you been feeling, Claire? You are looking quite well.

A little tired, but good. Thanks for saying so.

Everyone is very polite here, kind and patient. It would be hard to offend anyone, I'm sure, but lately I just don't feel like putting in the effort. At the ice cream stand, I wanted to be invisible or leave it to Rachel to do the talking. I liked listening to her explain our relationship. It made me feel tied to a past that I at least somewhat remember. We all met in grad school, she told the stranger at the picnic table. We renovated my parents' house, an old brownstone in Boston, and lived there for several years. We have been best friends for as long as I can remember, she said. We are a mismatched family.

Rachel ordered mint chocolate chip and I got my strawberry cone. They had run out of sugar cones and I was disappointed by the Styrofoam sogginess of whatever kind of cone I was eating. We sat at a picnic table and kissed our ice creams against one another so a splash of green colored my pink. It was easy to be quiet with Rachel. I hope she realized how grateful I was for this.

AFTER A WHILE, Rachel said that it was probably time to be heading back. It had cooled off a little bit and the ice cream had made us both chilly. On the way home, Rachel told me that sometime soon she'd have to be getting back to Boston. "I have been away a long time. I miss my plants," she said. "Isn't that stupid? And I miss the smelly trolleys on the way to work." It took everything in me not to pull on her arms and demand that she take me with her. But I didn't have to, because she had read my mind as she always seems to.

"You'll come and visit soon, don't you think?" she said.

"I do. And I will. Charlie will be happy to get rid of me for a while." I meant it as a joke, but we both knew I was right. He needs to get back to his life too.

"And I think it would be good for you to get back into some kind of work project. Maybe when you come, we can think about some possible stories, some features you could pitch to Susan. Susan—your editor."

For a moment I was irritated. She thought I didn't remember Susan, but I do. She thought I hadn't been thinking about new story ideas on my own. I am way ahead of her. When Rachel and Charlie go to bed, I am often restless, still bored from the day, so I tiptoe to the office and open my files and do my own version of research. It feels stealthy and secretive, to be awake when I'm meant to be sleeping. I stare at the computer screen and I try my hardest to memorize my own words. There is a half-finished story about a utopian community in Pondicherry called Auroville. My last notes are from five months ago. I am fascinated by the people who have moved to this place from so many different countries. They barter and learn trades and are self-sufficient and secluded from the rest of the town—from the rest of the world, for that matter. I read my notes.

Their edicts:

> Auroville belongs to nobody in particular. Auroville belongs to humanity as a whole. But, to live in Auroville, one must be the willing servitor of the divine consciousness.
>
> Auroville will be the place of an unending education, of constant progress, and a youth that never ages.
>
> Auroville wants to be the bridge between the past and the future. Taking advantage of all discoveries from without and from within, Auroville will boldly spring toward future realizations.
>
> Auroville will be a site of material and spiritual researches for a living embodiment of an actual human unity.

I sometimes think I would be very much at home there. There are so many questions I would want to ask this group of people. There are secrets here, I am sure of it. I have started a new notebook. It is filled with questions and story ideas and memorization quizzes I have set up for myself. I have been in contact with Susan. Charlie and Rachel don't know about this. I have convinced her that I am on the mend and there has been no one to contradict me. She worries that this story doesn't merge with the research I've been doing on environmental conflicts. I tell her that this community's self-sustaining and environmentally conscious mission could be a model for the rest of the city, and I will be close enough to Salem to finish the story I had begun there. She tells me I have always been good at persuading her to let me follow my story instincts. She has told me that whenever I am ready to start on a new project, she can try to help me put a plan into motion.

In these stolen moments, the house is quiet and there is finally space to breathe. The howling in my brain stops for a moment as I read in front of the computer's blue, illuminated worlds.

Charlie

Rachel and I brought Claire back from the hospital five days ago. Claire has been sleeping downstairs on the couch. Her balance is wobbly and the doctors have told us that she shouldn't exert herself for several days, only small bits of exercise, a short walk every now and then. Claire listened to this news with a blank expression. When I brought out the sheets and blankets tonight, she was staring into space. "I guess I'm trapped, then." She attempted a laugh. After a few moments, she said, "Maybe you and I should go on a trip once things have settled down again. It would be nice to get out of this house." I smiled in response and told her that we would see how the next weeks went. I have already taken so much time off from work; secretly I know that a trip would be impossible. Perhaps she could head down to Boston with Rachel, though Rachel, too, has put her life on hold for so many weeks now. We are all trapped, I want to say to Claire. Please don't think you're the only one who feels this way.

Instead of directly answering her questions about travel, I ask her, "Are you feeling weak? Would you like me to make you some tea?" She answers, barely, with a shrug of her shoulders. "Perhaps just some sleep, then," I say helplessly. I am not used to this kind of quiet from Claire; she has retreated somewhere inside herself. I am no good at trying to bring her out. In fact, I look at her face, bruised crescents under her eyes, her skin splotchy and gray, and I am frankly terrified. So instead of doing nothing, I fluff up her pillows and tuck the sheets into the sofa and squat down beside her, holding her limp hand. There are scars on the insides of her forearms; she has difficult veins, the nurses have repeatedly said by way of apology. They stick her and stick her again, drawing blood or inserting IVs, and I want to kiss each and every one of these marks of intrusion. The scar on her neck has started to heal, but there is a pink line at that most vulnerable place where the skin softens and dips just above the clavicles. Claire doesn't want to be touched and I can't really blame her, so I move aimlessly around the room.

Claire doesn't feel much like reading, but I've left some magazines on the table for her. She explains that she can't hold the information in her head long enough; she'll read five pages and then doesn't remember a thing. "I've lost my way again," she complained earlier this afternoon. "Just give me the remote. I'm giving myself up to the television." Rachel had been sitting with her for much of the evening, coiled up in her usual ball in the oversize chair. She read her manuscripts as Claire flipped through the channels. I watched the two of them, here in my living room, and I almost broke down there and then. I've become far too emotional, but I can't help seeing our past in their quiet company. I want to take that remote and hit Rewind and bring us back to that place where we were all tangled up comfortably in each other's lives, healthy, so very young, pushing our way into our futures.

Claire has quite suddenly taken an interest in sports. Tonight some NBA games were on, and she sat up in her chair, transfixed by the play. "I have no loyalties," she explained. "So I just get to root for whoever I feel like." On Sunday she watched three NFL games in a row. I busied myself in the kitchen. I'm not used to the buzz of the TV throughout the house. I really only use it to watch rented movies. Rachel, always thinking ahead, signed us up for cable sometime last week—I have no idea when she did it—but the TV now holds over one hundred channels, and I listen to the pulse of channels changing, having no idea how to turn the damn box on.

Claire's attention span is comparable to a toddler's these days. I'm not sure how Rachel can stand the incessant transitions. Before the detectives can solve a child's murder, the channel shifts to a comedy with an aggressive laugh track.

Someone has found a monkey in a laundry chute. The anonymous audience seems to find this hilarious. A news reporter's monotone voice tells of an earthquake in South America. The old version of Claire would pause here to listen to the story. She might project herself into the landscape, think about how she would cover the story, who she might interview, what combination of devastation and hope she might weave together to get people to pause from their daily lives and listen to news from another part of the world. But there is the flip again, and a crowd cheers for the home team. It seems the Patriots are beating the Jets. Claire has become a sports fan.

Since we've returned from the latest round at the hospital, we cook bland food, healthy and mundane. No exaggerated spices. Nothing fatty or difficult to digest. Whole grains and steamed vegetables and broiled fish with a quick spray of lemon. This is partly Rachel's doing—she's been researching—and partly the doctors' suggestions. Nothing to disrupt her systems, they say. The least stress possible, and this goes for her food too. Our house smells bitter—steamed broccoli and bubbled-over brown rice, charring the bottom of our old pots. Rachel went out to do the grocery shopping just after we first returned, perhaps thinking she should give us some space, some time alone to let Claire and me get our bearings. I have to admit, I get anxious when Rachel isn't here. I look at Claire, and more and more she appears to me as a familiar stranger. I recognize that I should know this person: perhaps we get our coffee at the same café every morning; perhaps we take the same subway car to work each day; perhaps we went to the same school, I a few grades ahead of her or she ahead of me. I have to tell myself: Look at her. It is Claire. Your wife. We are home from the hospital. Touch her hand. Reach out and caress her shoulder. Remind her that she isn't alone. There is too much darkness taking up space in her brain. I force myself to move toward her. I force myself to say her name again and again. "Claire, is there anything you need?" "Claire, would you like to take a bath?" "Claire, you look confused. What is bothering you?" And in my head too. This is Claire. This is still Claire. My Claire. I try to match her to my memories.

There are moments when I am overcome with impatience. I miss my buttery biscuits from Café Diva. I miss the bacon of my Sunday morning breakfasts. I miss my tubs of gelato in the freezer. Rachel says we can't take any chances. Claire might not remember what's off limits, plus she could do without the temptations herself. I'm growing plump, she says, puffing out her cheeks. This is not true. Rach goes running every morning, up into the hills, and her cheeks keep their rosy flush for most of the day. Her body is soft and folds into easy angles, but she is not growing plump. Unlike Claire, whose skin holds the creases of an Indian sun and desert landscape, Rachel looks much as she did when we first met—neither dark nor fair, thin nor fat. Thick eyebrows over changeable eyes. Just the faintest wrinkles in the middle of her forehead that crinkle when we talk about Claire, when we talk about Rachel going home. At some point she's going to have to return to her own life. But I want her to stay. I need her here with us. I am being selfish, but I can't bear the thought of her leaving.

It is only now that I think about what our leaving must have felt like to her. I was selfish then too, I suppose, but it seemed natural that Claire and I would eventually have to leave, set up our own house, now that we were married. And Rachel always seemed so solitary, somehow, even when we were all together. When the Burlington job came through, everything moved so quickly. Claire didn't want to leave the city, but she insisted that we could make it work. She could always commute back and forth every now and then, which would give her an excuse to see Rachel. She was keeping her job with the AP and we knew that she'd be going on assignment from time to time, but she hoped that she'd have more time to work on longer pieces. She'd query magazines. There were stories to be found in Vermont; there were stories to be found everywhere, she insisted. But looking back, I think she was trying to convince herself as much as she was trying to convince me.

And what about Rachel? Looking back now, it seems obvious that she was trying to ignore our leaving. When Claire and I were in the throes of packing, she made sure to leave the house on some errand. As the month when we'd be moving north approached, she stayed later at work. She slept in boyfriends' apartments and might return for breakfast or a quick shower in the mornings. When we bought our car, a used Subaru with its dependable four-wheel drive, Rachel scoffed.

"I've already lost you," she said. "You've become mountain people." I remember that Claire had put her hands on Rachel's shoulders then and looked her directly in her eyes. None of us had been doing that lately, really looking at one another, and I felt myself squirming.

"No one is lost to anyone. We are still a family." Claire tried to pull Rachel into a hug, but I could sense her lifelessness in Claire's arms. Rachel, for one, refused to participate in the fantasy Claire and I were cobbling together. If I think about it now, I can admit how angry she must have been with us. We were abandoning her; there was no other way to see it.

She had dutifully come to our "wedding," a quick exchange of paperwork and vows in front of a justice of the peace who moonlighted as a taxidermist. He wore his hair in a thin, graying ponytail and wore one emerald earring in his left ear. His face was leathery; the skin crumpled into folds as he smiled, and he smiled a lot and slapped his thigh and exclaimed how much he loved his job, getting to meet such happy young people just starting out in their lives together. The man's lair—there was no other way to describe it—was filled with animals, stuffed and glassy eyed. They were our witnesses, along with Rachel and Bernard, who stopped coming around just a few weeks later. Rachel never talked about his sudden absence. When Rachel got quiet, I had learned not to press. She kept her secrets coiled up within her.

We had celebrated with a decadent dinner in Harvard Square, drinking fancy cocktails at a restaurant splotched with bright colors and a sense of exuberant decadence. I was drunk by the second course, and so completely unmoored by stupid happiness. I think I must have caught everyone by surprise as I lifted Claire up off her seat and made her spin around the room with me in a clumsy waltz. Bernard whispered something to the bartender, who led the whole restaurant in a toast to our marriage and future. Rachel watched all of this from our table, tucked into the corner. She had looked so small sitting there. She lifted her glass and drank to us. Before too long, she was drunk too. I remember it as a happy night, but something lingers in my memory, just at the corners. If I could pinpoint it, this hesitancy I feel all these years later when I think about it, perhaps I could identify the warning signs of what would inevitably go wrong with all of us. I try to picture Rachel there, her expression: Did she really look happy or was she just pretending? What might this former Rachel have been wishing to say to us there and then? Where did Bernard go? Why had she gone so silent and distant? It took many years to feel at all linked to Rachel again. When we began sending those postcards. Those little scribbles of other people's words were more than we'd said to one another in many, many months. For all Claire's secrets, it is only lately that I've been realizing that Rachel has just as many.

TONIGHT I CLEANED the dishes and put away the leftovers, realizing I wouldn't want to touch them tomorrow or the next day, though I won't protest when Rachel insists on putting them together for me to take to work. When I walked into the living room, Claire was already asleep, the

TV flickering with its sound muted. Rachel had a pencil in her mouth, frowning over the latest chapters of a high school textbook. I reached out my hand to Rachel. "It's been a long day," I said. "Why don't you put away your work?"

Rachel kept the pencil in her mouth and mumbled, "Just a few minutes more."

But I grabbed the pencil out of her mouth, soggy with her spit, and tossed it onto the table. "How about some cards? Scrabble? Something mindless?" So we retreated into the kitchen and poured out some red wine and I found an old deck of playing cards and a cribbage board and we sat across from each other, quiet in the suddenly calm house.

After a few rounds of play, Rachel had pegged and pegged her way ahead of me, scoring triple runs and combinations of fives and face cards, and I was staring a skunk in the face. Rachel's eyes were wide and taunting; I often forget how competitive she is. She kicked me a few times under the table. We were both trying terribly hard to keep silent so we wouldn't wake up Claire, but when Rachel turned up a Jack and later revealed three fives in her hand and another Jack, she leapt up from the table, almost overturning our wine. At this point we were both giggling; something in us had turned giddy. I put my hand over her mouth as she struggled through her laughter. "Okay, okay," I said. "How about we head upstairs and you give me a rematch?"

Rachel nodded and left her shoes under the table as we gathered up the cards and the wine and tiptoed through the living room. I ask myself now, would I take it back? When

Rachel placed her hand on the small of my back, pushing me up the stairs, my body had warmed and I leaned back into her touch. When she poured out our wine and smirked at me from across the bed, only the cribbage board between us, of course I saw what would come next. I would win the next hand or two and squeeze Rachel's ankle. She would come back with some double runs and wink at me. "Don't think you're going to beat me, Charlie." But I did win the next game and we poured out more wine and then there was the rubber match and I lost my concentration. My head was buzzing with sleeplessness and wine and the sudden proximity of Rachel's body on my bed.

She touched my cheek and then flattened her palm against my forehead and closed her eyes. She pressed her own face against her hand and I felt her hair graze my neck and shoulders. She smelled of wine and lavender and detergent and chocolate. I was surprised by how familiar her body felt alongside me. I often forget there was a time when she would let me crawl into her bed, how her body warmed my cold feet and hands during the winter months when I first arrived in Boston. I placed my hand against her neck and felt her pulse racing under my fingers. She took a deep breath and sighed. For a moment, I thought I saw a shadow cross the doorway, but by then, Rachel had kicked the cribbage board out of our way and she fell on top of me. She looked down with a sad smile. "Oh, Charlie," she whispered. "Do you remember me?"

Rachel

Was it always my intention that Charlie and I sleep together? If I admit to wanting him, if I was out to sabotage things from the outset, then I would have to admit that I had been planning this all along, and then I might really start hating myself. These are my best friends. I have admitted that I am a dangerous person, but I would never have believed I was quite that vindictive. I love Charlie and I love Claire just as I have always loved them. But perhaps there was a part of me that was savoring the inevitability of my own leaving. This time, I would be the one leaving them alone. Alone and frightened, unsure of one another.

The truth is that Charlie and I had drunk too much wine and we were both exhausted and filled with worry. Claire had not been herself, and we had been trying to be so careful around her. There had been mutual relief in our laughter, and we clung to each other for comfort and for a sense of normalcy. I can rationalize all of this. But when I touched Charlie's face, it was like watching the actions of a stranger. I am doing this, I heard my mind saying. I am touching him and I can see in his eyes that he will kiss me. The door is open and Claire is asleep downstairs, but she could discover us at any moment. We know this, but it will not concern us. We are too far gone.

Charlie is older, his skin a bit rougher and his eyes more tired, but I remember the curves of his face and I remember the hesitations in his touch and I wonder if I am as familiar to him as he is to me. As in our earliest flirtations, I am the one to touch him first. I am the one to press my body into his and whisper his name. But I have changed. I no longer wait for things to come to me.

Afterward, when we were lying on their bed, I couldn't help myself. I had a terrible desire to harm him in some way. Here it was again—all this love and anger and desire and resentment churning inside me, the better me competing with the meaner me. He was calm and gazing up at the ceiling, and the window was cracked open a bit and I could hear the sounds of branches rubbing together just outside. Everything was still and peaceful and I wanted so very much to disrupt this undeserved moment of quietness.

Charlie walked to the bathroom, and for a moment the slant of light crossed my body and I felt exposed. My skin was pale, it always has been, but lately it's grown splotchy and translucent. I can see the blue of my veins pushing up from under the surface and I am never unaware of pulsing underneath.

Charlie, just before he shifted out of bed and toward the bathroom, told me that I had calmed him. He didn't think it was possible, he said, but I had done it. I got him to think of something else for a while. In fact, he said, you helped me think of nothing. I was sure he didn't mean anything cruel by this, but his words had twisted me up in anger. I wanted a fight. If I couldn't have one with Claire, I could have one with Charlie.

When he returned, Charlie brought me a glass of water and placed it on my chest gently and leaned over to give me a kiss on the forehead. A friendly, kind kiss, but one that might have been offered as a means to erase what had just happened. Charlie is a coward, just as I've been a coward. And then I started it; I couldn't help myself. "Claire thinks you've been having an affair with Sophie," I said without looking at him.

"She what?" Charlie leaned up on his elbow. He had put his pajama bottoms on, flannel and plaid. I felt bad for him for a moment, bad for what I was about to do.

"Claire thinks you and Sophie are sleeping together. She has set up traps to try to expose the two of you, but she feels thwarted."

"Well, that's absurd." Charlie turned onto his back. He wasn't looking at me any longer, which made this all the easier for me. "She's the one; she's the one who—"

"Oh, please, Charlie." I turned to him. "You just slept with me, didn't you? It's not an impossible thing to believe. And Sophie is quite lovely and obviously thinks a great deal of you."

"Are you telling me that you think I've been having an affair with Sophie too?" Charlie continued to face the ceiling.

"It doesn't matter what I think. But if I were to guess, I think you talked yourself out of having an affair with Sophie so you could keep all your righteous judgment."

I could hear Charlie breathing beside me. He was angry and hurt and it would have taken so little to reach out my hand and apologize, reassure him that I believed him. Instead I said, "I suppose sleeping with me is a slightly different case, though, since we have a past and we have always loved each other in our ways."

"I don't understand why you are so angry with me, Rachel." He finally turned his body back toward me. "Do you want me to apologize for sleeping with you? Would you like me to take the blame for that? Perhaps you'd like me to walk downstairs, wake Claire, and tell her that we are both very and truly sorry for fucking each other while she was sleeping on the couch. We can all come clean!" Charlie began to raise his voice and

I felt a wave of exhilaration race through me. "And perhaps this might jog her memory a little and she can cry in relief and say, Thank God! We're even! I have been keeping my little secrets too! Let me get the picture I've been keeping in the folds of my book on the desk. Do you remember this man, Charlie? You met him once, on one of your visits."

I couldn't help it. I started laughing. My entire body was shaking and I could tell that Charlie wanted to hit me, slap me across the face, but instead he punched the mattress several times and repeated, several times, "Please shut up, Rachel. Please shut up. Please."

Eventually, I felt myself calm and managed to say, "I'm sorry," and quieted Charlie's fists. I sat up, naked in their bed, my arms crossed against my chest. Charlie wouldn't look at me, but I needed him to see me here, see the two of us here and acknowledge what we had done. "We all have our secrets, Charlie." I touched his forehead, now damp, and he flinched. "It's always been easier to blame Claire. I've done it for years."

Charlie was as still as stone. Perhaps he wanted me to keep just as still and quiet as he was, but I kept on talking. I told him that I blamed Claire for taking him away, even though it was his job and his sense of their future that took them north and away from our home. I blamed Claire for the distance that had grown between us. I blamed Claire for lying to him and forcing me to keep her secrets. I blamed Claire for forcing me to keep my own secrets.

But I could have easily blamed you, Charlie, for taking

a job that would bring Claire to a place far too quiet and unexceptional for the kind of stories she wanted to pursue. I could have blamed you, Charlie, for falling in love with Claire and having such an easy time of it, walking away from me. I could have blamed you, Charlie, for not trying harder to pound on my door and shake the truth out of me that weekend when you returned and I had just gotten back from the hospital, yes, the hospital, Charlie. I lied to you about that. I could have blamed you, Charlie, for knowing about Michael and just letting things go on as usual, for your cowardice and your moral high ground and righteousness. I could have blamed you, Charlie, for those postcards you sent that made me think about you more than I wanted to, for making me think about the things I have never told you and knew I never would because I am a coward too. It was my secret to keep, but Claire made it seem as if it were ours, all of ours, so really it is my fault.

I wonder sometimes, Charlie, how you would have reacted to the news if I had told you from the start. Would you have said that we could keep it, that we could have a go at it, make a little family? Why is it that you and Claire never talked about having children, Charlie? It is something I never could ask either of you. Again, I assumed this was Claire's choice, her career was more important than motherhood; she was away too much and didn't want to give up her travels, her passport, her stories. You see, I blamed Claire on your behalf for this too, but for all I know, you never wanted to have children either, Charlie.

Or would you have left it all up to me with your typical politeness disguised as care? Would you have held my hand on the way to the hospital and on the way home? Would you have crawled into bed with me and brushed the hair out of my eyes the way you did whenever I got sad? Would you have stayed with me and been patient with me, and then it would have been Claire, only Claire, who would have left? It was always going to be Claire who left, Charlie. We could both see that, even all those years ago. I don't think it was ever any of our intentions to hurt one another, Charlie, but look at what we've done. You have always trusted me, but I am the one who has now perhaps hurt you the most. I must never have trusted you, Charlie. Otherwise, I would have told you all of this a long time ago.

Forgive me, my dear Charlie. I am a dangerous person, but I love you, and I love Claire. Tomorrow I will pack my bags and say good-bye. I will never tell Claire any of this; as you now know, I am very good at keeping my secrets. Maybe one of these days, you can get Claire a train ticket and let her stay with me awhile in Boston. I think it might do both of you some good. You don't see it, but she feels trapped in this house; it is no longer filled with her life. Perhaps you can forgive her a little bit too and let her breathe some, no matter what the doctors say. If not, I believe you will lose her all over again.

Claire

It was all surprisingly easy. Charlie had gone back to work, and Rachel had quite suddenly packed her bags and headed home, and the house was mine again. Charlie had asked me not to go on any wanders until he got home, which was fine with me. Most of what I needed to do I could do from the computer or over the phone. My passport was still valid, good for another three years even. Susan was handling the details of my visa; she would arrange the flight and she had rented a room for me for the first month of my stay in Pondicherry, and we would see how things went from there. I had pitched her my story ideas about Auroville. I read from my fragmented notes and mustered some strength in my voice, which I hoped would project whatever confidence people were used to me possessing.

Susan had called my ideas "promising"—I have this word underlined several times in my notebook—and said she would get back to me. She was concerned. Was I really well enough to travel? Was I really up for being on my own again so soon? You know, Claire, she had said, the hospitals where you are going. . . . But I interrupted her and told her I wouldn't stand for being treated like an invalid. I laughed a lot during those first conversations and stuck to the facts. My meds are keeping me stable and I can set up a three-month prescription with my doctor. There was a new controversy brewing about the way the children were being treated at Auroville. With my contacts, I would be able to get her a good feature. I told her I could simultaneously write a travel piece on Tamil Nadu. Oh, what the hell, she said. If you want to do it, let's do it. Over the years, Susan has become one of my closest allies. I knew she would help me.

Over the next days, I took taxis to the post office, to the pharmacy, to the bank. I bought some new notebooks, some practical shoes that seemed light and durable enough for the Tamil Nadu heat. I printed photos from the machine at the pharmacy. Rachel and me on the porch swing. Charlie and Rachel picking some berries at the edge of the property. The birthday party and Charlie's look of surprise.

I am not angry with you, Charlie; please don't be angry at me. If I don't get away from here, I will never be myself again. I hope you understand. I left copies of the photos along with a scribbled note on the kitchen table. I took a taxi to the Burlington airport. By the time Charlie got home from work on that Tuesday evening, I was already in London. And then Chennai. And now here.

There have been some difficult phone calls. Charlie called Susan, furious with her for letting me take this risk. He has threatened to come fetch me, put me back on the next plane to the States, but his words are fueled by worry more than action. Susan, in turn, was livid that I had kept so many details of my health secret from her. Rachel is the only one who has talked to me with patience and understanding in her voice. She knew I needed to leave, she said, though she never thought I'd journey quite so far away so fast. For now, at least, they are all leaving me be, and I am sure to check in with each of them at least once a week so that they know I am alive and well and hard at work.

I LIVE ON a quiet, dusty street in the old French Quarter of Pondicherry. In fact, I live above a French-language bookstore, and from my open windows I can hear the owner speaking in her lilting and lovely French to the few customers who come by each day. Here is a view from my building.

And here is another one. The city is "resurfacing the road," but these piles haven't been touched in days.

There is so little in my room. I have a bed with a mosquito net, and a desk and wardrobe. There is a small bathroom in the hallway that I share with my landlady's cousin's family. There is a bucket on the floor and a little spigot. I fill the bucket with cold, silty water and dump it over my head each morning and each night before bed. The water is always cool and startling, but it is also a relief. I am limited to five buckets a day.

My notebooks and pens cover the small desk and I have several photographs on the windowsill. Boston, the road stretching from Charlie's house. And one of Rachel, me, and Charlie. It is an old picture, taken when we all lived in Rachel's house. We are young and smiling and I like to think of us this way. I don't know who took the picture. It looks like autumn is just beginning. We are all wearing light sweaters and I can tell we must have been growing a little chilly as the image was snapped. It is a beautiful picture: the light just turning into shadow, a tree's leaves superimposed on our shoulders. I don't remember this day, but I can feel it. It cools me off when the afternoons grow hot and the ceiling fan's irregular motions do terribly little to offset the dusty heat coming in through the windows.

I am taking care of myself. I wear a hat and sunglasses and lots of sunscreen every time I leave the house. I always remember to tell my landlady, who lives next door, where I am going and when I will return. She often has me sit with her and share a sweet or some tea. She is happy to look after me and worry about me and I am happy to let her. She has a big family and they occasionally invite me over to eat with them, but I also spend time at my favorite restaurant on the corner, where I can order French dishes like bouillabaisse and feel the strange collision of times and places in this small city.

I have a to-do list on my wall to remind me of the small and larger things of my day-to-day. I have my own codes.

- 7:00 a.m.: Morning meds 1 × F, 1½ × P.

- 8:00–11:00: Interviews if possible before the heat of the day kicks in.

- 12:00: Lunch meds 1 × D, 2 × T.

- 12:00–2:00: Nap. Get out of the sun. Drink something cold.

- 2:00–4:00: Write.

- 4:00: Afternoon meds 1 × F.

- 5:00–7:00: Evening interviews if possible.

- 9:00: Night meds: 1 × P, 1 × D.

I keep a map with me at all times so that I never lose my way. Or if I have to I can point to the X on the map that shows my house, and a stranger can take me home. There is an emergency contact card in my purse, laminated, in Hindi, Tamil, and English. I have a copy in my apartment too.

In an emergency, please contact Champa Gopolam, landlady and friend: 91 413 222 6591
Other contacts: Susan Halloway +1 2125557896
Charlie Scott +1 8024328933
Rachel Haves +1 6173238211

My other contacts:
At Auroville: Pierre Dessain 91 413 652 001
Gayathri Jayaraman 91 413 652 786

Susan's contacts for me:
Fixer: Sunil Nair 91 222 652 1295
Driver: Arun Rangan 91 222 652 9982
Photographer: Michael Tillman 91 222 433 9854

THERE ARE MORNINGS when I wake up terrified. I look around my room, and everything in my mind jumbles. I have to step slowly out of bed, my feet planted first on the cold marble, before I stand. I count to ten, to twenty, sometimes to five hundred. I am in India, I tell myself once I sit at my desk. I am in Pondicherry. I look over my notes. I am doing a story on Auroville. Susan, now that she's talking to me again, thinks a whole book could come out of this project. The mother gurus of India. The photographer will come to join me in a few weeks. Michael. There are many Michaels in the world, but I wonder if this one might match the photo I used to keep in my pocket, the one that now acts as a bookmark in my travel guide.

I have a calendar on the wall with the dates x-ed off. I have been here for one month. The calendar has told me that I have been to the clinic twice. My notes tell me that I have had at least one seizure. I fell down on my way home. There is an ugly scratch on my cheek and a bruise at my temple, still yellowish green, and there are stitches underneath my chin. Champa took me to the doctors and has been scolding me since we returned. You are not from here, she says. You don't know this kind of heat. You must stay inside in the afternoons. The doctors can refill my prescriptions here. No one else knows about my misfiring brain or my seizures. I stare at my face in the mirror, sometimes for minutes on end. It is not vanity. I am trying to remember myself.

I am keeping my hair short and I bought myself some bright skirts and tunics at the shop down the street. My clothes from Vermont have stayed packed in my suitcase. Every water bottle I buy has a different label on it, and I am collecting them, fastening them together with tape. I will cover my desk with this plastic tablecloth. It will keep the dust at bay. It is very dusty here and dry and my ankles are always filthy.

I think about Charlie and Rachel. I think about their worry, and there are times I am sorry that I left so abruptly and hurt them all over again. Charlie will think that I'm crazy for doing this, that I am killing myself with my stupidity. Rachel might understand my decisions better, even though she would have counseled me against this too. How can I explain it to them? I could tell them that I was tired of listening to other people tell me who I was, but I was also tired of what people refused to share with me. I could tell them that I was tired of feeling guilty and watched over and cared for. I could tell them I didn't know how to live the way I was living in Charlie's house, stuck on a couch in a living room with the seasons changing outside without me. I'm not sure I know how to live here either, but I prefer feeling frightened or uncertain to feeling nothing at all.

I would like them to understand that I was trying to give us all a gift. Without me there, they could both settle into their lives again, be in each other's company without me always being the focus of concern and worry and, yes, anger as well. Leaving was selfish, but it was for their happiness too.

PERHAPS YOU CAN forgive me, Charlie, and you, also, Rachel. I don't think I'll be coming home. For now, I am going to stay put in this small room. Soon I will send you some pictures and you will see that I am doing fine. Maybe without you I'll be forced to remember things on my own. I'll be able to tell you my versions then. I don't want you to worry. There is so much to see here. I see myself and I see you. When I close my eyes, we are all sitting on a porch, laughing. The air is golden, the way it is in this afternoon light.

Acknowledgments

When I first started thinking about writing this book, my mother welcomed my questions about her own memory loss and told me once how strange it was to have to borrow other people's memories. Her words became the kernel of my novel's central questions. It is my hope that this book honors her courage and good humor, her generosity and kindness, her resilience and intelligence. I miss her and feel grateful for her every single day.

I am also grateful to the family, friends, teachers, and readers who have encouraged me over many years and many drafts. I want to thank Sox Serizawa for always being my first and most trusted reader. Her insights, her thoughtful questions, and her conversation motivate and challenge me. I am also grateful to the support I received at the University of Missouri from the excellent friends and fellow writers I was lucky to meet in Columbia, and particularly from Trudy Lewis, Marly Swick, Sam Cohen, Andy Hoberek, and Carsten Strathausen, all of whom helped guide my writing and research. Thanks also to Dan Chaon and Melanie Rae

Thon, who offered feedback to early pages of the book. And to the many friends and colleagues from Boston to Potsdam to Denver, thank you.

Christopher Vyce is not only a tireless and trustworthy agent but also a generous, smart, and loyal friend. Thank you to the Harvard Book Store for bringing us together many years ago. I have been grateful for the support of the wonderful people at Algonquin Books, especially my editor Chuck Adams. I also feel lucky for Rachel Careau's meticulous eye and for Brunson Hoole and Brooke Csuka's dedicated work. I'd also like to thank the *Hawaii Pacific Review* and *Locomotive* for publishing excerpts from this novel in their pages.

My family is my heart and my memory. Dad and Greg help me remember all of the most important things; I rely on their memories as much as on my own to know the ground I stand on and to trust it. Thank you to Greg for bringing Erin, Nora, and Sam into my life. My world feels bigger and more hopeful with them in it. I am grateful to the Buck-Abels—Spike, Carolee, Nina, Scott, Piper, and Charlie—for their good cheer and kindness. And I would be a lost cause without the ever adventurous, the ever smiling, the ever imaginative Will Buck, who makes anything and everything seem possible.